FLIGHT OF THE WREN

Atthys J. Gage

Flight of the Wren

Copyright 2015 Atthys J. Gage

ISBN: 978-0692469460

Ten digit ISBN: 069246946X

Cover Artist: Victoria Miller

Editor: Jennifer Herrington

Feckless Muse Press

For Jen, of course.

And also Ben, who keeps teaching me things I never wanted to learn.

Special thanks also to Ilona Bray, who first flew the whole idea of kids on flying carpets past my email window so many years ago.

One

"I suppose I ought to tell you, insanity runs in my family."

"Pardon?"

"Yeah. On my mother's side. I guess it could be on my father's side too, but he didn't stick around long enough for me to find out. I guess that says something for him, right? I mean, at least he wasn't crazy enough to marry my mother."

I'm talking too much. I'm nervous. Why the hell am I nervous?

The man reaches over and stabs a little round potato with his fork and makes it disappear into his mud-colored beard. Mouth full, he says, "I'm sure it's nothing to worry about, Miss Drake."

I, on the other hand, am not so sure.

He spears a scrap of meat and dips it in drippy brown gravy. While he chews, I keep right on talking too much. "I'm only telling you this because if it turns out this is my first full-fledged psychotic break, and you're really the doctor in the loony bin, well, you know, then it seems like important information."

He looks up again, one brow raised, the fork hovering near his mouth. "Miss Drake, I can assure you, I am not a doctor."

I admit he doesn't look like a doctor. He has gravy on the front of his purple dressing gown, and I don't suppose most psychiatrists interview patients while eating their dinner. Plus, the room doesn't look anything like a hospital ward, and I've seen my share. They don't usually have stone walls or high wood-raftered ceilings. I've certainly never seen one with arched, stone-framed windows. This place looks more like the inside of a castle than a hospital room.

He smiles again. "My apologies, Miss Drake. I know how disorienting these meetings can be." He takes a napkin from his lap and dabs his lips. "Let me start again." He touches his chest. "My name is Parnell Florian. I know, it's a funny name. You may call me Parnell if you wish. I'm afraid a lot of the ruggers call me Flo behind my back." He chuckles and arches his eyebrows. "Very amusing."

"Ruggers?"

He scratches a tooth with his fingertip then examines the nail. "Yes. That seems to be the current jargon."

This gets me exactly nowhere. "Okay. Well, Parnell, here's my problem. Either this is all a dream, or—"

"Well, of course it's a dream! This is a dream meeting. I'm fairly certain I told you that already."

He may have. He said a lot of stuff, but most of it kind of blurred together in my brain. "This whole experience," he continues, "has been put together for you because—well, because you have been selected for a very rare opportunity."

My stomach tightens. It seems like my delusional dream is about to turn into an infomercial. He picks up his fork again and spears another potato. It goes the same place as the last one. "Do you remember," he asked in a muffled voice, "what happened earlier this evening? Before you came here?"

He gives the word *earlier* a little lift, like it should have some special meaning for me. It does. I chew on the idea for a lot longer than I need to. "You mean the flying."

Of course he does. Up until that moment, I hadn't put the two together.

"You do remember the flying, don't you?" he asks.

I remember all right. He puts his pudgy fingers together and gives me an owlish stare. "Tell me about the flying, Miss Drake."

I know that look. My dream is turning into a therapy session after all. Screw that. Why should I tell him anything?

Instead, I tell him everything. I tell him about riding on a curl of wind, a thousand feet up, floating on nothing. I tell him about the light, about the color of the sky, about the little voices burbling all around me—giddy, giggling voices, bright and happy: *Now Renny? Now? Yes? Are you ready?*

And I know exactly what the voices are waiting for: they're waiting for me to fall.

So I fall. Darkness comes rushing up at me. The nap of the land becomes bristle, becomes stubble, becomes a forest of pine trees, growing, spreading, getting closer and closer. The wind tears through me, rifling my clothes, whipping my hair back, and the voices are everywhere, all shouting: *Good Renny! Oh, good!*

The trees leap up, like spears, like daggers.

Pull up, Renny! Pull, oh pull!

I slam back, grabbing the air. I pull until my knees are doubled back to my ears and I'm digging my heels into the sky. Up turns for down and, for a second, everything is silent. Above me, in the great open sky, the stars are shaking.

Then I hit level. The sky shouts and flings me over the treetops. Laughter scatters, and I'm skipping over the wind. When I finally coast to a stop, the voices catch up with me again. *Good Renny. Yes! Oh, well done.* The words keep jumping about, jostling, nudging. *Will you again? Yes?*

Five times I make the dive, cutting it finer every time. On my last go, I don't pull out until I'm brushing the treetops, like I could reach out and grab a handful of needles. The moon is out now, and I sweep up into the light—banking, stalling, dipping, rising.

I tell it all.

He looks at me, coughs into a fist, and says, "These voices you, uh, heard. Can you tell me more about them?" There's a look on his face I don't like, all narrowed eyes and pursed lips.

"Well, like I said, they were—high. Like little girls." I bite my lip.

One bushy eyebrow goes up. "Really?"

"Yeah. They were coming from everywhere. Like a bunch of little girls, laughing." I feel my own eyebrows draw down. "Is there something wrong with that?" My tongue is thick in my mouth. *Something* sounds more like *shumthing*.

"No, no." He shakes his head. "No, I'm sure it's fine. Just unusual is all. I need to do a little research, but I wouldn't worry about it. I'm sure it's nothing."

I'm staring at him even harder now. His face is changing even as I watch. It's fading, becoming gray. The whole room is flat and gray now, like it's all turning into some ancient black-and-white TV show. "Whatsh happening?"

"You're waking up," he says. The room slips sideways, leaning hard to the left. "It looks like we don't have much time. It's my own fault for letting you fly for so long, but you were so enjoying it. But I'm afraid I do need an answer."

"Answer?"

He nods. "Yes, Miss Drake. An answer. Do you return to your land-bound state of ignorance, or—" he gives the fingers of his hand a little flutter, "—do you continue what began here tonight?"

A shiver trembles my spine. "You mean the flying?"

His face slides into a grin so broad no thickness of beard can hide it. "You have certainly passed the first tests." He leans in a little closer to the table, as close as his considerable belly will allow. "You have a gift, Miss Drake. A special gift. But it must be cultivated. Naturally, you will have to stipulate to certain other parts of the agreement, but compared to the real thing, the flying you did here tonight will seem a pale imitation. A mere—*dream!*"

The room fades out and back in again, and everything tilts back hard to the right. Parnell's face is dimming fast. He looks deadly serious. "Miss Drake. It's really very simple. Do you or do you not want to fly?"

My mouth feels like it's full of dry crumbled crackers. I swallow hard. "Yes. Of course. Of course I want to fly."

Big hands grab me and throw me at the ceiling. "No!"

I wake. For real this time. It's still dark. I make myself sit up and pull the sheets loose. My legs are tangled. "Mr. Florian?"

My voice is tiny. I try again, louder. "Flo?"

The window rattles once, like a cough. Then everything is silent.

Two

When I wake up the next time, it's morning. All I can think is: Wow. Stupid dream. Of course, I'm glad it *is* a dream, since the alternative is waking up in the psych ward talking to some guy named Doctor Florian. But still. Stupid. Parnell Florian? From what bleak corner of my tortured subconscious did I dig that guy up?

I know a little bit about the subconscious mind, and I am no stranger to therapy. For instance, hearing voices nobody else hears? That's not good. In my particular situation, I don't think anyone would call it "nothing to worry about."

But it was just a dream after all, so I guess my psychotic break will have to wait another day. That guy Flo even said so. *"Of course it's a dream. This is a dream meeting."* But maybe that isn't much to go on. I mean, if you ask a guy in your psychotic delusion if he's really just part of your psychotic delusion, what's he going to say? And why should you believe him?

But I really don't have time to think about it anymore. It's late, and reality is reality after all. Which means I have to get ready for school.

***

"There she is," Lee announces.

I slide into the empty chair and take a piece of toast, diagonally sliced, already buttered. Gretchen is going on about some science fair project, and, after announcing me, Lee gives her his full attention. Amy—reading her phone, keying in messages—doesn't even look up. I chew on a toast corner while Lee tells Gretchen something about controls or variables or whatever. She's pretty much his last chance to produce a world-class scientist. Of course, she's only eleven. Never having been to middle school, she hasn't had all that love-for-learning stuff crushed out of her yet.

"I just want you girls to get the basics," he says. "What you do with it afterwards is up to you."

Lauren pushes a plate of bacon at me, but I wave it off. "You guys need to hurry up," she says. "Getting late."

I nod. Lee says, "Really ought to eat more than that, Renny. Half a piece of toast isn't much breakfast."

I give him a sort of half shrug. "Not hungry. I'll eat later."

He rolls his eyebrows and takes another forkful of pancakes. "Only saying, if you went to school with a good meal in you, you might find your day going smoother."

He doesn't say what he's really thinking: I might get better grades. He doesn't have to say it. When Lee and Lauren first fostered me almost three years ago, there were two provisions—my end of the bargain, they called it. One was to go to drug counseling and stop smoking weed. The other was getting my grades up. Giving up weed wasn't really that hard. I didn't care about it all that much in the first place, and all the people I used to smoke with were still back in Tucson. Problem was I didn't care about school either. That made the second provision pretty much impossible.

"You're obviously a smart girl, Renny. It's just about trying a little harder."

People always say that, only I'm not that smart. And they know it.

***

Amy drives me to school. We don't talk much. At least, I don't, but Amy's always been good at keeping conversations going all by herself. First day I came to their house, there she was, all ready to be my brand new big sister and best friend forever. I still remember sitting in the living room. Everything was real awkward. Lee made jokes. Lauren smiled at everything. They were all nice as hell, and I kept thinking maybe this wouldn't be so bad. I'd done worse. Three families in five years and you learn not to set the bar too high.

Anyway, while Lee and Lauren are getting chips and dip in the kitchen, Amy slides over to me like we're old pals already, flashes the beautiful smile and says, "I gotta go meet someone. We'll talk tonight." She leaves, and I'm left with the horrifying thought that we're going to be roommates.

That, mercifully, wasn't the case. I have my own room. It's pretty small, but it's fine. It's better than fine. It's got a door, anyway. It doesn't have a lock, but that doesn't turn out to be a problem. Lee and Lauren have a healthy regard for privacy.

Even Amy, it turns out, is pretty good at leaving me alone. There's nothing really wrong with her, we just don't have anything in common. Her idea of fun means shoe shopping at the Covey Creek Mall, or scoping out hairstyles in the fashion mags.

"We should do something like this with your hair," she says, stabbing some unlikely model with a fingertip.

My hair is a problem Amy needs to solve. Blonde—but not the sort of blonde you'd find in the Clairol aisle. All the words people use to describe blonde, like honey or ash or golden, these aren't mine. I'm dirty yellow Labrador. Wash it and it gets dull and frizzy. Or don't and it goes limp and flat.

"Or maybe that one," Amy tries, pointing out a model who I'm pretty sure is actually a man.

Amy has Teller hair, like Lee and Gretchen: thick, wavy, dark auburn. Lauren jokes that I have Beale hair, like hers. "Beale hair is straight and fine," she says, as if this is an accomplishment.

But I know perfectly well who I look like. If there was any doubt about whether I was really Miranda Drake's daughter, one look would erase it. Same lank blonde hair, same deathly pale complexion, same oversized gray-blue eyes. If I'm not careful, I sometimes catch a glimpse of her in the bathroom mirror: a crazy lady off her meds staring back at me. I see the tatty terrycloth bathrobe, the pack of Marlboros, the grimy glass of vodka in her hand.

Only I don't even need to see her. I know she's always there.

***

The day floats by like a glacier. Nobody calls on me in class. They all know me too well by now. Which is fine with me. Even compared to my usual school stupor, today is bad.

I blame that dream. A flying dream. What could be more ordinary? And that Parnell guy. He was strange, but you meet all kinds of strange people in dreams. But the strangest part is him *telling* me he's a part of my dream. I don't think it's ever happened before that a guy in my dream knew he was a part of a dream. That kind of bothers me.

And the voices. The voices definitely bother me. I said I was no stranger to therapy, and that's true. When I first moved into the House of Teller, I spent six months getting weekly sessions with Dr. Ivan Gananian. "You can call me Ivan," he said, "or doctor. Whatever makes you more comfortable." I did my best not to call him anything. I wasn't interested in being comfortable. Therapy was Lee's idea, of course. We made a deal that if I tested clean for weed for six months, I could quit. I did. To the day.

God, what a lot of money they must have dropped on that quack! But they can afford it, I guess. The Tellers are pretty rich.

13

Lauren is a real estate agent. Lee is a motivational speaker. He sells advice books. *What You Believe is What You Achieve. Hope for Hope's Sake. Amaze Yourself!* The only truly amazing part is people actually buy them.

One day when he was in a sharing mood Lee told me about his past jobs. "It's all just selling, Renny. I used to sell houses. Before that, insurance. I even sold used cars. Now I sell my books and my programs, which is like selling me!" He laughed his professional laugh. "Trying to sell something you believe in is easy. Trying to sell something you don't believe in is misery."

I guess he has that part down. Lee Teller believes in Lee Teller.

And therapy. Six months wasn't enough for Doc Gananian to crack me. I went. I answered questions. None of it seemed to go anywhere. Mostly he wanted me to talk about Miranda. He was convinced I was full of bitter feelings about her and I needed to talk about them. She was fucked up. Bat-shit crazy. What more did he want me to say?

He actually made me keep a dream journal for a little while. I tried writing down my dreams, but I could never remember very much, and I thought the whole thing was bullshit anyway. Finally I just made stuff up and wrote it down. It didn't matter. He never even looked at it. "That was supposed to be for your benefit, Renny."

Like I said: quack.

What would Doc Gananian think if I told him about the dream I had last night?

I spend way too much time thinking about all of this while dozing through seventh period. Amy goes over to her boyfriend's house after school, so I ride the bus home. All the way there, I keep going over it: flying, Parnell, voices. I finally realize just exactly why it's the voices, the ones Parnell told me were nothing to worry about, were worrying me most of all. Miranda, my mother, is a schizophrenic, and hearing voices in your head is like the most classic sign ever of schizophrenia. And what are the voices telling me? *Very good, Renny! Yes! Again! Again!*

They're telling me I can fly. So what the hell is next? Go ahead, Renny. Jump off that bridge! Leap off that rooftop! You can fly, girl!

By the time the bus wheezes to a stop, I'm okay again. I mean, it was just a dream, and I don't even believe in dreams. Dreams are just a bunch of random memories and stuff, all mushed together. It's like your brain is running the garbage disposal before flushing it all down the drain. They don't mean anything.

The bus lets me off about two blocks from the Tellers. The house is empty.

Upstairs, in my room, it's already waiting for me.

Three

My room at the Teller's house is on the top floor. It was converted from attic space sometime long before I arrived. It's long and narrow, and the ceiling cuts in at a steep angle. There's a single dormer window with a little seat in front of it, plus a bed and a chair, a lamp, a closet, and a desk I don't use very often.

And something else. A tube of heavy brown paper lies among the rumpled bedclothes. At least it looks like paper. It clings when I drag my finger across it, like soft leather. A thin ribbon of brown silk holds it tied around the middle. There's no mailing label, no return address, no stamps.

I kneel down beside the bed and slide the ribbon off the end of the tube. Before I've unrolled more than a single turn, a piece of white paper appears. This isn't ordinary paper either. It's crisp and heavy with little colored flecks stuck in the page, like the handmade stuff they sell in arts and crafts stores. In flowery purple cursive, it says:

Dear Miss Drake;
Please find enclosed the item of which we spoke the other night. I think you will find it most suitable. I shall be in touch soon.
Sincerely,
Parnell E. Florian

People say a lot of strange things about being crazy, like *the crowd went crazy*, or *that chick is crazy*, or *I may be crazy but I'm not stupid*. As if being crazy is just like being a little different, and maybe it's not even such a bad thing. I don't think the line between being eccentric and being certifiably insane is as fine as a lot of people seem to think it is. I think there's a real, unmistakable difference.

I only mention this because right now, something very odd and uncomfortable is happening inside my head. If I had to pinpoint the spot, I'd say right between my eyebrows and about half an inch inside my skull. It isn't exactly pain, but I don't know what else to call it. I reach up and squeeze the bridge of my nose, and wait until it passes. When it does, I do the only thing I can think of doing: I read the letter again.

Yes, it's still there. Yes, it still says exactly the same thing. I sit for a minute, just breathing. I should just walk away now. Go downstairs, wait until Lauren comes home, tell her everything. She's a reasonable person. She cares. And, with enough doctors, hospitals, and little plastic cups full of pills, maybe I'll be all right.

That's not what I do. I put down the letter and unroll the bundle. Dreams don't send you letters, and they don't send you packages. It takes me a while to pull it free from its wrappings. It's as long as the bed and just as wide. It's blue. It's also purple and silver and black. And shiny.

I spread it out on the floor, smoothing away the wrinkles, straightening out the pale lavender fringe. Blue? Silver? With every new view, the colors shift. A border of blue-green ivy runs all the way around, twisted with silver vines. On a field of lilac that fills most of the center, a tree stands with thick silver branches and indigo leaves. Tiny rainbow birds perch among the leaves. When I lean in close, I can see my own breath stirring the fine, shiny fibers.

It's a rug. Why the hell did he send me a rug?

Memory clicks. *Ruggers.* He said something about ruggers. So what does a rug have to do with flying?

17

For a moment, I think I stop breathing. When I start again, my tongue is dry. My mouth is open.

I go back to the bed and paw through the long coiling sheets of wrapping paper. I missed it the first time: a thin scroll of brownish parchment covered with careful fancy writing. It says:

> *Greetings!*
> *The enclosed carpet entitles the recipient to all rights*
> *and privileges associated with membership in the*
> *Arcane Order of Carpet Flyers, also known as*
> *the Fellows of Shaheen, sometimes called*
> *the Sublime Society of Scudders.*
> *It carries our assurance as to its flight-worthiness*
> *and reliability, though this should in no way be taken as*
> *an admission of any sort of liability on our part. Life offers*
> *no guarantees, and we would not presume. But rest*
> *assured, given the proper care and respect, your*
> *carpet will perform according to your wishes and,*
> *in all likelihood, last longer than you do.*
> *Volatilis vestis aeternum!*

I rub my eyes again. This time they're wet. Fuck! I'm crazy and I'm crying. Why the hell am I crying? It's not like I didn't see this coming. I've been expecting it my whole life.

After a few minutes, I stop crying. I take off my shoes and crawl out onto the center of the carpet. I sit cross-legged. Maybe I'm crazy now. Maybe my mother's defective genes have finally taken hold, but there's no way I'm not going to try this out.

"Fly!"

Nothing happens.

"Up!"

"Rise!"

"Hover!"

Nothing doing. Finally, I roll over and lie on my side. I'm not crying anymore. I'm not anything at all. But it's kind of comfortable lying on this rug. The fibers are cool and smooth and soft.

Is this what crazy feels like? I don't feel any different.

I lie there for a long time. Then I sit up. Someone is home. There are voices—real voices—down in the kitchen, cupboards banging shut. I check the bed. None of it is there anymore—the wrapping paper, the scroll, the letter. They're all gone. A brief flood of hope rises in me, but no. The carpet is still here. I'm sitting on it.

"Renny?" Lauren's voice calls from the foot of the stairs.

I kneel beside the carpet and smooth away the imprint my body has left. Then, even more gently, I smooth it again, as if I can smooth away even the signs of my own smoothing. Then I roll the whole thing into a tight bundle and shove it under my bed.

Four

Across the table, Parnell Florian digs a fork into an enormous potpie. He gets a full mouthful before he notices I'm there. "Miss Drake!" he mumbles, "How good to see you!"

Great. Another dream. Well, crazy people dream too. Maybe I really should keep a dream journal—*My Descent into Madness* by Irene Drake. I can't think of anything intelligent to say, so I ask a dumb question instead. "How come you're always eating?"

He looks up, a flake of piecrust in his beard. "I cannot help it that you always arrive at the supper hour. We are not in the same time zone, you know."

"You have a time zone?"

"Naturally I have a time zone. Did you think I lived on a cloud somewhere?"

I shrug. "Normal dreams don't live anywhere."

"Ah." He nods. "Well, Miss Drake, while this may be a dream, I promise you *I* am not—any more than that tapestry you received today is." He spears something brown and dripping and steers it into his mouth.

"I suppose it'd be pointless for me to ask how it got into my bedroom."

He finishes his mouthful before answering this time. "I could go into all of that but yes, I suppose it really would be, for the most part, pointless. What matters is you received it in good order, yes? No problems I hope?"

I stare, probing his coffee-brown eyes. "Uh, no. I mean, it looks fine."

"Good, good!" He grins, waggling his fork.

20

"Does it really fly?"

"Oh, assuredly. Your carpet was, for the last two-and-a-half decades, the property of one Cyril Longbow, late of Manchester, England. It served him admirably. Whatever complaints he had, they were not about the carpet. And of course, it has been thoroughly checked. I promise you, it is in perfect working order."

I watch him maneuver another forkful into his mouth. "What happened to him?"

"Mmm?"

"The Cyril guy from England."

"Ah, yes." He retrieves his napkin and pats his lips. "Cyril Longbow. He died, sadly. Nothing to do with the carpet. A street accident. Something with the number seven bus, I believe. We had quite a time getting the rug back, actually. Locked in a bus station locker. Curious tale." He waves his fork like he's erasing a blackboard. "But really, I'm not at liberty to say. Confidentiality and all that." He puts down the fork. "I can promise you, we shall always regard your privacy as a sacred trust."

"Uh huh. Who's we?"

"Miss Drake! The Arcane Order of Carpet Flyers! The Fellows of Shaheen! The Sublime Society of Scudders! Didn't you read the contract we sent you?"

"A contract? Is that what that was?"

"Well, not in the conventional sense. I mean, there's no actually signing involved." He smiles and does a flexing thing with his eyebrows. "Our contract exists on an entirely other level."

"You mean it only exists in my head."

This makes him frown. "Well, no, I wouldn't go that far."

"It's all right. I'm okay with it all being in my head. I mean, it's probably all going to go *pop!*" —I mime something popping with my fingertips— "any minute now, and I'm going to wake up in the lockdown ward with a little cup full of pills to swallow, but in the meantime, I've just decided to go with it." I don't know why I'm telling him this. Apparently I'm going to be one of those chatty psychotics.

He stares at me, brows scrunched, lips pushed out. "You are an unusual person, Miss Drake."

That's one way of putting it. "I gotta tell you, though, I may not be far enough gone yet, because the thing didn't work for me."

"Pardon?"

"The carpet. I tried everything. It never moved an inch."

"Oh, well, naturally. That's because you haven't been introduced."

Introduced. Naturally.

"No carpet will fly for you until you've been properly introduced. They're very fussy about that sort of thing. You must use its proper name, or it will tend to ignore you."

"It has a name?"

He sighs. I get the feeling he's not going to be one of those adults who tells me how bright I am. "Of course it has a name. Why would you think it wouldn't?"

I'm not sure how to answer this. "I don't know. I guess maybe because it's a carpet?"

"This is not your ordinary carpet."

I could have told him that so far, it looked exactly like an ordinary carpet, as least as far as the not-flying thing goes. But I don't say anything. If I'm really going to "go with it" like I said, I suppose I need to stop being so difficult. I try to put something like a smile on my face.

He gets a worried look, and when he speaks again, it's in a low, comforting sort of voice. "Miss Drake. It's normal to have doubts. It's only to be expected. But I can promise you are not having a nervous breakdown or anything like that. You are not delusional."

I consider mentioning that if he's part of the delusion, then he'd hardly be in a position to tell me if I'm deluded or not, but I don't say that either. Instead I say, "How do you know?"

"Pardon?"

"How do you know I'm not crazy? You just met me."

"Because," he says, as if it's all quite obvious, "the Orb would have told me."

He takes a dinner roll from a basket, rips it in half, and dunks the larger half into the wreck of his pie crust. I wait until he finishes chewing and swallowing before I ask. "Okay. I'll bite. What's the Orb?"

He gets a smile on his face. "Mere words," he says, "cannot do it justice."

He stands and crooks a finger at me. I swear he almost giggles like he's about to show me where the cookies are hidden. He's a round little man, not much taller than I am, but there's well over two hundred pounds of him packed into that lilac dressing gown. He pads across the flagstone floor and leads me to a little curtained alcove set between two big, floor-to-ceiling bookshelves. The curtain is printed with tiny flowers and little purple butterflies.

"Now *this*," he says, with a dramatic pause, "is, beyond a doubt, the only one of its kind in the entire world."

He whisks back the curtain. A glass sphere—smaller than a volleyball, larger than a grapefruit—sits on a small wooden table. Its glow warms the tiny space.

"This," he announces with obvious pride, "is the Orb of Descrying."

It could be a crystal ball from a gypsy fortune-teller, but it isn't filled with swirling mist. Sparkling flecks of metal—gold, silver, brass—swarm about, reflected in the curved glass. Parnell runs a fingertip along the top of the globe, and some of the flecks brighten and swim upward like feeding time at the aquarium.

"Those are your flock-mates, Miss Drake. Each speck represents a unique member of the Order. I can see L.G. Arne of Falls Church. And that is K. Smout of Darbyshire. There's M. Ahubudu of Anuradhapura, and Z. Fellows of Johannesburg."

"How can you tell one speck from another?"

"Ah." He beckons me over and steps aside. High up on the side of the sphere a circular lens sits, a magnifying lens. While I'm looking, a disk of cut gold floats by, glittering, paper thin. Behind it, a ten-pointed star of silver-blue metal spins slowly past.

"One of our oldest members, S. Valdemar or Cairo. Illinois, that is. And there is J. Ulara of Belem."

"You really know them all just by looking?"

"Some. Some not. But I have help." He holds his finger out again, and lowers it until it just touches the sphere. A thread of white light drops through the clear liquid until it finds one of the tiny flakes. The flake lights up copper red and begins to rise, still connected to the bright thread. "G. Tansing of Bharatpur."

He pulls his finger back and the thread vanishes. G. Tansing drifts into the frame of the magnifying lens. He, or she, is shiny white with a lot of complicated branches.

Parnell touches the globe again. "R. Figgisdottir. Reykjavik." This one is a blue disk of interlocking hexagons.

"Can you talk to them like this, when you touch the glass?"

He shakes his head. "Not exactly. Through the Orb, I can initiate a dream meeting. It's far easier to make a connection this way than trying to speak directly. In dream-sleep, your mental defenses drop. You are open to things your conscious mind cannot accept, not entirely anyway. It makes communication much more straightforward because your mind is not simultaneously telling you what you are hearing cannot be true. It allows me greater access. I could even plant suggestions, ideas you would accept entirely as our own once you awoke. Rest assured, Miss Drake, I would never do that. That is not the Orb's purpose."

"So, am I in there?"

"Absolutely. Just give me a moment." He adjusts the lens and peers into the depths. When he prods the glass with a fingertip, a tendril of light catches a tiny flake of floating bronze.

Something really odd happens. I'm standing on the floor in Parnell's dining room, but I'm also lying in bed at home. I'm staring up through the curved lens, watching my own distorted face stare down, watching my own sleeping face. I've never seen myself sleep before.

My mouth is open. I look like a dimwit. Parnell coaxes me up toward the viewing lens, but my little flake keeps sinking back.

He smiles. "You are a little reluctant. Not quite decided, *n'est-ce pas?*"

There's sludge at the bottom of the globe. When I look close, I can see it's made up of flakes—like the others, only dull instead of shiny, and not moving.

"What happened to those?"

He gets a weird look on his face. I hardly know him, so maybe I can't judge, but there's something uncomfortable, almost painful, behind his eyes.

"Those, well," he coughs, "those are out of circulation. Things happen. Carpets don't last forever. Though," he brightens, "some are phenomenally old. Did you know your own carpet is over five hundred years old? It dates from the Safavid dynasty, one of the last great periods of carpet making." He puts a soft, heavy hand on my shoulder and turns me back into the dining room. "Some are twice that old, even four times that old." He whisks the curtain closed again. "Carpets are amazingly durable. They are really only vulnerable to a few things—fire, of course, and moths. Mice too. Mice are curiously attracted to enchanted silk."

We're back at the table now, but he does not sit down. "Do you have any other questions? Your REM cycle will be ending soon. There are certain signs."

I have a pretty good idea what he's talking about. He's drifting out of focus, blurring at the edges. Everything seems somehow a little bit further away than it ought to be, like I'm looking through one of those fish-eye lens things.

"Wushin't there—" I give my head a hard shake, "—wasn't there shumthing about a name?"

"Yes! Yes, a name. I'd better hurry before you fade. Let me check the registry."

He goes to one of the bookshelves and pulls out a big leather volume. I sit, or stand, or maybe just float. He's getting smaller and smaller, and grayer and grayer. "Can't you make this stop?" I ask. "Ishn't this your meeting?" Some part of my addled brain thinks this is a pretty good observation. "I've heard about people controlling their own dreams."

He looks up, puzzled. "You mean like lucid dreaming?"

I nod. It takes a lot of effort. The ceiling and the floor are having a hard time agreeing which is supposed to be up and which down. "Right," I say. "Lushid."

He pushes his lips out and shakes his head. "This isn't that."

Then it's morning. I open my eyes. I'm lying in bed.

Damn! I didn't get the name. Now I'll have to wait for Parnell to connect with me again. Downstairs, I hear the clunk and gurgle of a water pipe. It's time to get up. I reach down to pull back the covers, but there's something in my hand already: a scroll. It's the same heavy parchment like before, but much smaller—a single, tightly rolled page. It says:

Dear Miss Drake;

My apologies for the rude termination of our meeting. These things happen. The carpet goes by the name of Maysa. Be polite. And please try to keep this information to yourself. A name, once given, cannot be lightly taken back.

Yours,
P. Florian.

Five

By the time school is over, I've decided one thing: there's no possible way any of this can be real. I'm not an idiot. I know there's no such thing as flying carpets. If it isn't real, then I really have gone crazy, just like I always figured I would.

The thing I can't figure is what I'm going to do about it. If I'm crazy, if I've really gone nuts, do I want to give into the pills and therapy, or do I want to see just how far crazy will take me? I saw my mom do some really messed-up stuff, and there was nothing pretty about it. When she wasn't bouncing off the walls, she was usually frightened and paranoid. Maybe I'm just as crazy as she is now, but the odd thing is, I'm not scared. I'm really not. I don't know whether that's a good thing or a bad thing. I don't know how much of this is real, but who does? I mean, who really knows anything? So what have I got to lose?

What have I got to lose is probably the worst reason anybody ever had for doing anything, but that's what I got.

I hurry home. The house is blissfully empty.

Upstairs, the carpet is right where I left it this morning, rolled up tight. I spread it out on the floor beside the bed, picking away the dust bunnies. It really is a pretty thing in an antique kind of way. The

27

colors pop and shift when you move around it. The tiny birds are amazingly detailed. In some places, it's almost as though you can see individual feathers, but I suppose those are just the carpet fibers.

Maysa. Her name is Maysa.

The letter didn't say how to pronounce it. Like all of the other documents, it did a disappearing act shortly after I'd finished reading it. May-sa? My-sah? I take my shoes off and kneel down beside it. "Uh, Maysa?"

I sound like an idiot. I try again. Parnell said we needed to be introduced. That's going to sound even stupider. "Hello, Maysa, my name is Renny. Irene. Irene Drake."

I'm right. I sound like a moron. Plus, nothing happens. I don't know what I should be expecting. I put my palm flat on the smooth, soft surface, and give it a stroke. It's nice. I like the feeling of it.

It's just an ordinary carpet.

I crawl out into the center and sit cross-legged. Maybe it needs me to be sitting on it. It? He? She? Is Maysa a girl's name? *It's a carpet, idiot! It can't be a boy or a girl!*

"Maysa," I begin again. "Hi. My name is Renny. I hope you don't mind me sitting on you, but that guy Parnell said you were— well, he said you could fly and, well, either you know this already or you don't, I guess."

And right there, between *I* and *guess,* something happens. A tiny trembling. Maybe. Maybe it's me who trembled. Maybe my leg is falling asleep.

"Are you there? Maysa, is that you?"

This time, I'm almost certain it's coming from the carpet. A little flutter, like in your stomach when you think something is about to happen. It didn't come from me, or at least it didn't start with me.

"Wow! You really are there, aren't you?" I stroke a silver branch, following it out to where it ends in a spray of violet leaves. A warm feeling nuzzles down in my belly. I wriggle my fingers into the weave.

She likes it. The *carpet* likes it. I know that's impossible, but I also know it's true. And even while I know this is all way too crazy to be real, another part of me has a different opinion: Who cares?

A little silk bird quivers. For a moment, I almost think it's going to leap off its tiny branch and perch on my finger. I'm smiling. "Wow." I say it again. "I guess all I have to do now is figure out how to make you fly—whoa!"

The floor bunches beneath me and flings itself straight upward. "Ow! Hey!" My head thumps the ceiling, once, twice. "Cut that out!"

Maysa drops and spins like a turntable. "Stop it!" I pitch forward, sprawled out flat, my legs tangled beneath me. "Just—stop!" Again we hit the ceiling. We bounce three times. "Ow! Ugh!" We reach the peak of the slanted ceiling, and Maysa hangs there, pressing me against the sheetrock.

"Maysa! Put me down!"

We drop. I hit the edge of the bed and lurch forward. Maysa swings back again like some demonic pendulum. We spin hard once, front for back, jolt forward, then freeze. When I open my eyes, I am about eighteen inches from my closet door.

"All right," I say, keeping my voice perfectly calm. "Just stay, okay? Just don't do that agaaiin...!"

The damned thing rams forward, hits the door, then swings around the other way. I see the window getting larger and larger.

"Maysa!"

Everything stops. I'm hanging, six feet in the air, just above my desk chair. "Don't move!" I bark. Slowly, I pick myself up, back to a sitting position. "Just stay."

She's hovering, swaying just a little. A shiver passes through her. It's not fear. She's happy. She's excited. She wants more.

"Slowly," I say, speaking very carefully, "*slowly.*"

We go *very* slowly. We spend maybe ten minutes, going in little fits and flurries, touring the tiny room, trying not to hit any more walls or ceilings. It's a clunky, awkward flight, but that isn't Maysa's fault.

29

She's ready and eager to show me what she can do. It just isn't possible in the confines of my bedroom.

"Okay. That's enough for now."

She lowers me to the floor and I climb off. My knees are trembling. I sit on the floor beside her, stroking the leaves of a silk tree. "Tonight," I say, almost whispering, eyeing my bedroom window, "after everyone has gone to bed."

A vibration pulses through the shiny fibers. It's unmistakable: a purr.

***

It takes forever for all of them to finally go to bed. I keep flitting around, from living room to kitchen, kitchen to bedroom. At one point I even go out on the front porch to check the weather. Lauren gives me a strange look. I couldn't look more suspicious if I tried.

Finally I just go upstairs and sit on my bed. I fake my way through some very real homework with my French-English dictionary propped beside me on my pillow, but it's no good. I can't think about homework.

A little after eleven, I hear footsteps trudging up the stairs. I switch off the bedside lamp and wait in the dark. I hear water in the pipes, the creak of a floorboard. When five minutes of nothing but silence pass, I snap on the lamp again. I tiptoe to the window and undo the catch. It's an old window, one of those kinds that slide up. It scrapes when it slides. At about three-quarters open, it sticks and won't go any farther. I walk soft-footed back to the bed and pull Maysa out and carry her to the window.

Her. Funny how she became a she. I didn't even decide, it just happened.

It's a small window, but I know I fit through. This isn't the first time I've sat on that sill. There's a big ash tree just a few yards away. During the summer, it pretty much crowds out the night sky. A lopsided moon hangs high, snagged in its branches.

Nice night for flying.

My stomach squirms like something's living down there. What the hell am I doing?

No. I'm not going to think about that. Either this *is* real, or that whole freaky thing that happened in my room today is a schizo delusion—including the bruise on my elbow. If I fall off the roof, well, there's grass and oleander bushes underneath. It isn't going to kill me. It's what-have-I-got-to-lose time.

I have a feeling I'm about to find out.

I pull myself through the window frame and squat on the roof shingles. Unscrolled, Maysa stretches out on the air at my knees. The invitation couldn't be any plainer if she said it out loud: *climb on.*

I test it with my palm. It's as firm and cushiony as an air mattress. I push down with both hands. Lightness fills me. The feeling of buoyancy flows up through the palms of my hands, up my arms, filling my chest. A tingling. It's hard to explain, and even harder to resist, I guess, because a few seconds later, I'm sitting cross-legged in mid-air. My heart beats fast, but it's a good feeling. I keep my hands pressed into the fibers. Excitement—her excitement—is coming right up out of the weave. She can't wait.

I take a breath. "All right, Maysa, just start slowly—"

We tear right through the branches of the ash tree.

"Hey!" I yelp. "Slow down!"

Twigs snap. A branch scrapes my face.

"Stop! Stop it, May—ugh." I spit out a mouthful of leaves. "Ow! What the—?"

She swings hard, straight up. I throw my arm over my face. She breaches like a dolphin, clears the highest branch, and sails out over the neighbor's garage. I push my face in close to her.

"Maysa! Slow down!"

She speeds up. We race up to the peak of the neighbor's roof and down the other side into their yard.

"Maysa!"

She leaps the back fence and into another yard. We slide across the patio, jump a glass-topped picnic table, and head straight for a structure of wooden beams and metal bars, a curving plastic slide...

"Maysa! Up! Up!"

She doesn't need me to tell her. Already, she's pulling up. She clears the jungle gym, clears the fence, clears the sweet gum tree that towers over everything. Up she soars into the dark sky, slowing—finally slowing. She levels off and eases into a long banking turn.

"Good," I croon, my heart pounding. "Good girl. Easy does it."

We're above everything now—trees, rooftops, power lines. When she swings around, I can see the Teller's house, my own window standing open. A cat runs along the backyard fence. It stops to stare, flashing amber eyes, then disappears.

"Maysa." I keep my voice low and calm. "Up. *Slowly.*"

The neighborhood drops away beneath us. The rooftops spread. I can see the whole division from here. A few windows flicker with blue television light, but otherwise, houses are mostly dark.

Way off, past the tops of the eucalyptus trees, Albuquerque is a yellow glow. Trucks are moving up and down the interstate, making all-night runs. Two years ago in eighth grade, I gave that answer for career day: truck driver. I wanted to be a truck driver. It was just a spontaneous answer. I'd never thought about it before. But as soon as I said it, I realized it sounded pretty good. Overnighters driving all alone, nothing but the road and the mind-numbing roar of the engine. I got some laughs over that one. Barry Peebles and some ugly kid whose name I didn't know baited me about it for days. Truck drivers were dumb rednecks. Women truck drivers were dumb, redneck dykes.

I didn't care. It was amazing, actually, how much I didn't care.

A roll of wind passes under us. Maysa ripples.

"Okay, that's good. We're high enough."

We hang there, turning—slowly one way, then back the other, like a lazy weather vane. I can see the highway now, a strip of crawling lights dividing one dark desert from another. If someone looked up, what would they see? Just an object, hanging in the moonlight, unidentifiable. A UFO.

My stomach gives a gurgle, and I laugh. I'm a UFO.

The wind cuts up and Maysa rides it like a wave, up one side and down the other. Without any warning at all, she dives. The sky tips upward. I throw myself flat and grab the front fringe. The wind rushes in my face. "Maysa. Easy."

Just like that, she pulls up, and once again, we're hanging in the gusty breeze, hardly moving at all. "What was that about?"

Her only answer is a shudder—a pleasurable shudder.

"You liked that, didn't you?"

She frisks to the left, then skids to a stop again. A swell of wind passes through us and we bob like a cork.

"Whoa, girl!" I hold the fringe more tightly. "You like flying fast, don't you?"

Again, the shudder.

"Well. Okay, then."

We fly—fast. The air is thin and crisp and full of wind. There's a whole texture to wind I never knew about before. It blows in layers. Narrow streams of wind are sandwiched between blankets of calm air. Riffles can form out of nothing. Sudden squalls, then sudden stillness—then wild, tumbling rapids. I have no idea what I'm doing up here. It's all Maysa. I'm just along for the ride. And I get it now, why she couldn't wait. This is what she wanted to show me: the high wind.

This is where she belongs. It's her home.

We ride for a long time, so long I'm not even surprised to see the sun starting to rise. Except it isn't. It's only Albuquerque glowing over the mesa. I laugh at the false dawn and then plunge into the night again. I brace myself for the wind and let the roar fill my ears.

Then I hear the bells.

Only they can't be bells. It's the middle of the night, and I'm miles from everything. We slow to a hover and I listen. It *is* bells. But it isn't. It isn't even a sound, really. I mean, there are bells, yes— beautiful bells, high and low, chiming and pealing in complicated patterns—but they aren't sounding in my ears. They're coming up through my knees and the palms of my hands.

"Maysa?"

The music swells up, with an off-kilter rhythm. The beat falls in a funny way, landing sometimes in one place and sometimes in another. It's strange, but it isn't the strangeness I really notice. It's the restlessness, the craziness, the excitement of the thing.

All at once, it stops.

"Maysa, was that you?"

A voice tickles my ear. *Fine, Renny. Very fine!*

I whip around. Someone giggles. Then someone else, behind me. I whirl around again. There's nothing. Two tiny voices out of nowhere are sharing a joke.

"Hey! Who is that?"

Whoo! Whoo!

That isn't Maysa. I twist around again. "Where are you? Who just spoke?"

Laughter gusts again, and a tiny voice repeats the word: *spoke!*

Then, from all around me: *Spoke! Spake! Spook! Speak!* The words spring like plucked metal, tinny and brittle. There's another little volley of giddy laughter, and then they are gone.

34

Six

Three nights later, I have one of those dreams again. I'm walking in a dusty stone staircase, winding my way up, step by step. I'm not alone. Right in front of me, a gauzy swatch of fabric darts and twists through the air, leading me on. Light spills from a doorway at the top of the stairs. The swatch climbs until it's just in front of the open door, turns like it's checking to see if I'm still following, then wafts through the door.

None of this even seems strange to me anymore. I follow the scrap of flying fabric through the doorway and I'm in that same room again. Parnell sits at the same table, eating a muffin. He doesn't notice me, but he notices the swatch. "There you are," he says. It circles twice, orbiting his head. He holds a hand up, fingers spread. The silk winds itself around his knuckles.

He turns and looks at me. "And there *you* are."

I enter the room all the way. The little swatch lifts itself upward and floats down again, landing on the sleeve of his violet dressing gown.

"Don't tell me. A flying handkerchief."

Parnell chuckles. "Such a scamp."

The handkerchief curls and stretches into a lazy yawn. Parnell scoops it up and holds it in his open palm. "Miss Drake, meet—well, meet my handkerchief. I can't tell you her name, of course."

"The handkerchief has a name?"

"Naturally."

The swatch extends a corner. I put my finger out. Its touch is just the faintest nuzzle, like a down-feather brushing my skin. Right away, I hear tiny music, like a pennywhistle playing a soft dancing tune. Parnell smiles. "Well, well. She likes you."

"Is that coming from her?"

"They all have songs. Your carpet too—though perhaps she hasn't sung for you yet."

"Sure she did. The very first night."

"Really? Well, excellent! That's a very good sign. It is just another of the mysterious, marvelous things about enchanted silk. It has awareness, you know. Personality, even. The better it gets to know you, the more it will reveal." He clucks twice with his tongue. The handkerchief scrunches down in his palm and then dives into the breast pocket of his gown, disappearing for good. Parnell breaks what remains of his muffin in two, and stuffs the larger bit into his mouth.

"So. You've been flying a lot."

There's no question mark at the end of his crumb-mumbled sentence, but I nod anyway. I have been—every night, in fact. On Wednesday I ran the dry river up to the Sandia Crest, then skimmed the dark surface of the reservoir at Jemez Canyon. Last night it was the weird lunar salt-flats out beyond Estancia and a wild ride through the treetops at Cibola. "You've been watching me? With that globe thing?"

"The Orb," Parnell corrects. "Not watching. I wouldn't spy on you. But it is necessary for me to keep tabs on you. You," his smile widens, "are one of the most interesting new members we have seen in a long while."

"I am?"

"Oh, assuredly! Your progress is being followed with great interest. But that isn't anything you need to concern yourself with. The carpet," he leans a little closer, "it is living up to your expectations, I trust?"

I laugh. What expectations could I have had, except for maybe falling off the roof and dying? The truth is, it's fantastic. It's the thing I look forward to. It gets me through the day. And it's not just the flying—it's Maysa. When we fly, she gets so excited, so happy, I feel it too. Like the greatest contact high ever.

I don't say all of this to Parnell. Instead I say, "It's great. I know it's all probably just some schizophrenic dream, but as long as it lasts, it's okay with me."

His frown twitches an eyebrow. "I must say, Miss Drake, you are persistent in your disbelief. But I guess time will tell." He gives his fingers a soft snap. "I meant to ask you. At our first meeting, you mentioned something about voices. Do you remember?"

I nod. "Of course."

"Have you heard them since? During actual flight?"

I'd been wondering if he'd ask. "Yeah," I admit. "Once."

"And was it the same as the first time? High pitched, gigging, full of—enthusiasm?"

I nod again.

He puts his fingers together in front of his chest. "I've been doing some reading on the subject. There isn't a lot of literature on flying carpets, but what there is"—he waves a hand at his bookshelves—"I've got. I believe what you have been experiencing are windsprites." He clasps his hands together and washes them in the air. "In the thirteenth century there was a priest, Monseigneur Raphael DellaPonte. A mystic. He had some unconventional views, but he was also a member of the Order, and riding a magic carpet is going to give you a unique perspective on things. There are several pages on him in Gilderscott's *A History of Enchanted Textiles*. Anyway, his description is much like your own. 'Merrie spirits' he called them. 'Laughing fairies from beyond our ken'—I believe that's the phrase he used. He

37

believed they were actual emissaries from the spirit world, and credited them with the power of prognostication."

"Like telling the future?"

"Precisely. Of course, he was excommunicated as a heretic, and possibly burnt at the stake. History is a little vague on that part."

He smiles like he thinks this story of his is going to make my day. It doesn't. "So aside from me and some crackpot priest, has anybody else heard these...?"

"Windsprites," he fills in the word. "And yes. Every now and then, history tells us of some rider who reported hearing something similar. Of course, there are those who insist that they can only be a figment of the imagination—an illusion brought on by altitude, perhaps."

"So they *aren't* real?"

"I didn't say that. I only said some folk believe in them, some don't." He yawns. "Either way, I wouldn't let it worry you."

I raise an eyebrow. "No?"

"Not at all. You've entered a new world, Miss Drake. You will see and hear some strange things riding on a carpet. Believe me, I've heard some mighty odd tales over the years. Though you—" he taps his own ear "—are my first *hearer.*"

I give him a long look. He looks ridiculously pleased. "I envy you, Miss Drake. You are finding a whole new you! Stepping free from your earthbound self! It is a privilege. And though you have earned it, it is still wise to regard it as such."

"Earned it?"

"Oh, absolutely! You wouldn't be here if you weren't inherently worthy."

I can't think of a single thing I've ever done to make me worthy of Maysa. I shake my head. "I don't know about that."

"It really doesn't make any difference. You have flown, several times now. You have bonded with the carpet. And more importantly, she has bonded with you." He drops his voice. "I hope you are not having second thoughts?"

I feel my eyes go wide. "What? No! No way."

"Ah well, good. Because frankly it's a wrenching thing for a carpet, bonding and then sundering that bond again so quickly. But I was sure you wouldn't want to. So everything is going well? I am glad to see you have been waiting until nightfall to do your flying. Sometimes our more youthful flyers get a little reckless and fly during daylight hours. But it's terribly foolhardy. A cloaking spell is always more effective in the deepest darkness, and that's especially true for a novice."

"Cloaking spell?"

"You did use a cloaking spell, didn't you?"

"Uh—I don't think so."

He makes a disapproving cluck. "It is not difficult. Didn't I tell you about the cloaking spell? No?" He shrugs, "Well, it's my own fault, then. But really," he says, rising from his seat, "it is the most basic spell. No flyer should be without it." He crosses to the nearest bookshelf and lets his eyes search. "Here we are." He pulls down a leather-bound volume, thumbing through it as he walks back to the table. "You'll have to commit the incantation to memory but I don't think it will give you any trouble. It is only eight syllables." He sets the open book on the table. I read:

> The Spell of Concealing, known more commonly—though less accurately—as a Cloaking Spell, is one of the simplest incantations and one every flyer should master. The particular combination of syllables: ro-sur-suh-suh-ob-scuse-ay-mor—spoken aloud or sub-vocally, shall call forth the desired response. Repetition may be necessary, possibly a great deal of repetition, but with time, the spell will become easier. It is, after all, within a carpet's nature to seek concealment. The Sub Rosa spell that attends to acceptance of membership in the Order is a part of this same tendency. Self-preservation depends upon secrecy. Every carpet knows this. Still, the term Cloaking Spell is somewhat optimistic. The Spell of Concealing depends on a number of favorable conditions for its

effectiveness. First and foremost, any awareness by an observer prior to 'cloaking' will render the spell useless. Awareness will endure the enchantment, allowing continuity...

I look up. "I'm supposed to remember this?"

"Cloaking is a basic precaution, Miss Drake. Restrict yourself to night time flying, always use a cloak, and the chances of your being discovered are very slim."

"Yeah, okay. Only—" I scan the page again. *Ro-sur-suh-suh-ob-scuse-ay-mor. Ro-sur-suh-suh-ob-scuse-ay-mor.*

"Yes?"

"Well, I've never done any spells before. I mean, I've never even believed in spells before."

"You've never had a flying carpet before. And it is much the same thing. The magic is in the carpet. Flying, being cloaked—you don't do these things, your carpet does. An incantation is simply a way of telling her what you want her to do. It takes a little practice, naturally, but before you know it you'll be cloaking without even thinking."

My eyes go back to the page. "If you say so."

He wrinkles his brow. "Is there a problem?"

Ro-sur-suh-suh-ob-scuse-ay-mor. "No, I guess not. It's just, well, how will I know if it's working? What will it feel like?"

He studies me, tapping his finger on the rim of his plate. "Hmm. That's a fair point. It is always advisable to have a mentor of some sort. Someone to help you over the rough spots." He gives me another long stare. "You know," his face brightens "I think we're in luck." He presses his hands together with obvious delight. "Yes! This will work out splendidly. We need to get you with some folks who can give you some help, face to face, walk you through the finer points..." he lets his sentence drift off unfinished and a broad smile spreads across his face. "The time has come, Miss Drake."

I stare at him. "Time?"

"Time for *you*," he gives a playful little chuckle, "to meet your flock!" He smiles in a very self-satisfied way and then stuffs the last crumb of muffin between his lips.

"Yes indeed," he says, chewing. "High time."

Seven

Ro-sur-suh-suh-oh-scuse-ay-mor.

I wake with the string of strange syllables in my head.

This is just getting goofier and goofier. Now I've got a magic spell. I get to be invisible. And my flock. Can't forget about that. Tonight I get to meet my flock and they'll teach me how to be invisible.

Ro-sur-suh-suh-oh-scuse-ay-mor.

I'd better write that thing down before I forget it. I flop over onto the side of the bed and dig around in the nightstand drawer until I find a pencil stub and a scrap of paper.

Written out, it doesn't look quite as goofy for some reason. A bunch of syllables that'll make me invisible. I say them out loud. *Ro-sur-suh-suh-oh-scuse-ay-mor.*

Probably I need to be sitting on Maysa for it to work. It's Saturday morning. Lauren will be downstairs reading the paper, drinking coffee. Gretchen is probably watching TV. Maybe it's not too risky. I pull Maysa out and spread her over the rumpled bed. She hums and gives an eager little toss.

"Sorry, girl. Not flying time."

I climb on and take a deep breath. "Ro-sur, Suh-suh, Ob-scuse-ay-mor!"

Nothing happens. I feel entirely ridiculous.

I try again. "Ro-sur, Suh-suh, Ob-scuse-ay-mor!"

It doesn't *feel* like anything is happening. But how is being invisible supposed to feel? I hold my hand up and try to see through it. That doesn't work either.

I try a third time, and a fourth, each time changing the length of the syllables and which ones I emphasize. From the mirror on my closet door, my very visible reflection studies me, muttering her own magic words. Can you be invisible and yet still be visible to yourself? If Lauren walked in right now, would she see an empty room?

I roll Maysa up into a bundle and stow her away again.

In the bathroom I turn on the water and look in the mirror. Pale eyes stare back, with grubby smudges underneath them. *Hello, Miranda. I figured I'd find you here.* I pull my lips back and examine my teeth until the steam makes the glass go pearly. Then I step inside the shower and let the hot rain needle my skin.

Tonight, at a place called Big Hatchet, there will be a gathering. Parnell called it a *kettle*. My flock will be there.

"Only the local chapter," he explained, "though they come from farther away than you might think."

"Will you be there?"

"Oh, heaven's no! But I will spread the word you might be coming. I'm sure they will be looking forward to meeting you."

Saturday night. Big Hatchet. Sounds loony. But reality has been keeping its distance lately. Why should this be any different?

***

Downstairs, Lauren's at her laptop, writing something. She looks up as I enter the kitchen.

"Well, there you are." She peers at me. "You've washed your hair!"

43

I'm not surprised she noticed. I also have on a clean pair of blue jeans and a mostly unwrinkled shirt.

"Do you have plans?"

"Huh? No. Well, actually yeah. Tonight. I'm, uh, going over to Caddy's. There's a party."

"At Caddy's?"

"No. At Stacy Brunswick's house."

Stacy Brunswick is a straight-A student and not the wild party type. And Lauren hardly knows her mom. For an improvisation, it's pretty good. Never mind that I haven't even talked to Stacy in probably a year.

"That's nice. You need a ride?"

"Uh, no. Caddy is going to drive." The offer kind of catches me by surprise. I haven't actually figured how I'm going to work the departure. "I'm going to walk over to her house and she's going to drive. She'll give me a ride home."

It sounds a little strange but Lauren is tapping keys again, only half-listening. "Okee-dokey."

When I open the fridge door, she says, "Try not to be super-late, okay?"

"Yeah, sure. No problem." Super-late. Roughly translated, that means maybe one o'clock on a Saturday. It also means no one is likely to be waiting up.

***

A little before eight, I look out the window. The sky is growing dark. I put a windbreaker on over my T-shirt and tie on a pair of tennis shoes. Downstairs, I can hear the television going. Someone is rattling around in the kitchen. Lee is in Santa Fe at a seminar. Amy, no doubt, is with her boyfriend Jeff.

All evening long I've been going over my plans—or at least thinking about how I *ought* to be going over my plans. Problem is, there isn't that much *to* go over. Step One: sneak out. Step Two: find Big Hatchet. That's all I got. I spend a lot of time staring at the map

44

on the computer. Big Hatchet is a long way away, down in the boot-heel of New Mexico, almost at the border. It could take hours to get there. And finding it on a map is one thing, but finding it for real and in the dark is another thing completely. But if one thing is clear after a week of flying, it's that Maysa is a lot more than a couple of yards of flying silk. She has an amazing sense of direction. I don't worry about getting lost with her. All I have to do is think *let's go home* and she always knows. She is also unbelievably fast. I've flown over highways, tracking the headlights. She can easily outrun the average car.

So that's my real plan in a nutshell: trust Maysa.

The only question left is how to smuggle her out of the house. She might fit in a backpack if I fold her up. I empty the backpack on to the desk, I even shake a year's worth of crumbs into the wastepaper basket, but it doesn't feel right stuffing Maysa inside like an old sweatshirt. Instead, I take her to the window and heave open the sash. I check the neighbor's windows, the sidewalk. No one's watching.

I say, "I'll be down in a minute, okay?" Then I drop her into the bushes below.

***

"I'm going now."

Lauren looks up from her newspaper.

"Okay. Have a good time."

She turns a page and keeps on reading. I turn for the door.

"Hey, you sure you don't want a ride over?"

"No. I'm sure. It's okay." I put a hand on the doorknob and then remember to add, "But thanks, anyway."

I find Maysa under the oleanders. "You okay?"

A silly question. I unroll Maysa, and climb on.

"Ready?" Another silly question—but of course it isn't Maysa I'm asking. We rise straight up, turning slowly.

"*Ro-sur, Suh-suh, Ob-scuse-ay-mor. Ro-sur, Suh-suh, Ob-scuse-ay-mor.*" It's barely dark. I have no idea whether this so-called spell is doing anything but I don't stop chanting. We keep on rising, going higher

45

than usual. There's still color in the sky, a faint trace of blue just barely resting on the western horizon. The moon is milky—nearly, but not quite full: an imperfect pearl.

West, I think, *and south*. I try to call up the pictures in my memory, the satellite images on the computer, the map to Big Hatchet.

"Okay, girl. Let's go."

***

An hour? Maybe an hour and a half?

The dark land unrolls below me. For a while we follow the path of Highway 25 and its trickle of headlights. Then, just when I see the glare of Truth or Consequences, we veer to the west.

The map in my head is barely a sketch—a few familiar points and then a whole lot of nothing—but Maysa seems to know where she's going. Ever since we left she's held a steady course, high and fast. I let her run.

After a length of unbroken darkness, we cross a quiet highway. A few trucks nose their way east to west, west to east. That has to be Interstate 10. The glow to the east must be a city called Deming. We're getting close.

Somewhere out in all that darkness a mountain is hiding. Maysa flies on without any sign of uncertainty. She's singing again— the same melody, a clanking, tumbling choir of bells and chimes. I stroke silk with my thumb. "I like your song."

She keeps singing. If anything, she sings a little louder.

Another twenty minutes and we begin to slow. It takes me a minute to be sure it's really happening. By the time I'm certain, I also realize we're descending. Maysa's gone silent. The sky brims with stars. As we drop lower, the wash of moonlight begins to pick shapes out of the darkness: rock and shadow; a dry gulch; a long silver stretch of sand clumped with desert grass. The moon catches the white of a startled jackrabbit. It bounds zigzag across the desert floor and then vanishes.

When I look up again, I see it. From above it would have been lost in the darkness. From this low angle, it cuts a jagged notch in the sea of stars. It's not all that big. In daylight I might not even notice it, but here, in the darkness and the silence, it makes my breath catch. "Is that it?"

The answer is already obvious. She's heading straight for it. In another minute we're sliding up the flank of the mountain, heading for a pass between the two highest peaks. We slide right over the top and down the other side. Maysa banks hard to the west, and I stop dead in the air.

Across the dark dessert, maybe a mile away, a light flickers. Firelight. Out here in the middle of what might as well be nowhere, there's a campfire burning.

Eight

This is it. That has to be them.

But what if it isn't? What if it's just campers—or worse, creepy backwoods types with rifles and skinning knives? I drop down low until I'm level with the tops of the yuccas. A yelp of laughter drifts across the sand—a woman's laugh, mingled with several less raucous others. Maysa gives an eager quiver. I'm chewing my lip, but I let myself edge closer. After all, Maysa brought me here. What could have drawn her here except for other carpets?

It's a theory, anyway.

Another loud splash of laughter. How many people are there? Five? Ten? It's a strange place for a party. There's no campground out here, just a dirt road. But if they are creeps, I still have Maysa. I can get away easy. And even if they see me flying, who's going to believe them?

Cloaked! I should be cloaked! I repeat the incantation under my breath. "Ro-sur, Suh-suh, Ob-scuse-ay-mor. Ro-sur, Suh-suh, Ob-scuse-ay-mor."

It still makes me feel ridiculous. And it doesn't make me feel invisible. A woman yells, "Longbill! Bloody hell!" and brays rough laughter.

48

About ten yards from the fire, a scrawny tree stands, black branches upraised. I drift forward until I'm crouching, almost on the ground, by its trunk.

In a circle of stones, flames dance up a crooked tripod of branches. People sit, gathered in the flicker, some on low stones, others on the ground. Perched on a particularly high stone, a girl with short black hair dangles a cigarette from curled fingers. She wears a jacket that might be leather and a short skirt over striped tights. Firelight daubs her face, showing dark-ringed eyes and burgundy lips. Someone gets up and starts digging around in the shadows. When he stands up again he's holding a bottle in one hand, working the cork loose with the other.

A voice, female, says, "That's what I'm talking about!"

The bottle makes its way around the circle. A man says something that sounds like "cereal order" in a deep voice. Someone else yells, "Hear! Hear!" The girl with the short hair snorts laughter.

"Oh, yeah!" she barks. "The sodding order!" Her voice cuts through everything else.

A lanky man with a lopsided buzz-cut and a biker logo on his T-shirt stands and wanders away from the fire, searching the darkness. "So where the hell is she?"

"Give her a chance," another voice drawls.

The girl with the accent says, "Don't waste your time, Longbill. If she ain't here by now, she ain't coming."

The man—still standing, still staring out—says, "Maybe not." He stares directly at me. "Hey!" he shouts.

I stay put.

"Hey you, by the greasewood tree!" His voice has more than a hint of West Texas twang. Moonlight shows a toothy grin. Two others come over and stand beside him. One is a boy wearing jeans and a pullover shirt. He has an amazing mop of curly black hair.

The other is a dark man with a mustache. "Welcome," he says. His voice is as smooth and friendly as a spokesman on a television

49

commercial. "You know, I'm afraid that tree really doesn't hide you. Why don't you come and join us?"

I let the breath out of my lungs. Without my asking, Maysa nudges forward from shadow into moonlight. When we're about five paces away I say, "Guess my cloaking spell isn't so hot."

The boy with the curly hair grins and says, "You faded out there, just a little. But mostly, yeah. Not so hot."

"Come and have a seat," the man with the mustache says, "Better leave the carpet over there. They don't care much for campfires."

A few yards from the circle, carpets are spread about on a broad stone at the foot of a hackberry bush. I put Maysa down with the others. She purrs with obvious contentment. "Be good," I whisper.

I turn back to the fire. People are talking, drinking, laughing— but they're also watching me. I pick my way into the circle, avoiding eye contact. There isn't a lot of room. A man wearing a strange purple smock over a pair of baggy trousers scoots over. He's delicate looking, with thin wrists and a hollow face. He smiles as I sit.

The guy with the mustache talks first. "Have any trouble finding the place?"

I shake my head. "My carpet took me right here."

He nods. "They're good at that. Uncanny sense of direction, like homing pigeons. Once they've been somewhere, they never forget."

"I don't think she's ever been here before. As far as I know."

He shrugs. "No way to be sure. Do you know who owned her before you?"

I prod my memory. "Cyril something. Longbill?"

The guy with the Texas twang and the funny haircut gives me an odd look. "Yeah?" *Longbill* is what the English girl called *him*.

"I mean something *like* Longbill. Maybe Longbow. I only heard it once. I know he was from England." I look at the girl with the cigarette, but she isn't paying any attention at all.

Redstart says, "Scaup?"

An older man, sitting low on a flat rock, looks up, his eyes red and tired. He twists his mouth and sucks at his teeth. "No," he says, his voice a rusty scrape. "Never heard of him."

"Doesn't prove anything. Ruggers have been meeting at Big Hatchet since long before Scaup was a lad."

It's a woman who speaks. She has a luxurious, sing-song accent—not English: Irish. She has straight, shoulder-long hair under a straw-colored Stetson. The hand resting on her knee cradles a straight-stemmed pipe. Mixed in with the fire-smoke, I recognize the sweet smell of pipe tobacco.

The older man gives a sleepy nod. "Hard to imagine, but true."

"Carpets," the woman says, "have long memories. And their own histories."

"A carpet never forgets," someone else adds.

"So they say," the man with the mustache says. "At any rate, welcome to Big Hatchet. I'm called Redstart."

We're too far apart for a handshake so I just say, "Renny."

Redstart gives me everyone's name, going around the circle. The man beside me is Whimbrel. The lady with the pipe is Raven. The girl with the leather jacket and the cigarette, who is still ignoring all of us, is called Budgie. The boy with the hair—the one who had told me my cloaking spell wasn't so hot—is called Stonechat. He has a wry, almost impish smile, and dark brown eyes. He catches me studying his face, and gives me a big grin that makes my cheeks go warm. I look away fast.

"So," Redstart says, "You haven't been flying long."

"No," I admit. "My cloaking spell—"

"Needs work," Redstart agrees.

"Sucks," Longbill adds.

"We can fix it."

"How old are you?" Whimbrel asks. "If you don't mind my asking."

"Seventeen."

51

"And you're from Albuquerque?" This is from a young woman seated on the other side of Redstart. "I went to college at UNM." She has big round eyes and high, enviable cheekbones—and a tattoo high up on her left cheek of a small bird with an up-ticked tail. It blends so well with her coffee-and-cream complexion, it's only visible when the light catches it.

"Hey. You have to try some of this." A stout man with a round face and a maroon vest pushes a plastic cup into my hands.

"Easy, Junco," Redstart says. "She's only a kid."

"It's only a little gossamer. I'm not going to corrupt her."

I take the cup. "Wine?" I don't like wine. Lee doesn't drink, but Lauren usually has a bottle going. I've helped myself a few times, when I thought it wouldn't be missed.

"Not wine—gossamer mead! The legendary drink of carpet-flyers since time immemorial. When conditions are just so, it collects as ice crystals in noctilucent clouds. I gather them myself, and then bring them down to earth."

"Nauti-lucid?"

"Distilled," Junco says, "from the darkest fruit of night! Caught in the upturned jars of dawn!"

A woman—thirty-something, with a wave of mahogany hair—gives a bright laugh. "Good God, Junco! How much of this stuff did you drink?" From her voice, I'd say she's had a fair bit herself.

Redstart still looks uncomfortable. "You don't have to drink it. It *is* wine of a sort."

It doesn't smell like anything. I raise the cup and tip it back. It fizzes on the tongue, filling my mouth with mist. Sweet—honey? plums?—but with a tartness that isn't like either. I swallow.

And I smile.

Junco beams. "Good, huh? It comes out a little different every time," he explains, holding the bottle up. "It's not usually this blue or this fizzy, but that comes from lightning storms. A few months ago it was purple and frothy as beer."

I help myself to a slightly larger sip. It's cool in the mouth but warm in the belly.

"It's good," I say.

"Fuck yeah!" Junco enthuses. "More?"

I extend the cup and he pours. I catch a scowl of disapproval from Redstart's heavy brows. The boy across the way with all the wavy hair says:

"Wine comes in at the mouth
And love comes in at the eye;
That's all we shall know for truth
Before we grow old and die."

I look up. He's watching me again. Of course, so is nearly everyone else.

"Beware, lovebird," he calls across the fire. His voice is unusual. He doesn't have an accent, but it's unusual in a different way—careful, like every word is important. Of course maybe it's just because he's reciting poetry.

Lovebird? I feel my cheeks warm again.

Maybe that's just part of the poem.

He has his elbows propped upon his knees, his chin resting on his long, linked fingers like they're a hammock. I take another sip, and hide behind the rim of my cup. The fizz wets my cheeks, my nose.

"Have you ever ridden the wind over Mavericks, Billy? Man! Un*real*!" A burly man named Crane with a shaved head rears back and carves the air with his hands, talking to Longbill. "I used to surf all over, you know? Mavericks, Pipeline." He shakes his head. "But on a rug? No waves, no boards—nothing! Like riding on the fucking wind!"

Next thing I know, Crane and Longbill are on their carpets and in the air. Avocet with the high-cheekbones follows a moment later. Junco rummages in a duffle and pulls out a huge flashlight with a beam like a car headlamp and points it up into the sky. In the

53

moonlight, they're shadows—flitting, wheeling. Junco rolls the beam about, catching the occasional glint of silk.

Whimbrel nudges my shoulder. "Watch Avocet!"

Avocet's carpet cuts tight spirals, climbing the beam of light. Longbill whips past her through the smoke. He shoots right over us and off across the desert floor, crashing through a shower of white yucca blossoms. Crane is right behind him. They're both laughing and shouting.

"He cuts it close," Whimbrel says.

I give him a confused look, so he adds, "The fire. Pretty close to the fire."

The uneven pyramid of branches is burning a little higher now. Flame licks up a white branch. Whimbrel shakes his head. "It's always a game of chicken with those two."

"You guys do this a lot?"

He nods. "A few times a month, weather permitting." He releases his knee and sits upright.

"Why here?"

"Big Hatchet?" He shrugs. "Mountains are powerful places. Holy places, even. The Apaches were here, the Chiricahua. Geronimo might have stood on this very spot."

"Geronimo?"

"His people said he had remarkable powers. That he could make himself invisible, move without leaving tracks, appear suddenly out of thin air. Sound familiar?"

I laugh. "You're telling me Geronimo had a flying carpet?"

"Sure. Why not? But mostly, we meet here because we always have. We need some place remote. You almost never see anyone out here. And if anybody does see us flying around out here, they're going to have a hard time proving it. More likely than not, they'll think it's just some UFO nut. I'd be willing to guess we've probably inspired our share of UFO sightings over the years."

Above, Longbill is chasing Crane, flanking him on the left. All at once, Avocet materializes directly in their path. Both of the big ruggers swing away, careening off course, laughing and yelling.

I gasp. "She came out of nowhere!"

"Neat, huh?" Junco says. "Shows what you can do with a first-class cloaking spell."

Stonechat leaves his perch and comes over. He sits beside me and hangs a finger in the air, tracing Avocet's darting movements. "See if you can follow her. She's cloaked again."

"But I can still see her."

"Sure, because you know where she is. If you lose track of her—there!"

Avocet picks up speed and dips out of sight below a rise studded with agaves. I scan left and right, trying to catch sight of her when she emerges.

Stonechat grins. "Lost her?"

"Yeah."

"She's out there somewhere. But by now she could've doubled around, gone behind us. Or she could still be sitting behind that rise, laying low. It's a tricky thing. Of course, Avocet's an ace. Someone not so proficient, and sometimes you can find them just by looking even if you're not sure they're out there. But a good spell-caster? You lose her for an instant and she's gone."

"Seems like you guys didn't have any trouble seeing me."

He gives his head a little tilt to the left. "To be honest, Lovebird, I didn't even know you were using a cloak. Like I said, there was one point where you faded out a little."

"I just don't have a knack for it, I guess."

"Takes practice. The key thing is getting comfortable with the incantation so you don't even have to think about it. It should be second nature to you. Let's hear your incantation."

I chew my tongue. "*Ro-sur, Suh-suh, Ob-scuse-ay-mor?*"

His lips push out. "It's not a question, you know."

I try again, but he shakes his head. "You have the words, but if that's the way you're saying it, I can see why you're carpet is confused."

"What's wrong with how I'm saying it?"

"It's got no music to it. No melody. You sound like you're reading out of a phonebook."

"There's supposed to be a melody?"

"Not a particular melody. Listen. It's like poetry."

He drops his hands onto his knees, and lets his head dip to the side:

"Oh, bid me mount and sail up there
A mid the cloudy wrack,
For Peg and Meg and Paris' love
That had so straight a back,
Are gone away, and some that stay
Have changed their silk for sack."

He cocks his head back to normal and gives me a wry smile. "You can't just say it, you have to sing it." He sings in a breathy voice, *"Ro-sur, Suh-suh, Ob-scuse-ay-mor.* C'mon, try it with me."

Wow. I so don't want to do that. But the only one watching us is Raven—and Budgie, who stares at us pretty hard. "I'm not very good at singing."

"It's not about how great your singing is. The notes don't even matter. Just try it with me," he coaxes. *"Ro-sur, Suh-suh, Ob-scuse-ay-mor."*

His second time through, I make a feeble attempt to follow along.

"Good! Again!"

My voice is a warbling croak compared to his easy croon, but Stonechat is all enthusiasm. "Yes! Again."

The next time around, he leaves me hanging, but I force myself to keep going. "Don't stop," he says. "You've got it."

I sing it solo, three more times. I'm in sad need of auto-tune, but he smiles. "Now, you see? You've got a good singing voice."

There's a huff and a snort from the other side of the fire. Budgie flicks a spent cigarette into the fire and tromps off into the darkness. A moment later, I see her shadow climbing into the sky. Longbill's boisterous cry—"Eyah, Budgie!"—rings out before dissolving in a gruff peal of laughter.

Stonechat watches her go. When he looks back at me he shrugs. "Well, *I* like your voice, anyway. Listen, you'll work out your own way of casting the spells, your own melodies. It just takes a little time."

Above us, Avocet and Crane are cutting long roller-coaster loops, matching each other move for move. Stonechat stares up and says: *"I know that I shall meet my fate somewhere among the clouds above."*

"Is that another poem?"

He looks at me with fire-lit eyes. "Yeats, dear girl. Finest poet of a nation of poets."

The only poet I can think of is Shakespeare, and only because they made us read *Julius Caesar* last year.

Stonechat snaps his fingers. "You need a name!"

"Huh?"

"A flock name. What do you think, Raven?"

The woman in the Stetson looks up. "She a little 'un. Sparrow?"

"I know a Sparrow, out in Baja." This is from Whimbrel. "Siskin? Tanager?"

"What about Wren?" Raven suggests. "Didn't you say your name was Renee?"

"Renny." It's a common mistake.

Raven gestures with her pipe. "There you go, then. Hasn't been a Wren in the flock in recent memory."

"What do you think?" Stonechat asks.

"Me?"

"Well it's your name, Lovebird. You can choose another if you want. Only it's generally considered bad form to take a name that somebody else is using, at least in the local flock."

I run my tongue against my teeth. They're all watching me again. Even the old man, Scaup, gives me the eye. I shrug. "Wren is okay."

Junco lifts a fresh bottle from between his boots and pulls the cork. "We have something to toast."

Cups are held out. Junco splashes gossamer into each one.

"Hey!" Junco hollers. Crane and Avocet have just landed. Junco waves them over. "Drink to the newest member!"

Longbill joins us. More cups are filled and raised.

"To Wren!"

"Wren," Longbill says, rolling the name around in his mouth along with the gossamer. "I knew a Wren once, in Portugal. Crazy old coot."

People sit, cradling cups. Stonechat doesn't take any. Longbill begins talking to Crane about cliff wind-currents, and within another minute at least three different conversations are going on.

"So that's the whole deal?" I ask Whimbrel. "I'm in now? No initiation?"

He smiles an oddly pained smile. Crane says, "There's an idea!"

Longbill laughs. "Now you're talking!"

"Wait. What did I say?" I thought I was only joking.

The several conversations all dissolve into one, and somehow I'm at the center of it again.

"Come on, Redstart! You're the expert on this," Longbill says. "It's tradition, right? We all know how you feel about tradition."

"It's not really necessary," Redstart says.

"Sure it is!" Longbill insists, and he flashes me a wink.

Everyone looks at me again. "If there's something I'm supposed to do—I mean, I can try. If it's not too..." My sentence dwindles off into lameness.

"That's the spirit!" Nightjar says. She turns to Redstart. "A questing run?"

Redstart gives a little tip of his head. "I guess."

"Need a harrier," Crane says.

"Yeah," Longbill agrees. "No point without a harrier. I could do it."

"No." The voice isn't loud, but the sharpness of it cuts through. Everyone gets very quiet. Just at the edge of the firelight, Budgie stands, a shadow on the darkness.

"Me," she says. "I'll do it."

Nine

The silence hangs on the air. Is this a joke? In another second they're all going to burst out laughing.

That's not what happens. There's a rustle of feet, the fire makes a loud pop, but if anything the silence only grows deeper. There's a lot of looking back and forth, eyes finding other eyes around the circle, but mostly I'm looking across the fire at Budgie. *Hairier?*

Whimbrel stands. "*I'll* be harrier."

"Oh, balls, Whimbrel!" Budgie spits. "You couldn't harry a freakin' butterfly!"

Crane gives a gruff laugh. Whimbrel says nothing.

Budgie gets a coy smile on her face. "Look, I mean, I don't give a rat's ass, but if you're going to do the initiation you may as well do it right." She looks at me, still smiling. "Let's see what you've got," she says, her voice almost sweet by now. "Don't worry, Ducks. I'll play nice."

I stand up with a wobble I'm sure no one misses. The gossamer—how many cups have I had? The stuff goes down like soda pop, but it's catching up with me. I'm not exactly sure what the hell's going on here, but it's obvious I've been challenged to something. I don't like it. I also don't like the way Budgie is calling me "Ducks." I take a deep breath, hoping some clever reply might occur to me, but when I open my mouth, all that comes out is a surprisingly loud and long belch.

That cracks me up. Maybe it's the gossamer but I can't help laughing. "Sure," I say sitting down again, "Whatever."

Nightjar is suddenly beside me, laughing and thumping me on the back. Everybody is talking and laughing again. Especially Longbill and Crane, who are whooping it up like—well, like cranes, I guess.

"Hey," Stonechat drops down in front of me and puts a hand on my shoulder. He smiles at me and, for a moment, I think he is going to start giving me pointers or at least a pep talk, but all he says is, "Go get her, Lovebird."

Redstart speaks. "All right then. Where are we going to hang the silk?"

"The snag across the ravine," Crane says. "That's the place, ain't it Scaup?"

The old man, sitting up now, nods. "That'll work."

"Yeah, but you gotta do the speech," Nightjar insists.

Others agree.

Scaup shakes his head. "I don't remember that stuff. Let Redstart do it."

"I'm not sure I remember all of it either," Redstart says.

"Come on Red. Do what you remember."

Redstart frowns. "Okay. I'll try." He holds up a hand and shuts his eyes. "Look! Look through the backward eyes of time! Uh, since Sulayman first strode the air. Since Saba's mage put needle to thread. Gathered then as—no, wait. Gather we as they did then, those who sought this place, this blade, underneath these skies."

"Go, Red!" Crane shouts.

Redstart holds a hand up for silence. "Now," he continues, "now this new one comes before us, ready to spread her silks on the wind. Let us gather her beneath our wings. Let her walk the skies in the company of the flock. Give her a name. Call her: Wren."

Cups are raised. "Wren!"

Crane says something I don't catch, and Nightjar lets go a loop of laughter. Longbill grins. Stonechat sits quietly, knees gathered in his arms. He's smiling too. Budgie, still at the edge of the circle, stands leaning, her face lost in shadow.

Redstart turns to me. "Fledgling. The time has come. Are you ready to face the ordeal?"

The seriousness of his question is decidedly undercut by Nightjar's giggling. When Longbill begins to chant: "Wren! Wren! Wren!"—very quietly, but like a crowd of fans at a football game—her chirpy little laugh breaks into a full-fledged cackle. I try to put a smile on my face, but it's a poor specimen. "Yeah, okay."

Redstart bows his head and turns to the circle. "Crane will fly across the ravine. There stands a snag of ironwood. To the top-most branch he will tie—" He pauses. "Did anybody bring something we can use?"

A murmur circles the group.

"Anything will do," Redstart says, "as long as it's silk."

"Hey, Avvy," Longbill says, "isn't your shirt silk?"

Avocet, without missing a beat, shows him the back of her hand, middle finger extended.

"Here." Whimbrel holds out his hand. A rose colored scarf dangles in the firelight. Redstart holds it up for all to see.

"This shall be the prize."

Crane takes the scarf. He gives me a quick wink and leaves the circle.

We wait. Junco holds out the bottle of gossamer. I shake my head. I definitely don't need any more gossamer. A moment later, a shadow flits across the moon's face. Crane touches down at the edge of the firelight. He steps into the circle and nods at Redstart.

"All right," Redstart says. He spreads his arms wide. "Let it begin!"

I wait. Everyone waits. It takes me a moment to realize they're all waiting for me. "What do I do?"

Redstart answers. "You go and get it."

I can see nothing out in the darkness.

"You'll see it," Crane tells me. "Just fly out over the ravine. It's the tallest tree over there."

"And Budgie?"

"She'll try and stop you," Stonechat says.

I look around the circle. Budgie is gone, all right. Sometime, between Redstart's speech and Crane's return, she has slipped away.

"You go, Wren!" Nightjar shouts. She gives a whoop and salutes me with her cup. Longbill begins his football chant again. "Wren! Wren! Wren!"

Stonechat's at my side, his hand on the back of my neck.

"Don't worry. You can do it."

I step my way out into the darkness and pick Maysa from the pile. Climbing on, I push my fingers into the nap. "You ready, girl?"

She purrs and lifts us up into the night. She is so much readier for this than I am.

Crane is right about one thing—away from the fire, I can see pretty well. Dark shapes stand out against the pale, silver sand: the yucca stands, tangles of mesquite, the same greasewood tree I tried to hide behind. I can hear pretty well too—Crane's gruff shout, Nightjar's goofy laugh.

I fly out over the ravine. On the far side, in a shaggy clump of tamarix, a finger of white wood points at the sky. It had been a big tree once, probably thirty-feet tall—big for the desert. Now it's a bony thing, ghost-white and twisted. Tied to a stub near the top, the scarf hangs, not moving. In the moonlight, it looks almost white.

Somewhere out there, Budgie is waiting, probably watching me even now. I look around, trying to catch the first thing that moves. The desert is still and quiet. I make a wide circle around the top of the snag. Crouching low, I make another, closer loop.

On the third loop I reach the snag. The scarf is tied with a loose knot that comes undone easily. I tuck it up in my left hand and turned back across the ravine. The campfire, the circle of stones—I can see them from here. And something else: a beam dancing up

63

against the sky like a searchlight. The beam winks and rolls, cutting arcs—Junco, playing with his flashlight.

Night drops down in front of me like a fist. I crumple hard against it. "Uhhn..."

Night has claws. It hisses hot breath into my face. "Give it!"

Night has a face too—pale, with angry raccoon eyes. "Give!"

"Nuhhn..."

Fingernails rake down my arm. She snarls something in my ear. I can't understand a word.

Maysa pulls up, straight up. My stomach drops, and I scrabble forward, clutching at smooth slipping silk. "No, no, no...!"

The next thing I know I'm flat out, my face pressed against Maysa's soft back. Harsh laughter scrapes the sky.

I lift my head. We're floating, high above the desert. I breathe again. Budgie's laugh is far away now. I find her with my eyes, circling the campfire, trailing the scarf behind her like a victory flag. Others are laughing too. Someone gives a loud clap. I can't tell what anyone is saying.

Hot tears spill my cheek. I smear my sleeve against my face, hard enough to hurt, and dive for the firelight.

Budgie perches on the highest stone again, still holding the scarf. She gives it a twirl. Everyone is laughing and talking. I drift in, taking Maysa as near to the fire as I dare to go and stop, inches from the ground. I stand upright on Maysa's back and steady myself. It's important I be steady. Every eye is on me now. The talking stops.

"We're going to try that again." My voice is calm and hard. Inside me, everything is quivering and soft.

On the other side of the fire, Budgie's eyes widen. Her face cracks into a grin. "Love to, Ducky. But it won't make any difference."

"That's what you say," I croak. "I didn't know we could use cloaking spells."

Budgie lets loose a delighted, cawing laugh. "A cloaking spell! A cloaking spell isn't going to help you, Ducks."

"Stop calling me—"

"One," she goes on, "because you can't *do* one, and two because I had you in my sights the whole time!"

I stare back at her, not saying anything.

"You do know how it works, don't you. You can't hide behind a cloak if I already know where you are."

"I know that. I said I want to try it again." I look around. "Any law against that?"

Redstart looks at Scaup. The old man shrugs. He looks more alert than he has all evening. Redstart looks at me and gives a shrug of his own. "Does anyone else want to be harrier?"

"No," I say. "Budgie."

"Too right," Budgie says.

We stare at each other. The fire pops. Redstart turns to Crane. "You know what to do."

The big man takes the scarf and disappears into the darkness again.

Maysa trembles. I drop to my knees. Her front edge is curled up, like she's trying to keep it as far away from the fire as possible. I let her drift back, stroking the warmed fringe. "It's okay girl. Sorry about that."

Crane returns and Redstart gives me a nod. I let Maysa take me up. Relief runs through her as we climb into the cool air. Budgie stands by the fire, watching me go, wearing her carpet around her shoulders. I turn toward the ravine, and pick out the bone-white snag of ironwood. When I look back again, Budgie isn't there anymore.

I grit my teeth and head for the snag. I consider dropping down into the ravine and seeing if I can lose Budgie, put on a cloaking spell of my own. But she's probably waiting for something just like that. And besides, annoying as Budgie is, she's right about one thing: my cloaking spell is lousy.

I fly across the ravine and head straight for the snag. I don't bother with a careful approach this time. Budgie won't strike until I've got the thing in my hands.

Down in the ravine, a bird calls: *"poor wheedo, poor wheedo."* A sad cry, but also irritated, like I just woke him up. But desert birds don't sleep at night. Night is when it's cool enough to hunt for bugs or whatever they eat. This bird is probably a hunter. Like Budgie. Budgie is the hunter, I am the bug.

Fuck that. I'm not going to be the bug. It sounds like one of Lee's motivational tapes. *Don't be the bug. Decide you are not going to be the bug.* It's dumb enough to actually be one of his slogans. Okay, then. I'm not a bug; I'm Renny. Wren. That's what this whole thing is about. I have to earn my stupid nickname.

I clear the far side of the ravine and flit up the trunk of the ironwood snag. I listen. No doubt Budgie is fully cloaked now, hanging somewhere near and biding her time.

I undo the scarf.

The night stays calm and empty. Way off, back at the campfire, Junco does his searchlight routine again, scanning the sky with lazy strokes. Will she attack here? No. We're too far away from the fire, too far from an audience. She doesn't just want to beat me. She wants to humiliate me.

Down over the rim of the ravine, the bird calls again, *"poor-wheedo, poor-wheedo."*

Poor wittle Renny all alone, with a crazed Budgie on my tail. I tighten my grip on the scarf. Okay, then. Here goes nothing.

I launch myself straight up, not circling, not weaving. Surprise! Or at least I hope it's a surprise. I call to Maysa, asking for all the speed she can give me. She doesn't disappoint. I make a hard loop and head for the top of Big Hatchet, away from the campfire, away from Budgie.

I lean out sideways, trying to catch some sound—the flutter of silk, an angry British curse—any sign that Budgie is now in hot pursuit. All I can hear is wind.

I head toward the mountain, cutting for a pass between two shoulders of bare rock. It all comes down to whether Budgie believes I can't do a cloaking spell. If she has any doubts at all, she'll have to

66

follow. She has to keep me in view. If she follows, I might be able to double back and get in front of her. I don't know much about Budgie's flying ability—she's probably been flying a lot longer than I have—but in a straight out race, I'll take my chances on Maysa being faster.

I rack my brain, trying to remember the melody Stonechat taught me. *It's not the particular melody, it's not about the notes.* Still, I wish I could remember it. I wish I could hear him singing it in my ear right now. Whose side is he on in this dumb contest, anyway? It seems like he's rooting for me. But why would he care? For all I know, it's just cheap entertainment for a Saturday night.

We slide low over a dry wash littered with rocks and broken branches, then shoot through the notch between the two hillsides into a valley drenched in moonlight. Careening hard left, we dive down the granite face. I bury myself in a single thought: *"Ro-sur, Suh-suh, Ob-scuse-ay-mor. Ro-sur, Suh-suh, Ob-scuse-ay-mor."*

Silently, I sing the syllables. Rounding the vowels, letting them rise and swell and fall. I want to feel what I felt when Stonechat sang it, his voice low and husky, his breath warm.

Something weird is happening. It starts at my knees and in my hands. The silk under my palms becomes warmer and somehow, even softer, smoother—more *silky*. It feels like my hands will go right through it, like I can sink all the way down inside it.

A silver voice titters in my ear. *Good, Renny! Very good!*

In my other ear, another voice sings, *Ob bop susy heyup rosy...* and then it falls apart into laughter again.

"Is that all you guys can do? Make fun?"

Both break into tinny laughter. Speaking at once, the voices tumble over one another:

Oh, no, Renny!

We can—

—much, much, more!

"Can you tell me if this is working? Am I invisible?"

The one in my left ear gives another sparkly little laugh.

Visible? Who is that?

"Not who. Am *I* invisible?"

Are you? Invisible who?

"Who?" An idea pops into my head. "You mean, who am I invisible *to*?"

Not us! Not us!

"I don't mean you. I mean Budgie." The air blinks in wordless confusion. "The one who's following me."

Oh!

Oh! Yes.

That one.

"Yes. Am I invisible to her?"

Her? Yes.

No.

Maybe.

"What d'you mean, maybe?" I hiss.

Time will show—

—soon. Yes, soon.

"Soon?"

She is close.

I sit up. "How close?"

Oh, very.

Very, very close!

I throw myself hard to the right. The wind slaps back across my face. A loud voice spits something unpleasant, and there's Budgie, filling the air in front of me. Her face cracks into a hateful grin.

"Learned something after all, Duckling? I almost lost you there." She laughs. "But you'll have to do better than that."

She lunges. I flip backwards, throwing the full flat of Maysa's underside into Budgie's path. Silk hits silk. Budgie grunts. I throw myself forward and grab the fringe. Like a kite I go up, straight up, one hand gripping scarf and carpet, the other clutching Maysa's edge. I glance back. Budgie digs hard for the top of Big Hatchet.

She isn't following. She's trying to head me off. My rocket launch strategy is only a temporary reprieve, not an escape. She'll be tracking me all the way, making doubly sure not to lose me now.

My cloaking spell: it worked! *I almost lost you there!* It only lasted for a minute before those windsprites interrupted, but it worked. I level off and head back for the campfire. Somewhere, Budgie is watching me, no doubt invisible again.

I'm too vulnerable. The scarf is too easy to grab. All Budgie needs is another mid-air mugging. I suppose I could tie it around my neck but she would probably just rip it right off. Probably take my head off with it.

I can see the campfire again. Somewhere—after I cross the ravine, probably—Budgie will hit again. I need a plan.

Just past the ironwood, before I've even cleared the ravine, a breeze blows voices up my back, tickling the hairs on my neck: *Renny! Renny!*

"I don't have time for you guys!"

Time, Renny!

Here. Now.

The time is here!

Now!

Almost too late, I get it. A ripple of silk comes at me sideways. I duck away and roll to the right. A dark wing looms overhead, passes beneath me, tails away into the darkness. I dig my fingers in. The moon drops, and the world stretches out above me. Then, in an instant, the world dives beneath me again, and the stars and the moon swing back overhead.

Maysa. Maysa did that: flipped us over, flew upside down. Somehow, she kept me from falling, kept me pinned to her surface. I throw us forward into a dive—spinning, spiraling—then pull up skyward again. Through every maneuver, Budgie stays right with me, sweeping forward, pulling back. Junco has his searchlight trained on us. Shouts ring up from the desert floor. I can't help but wonder who they're cheering for.

I fake a run to the left.

I dive and whip hard to the right.

Budgie gives way, but stays always right in front of me, always keeping herself between me and the firelight.

She skids to a halt, right in front of me. In the moonlight her face is white, her eyes dark, her mouth angry and red.

"Give it up, slag!" She's breathing hard.

I raise my hands slowly. Budgie stares.

"Where's the bloody scarf?" she snarls.

I stare at my own empty hands, each in turn. I look at Budgie again, my eyes wide, still saying nothing. I put on my best look of horror and lean forward, peering over Maysa's edge, searching the darkness.

Budgie looks too.

In the instant her gaze drops, I bolt. Up first, over her left shoulder, then down, headfirst. Wind pounds in my ears. The firelight, growing closer, blurs between my eyelids. I skid to a halt in the sand beside the fire-pit. Everyone is standing, jumping around, laughing, yelling. Longbill hollers something, an idiot grin spread all over his face. Nightjar cackles, filling the air with laughter.

Stonechat, hands in pockets, beams at me saying nothing.

Not two seconds after I land, Budgie comes crashing in behind me, kicking sand. Crane puts an arm around her shoulder, and roughs up her hair.

She shoves him away. "Hey!" she yells.

No one listens.

"Hey!" she tries, even louder. "She doesn't have it!"

Now people listen.

"Look!" she insists. "She hasn't got it! She dropped it out there!"

They all fix their eyes on me.

"Wren?" Redstart asks. "Have you got it?"

I give him a very puffy-cheeked smile. Then I open my mouth and dig thumb and finger between my teeth. It comes out slowly, an inch at a time. When it's all the way free, I hold it up, letting it dangle, and hand it to Whimbrel. "Sorry. It's a little wet."

Whimbrel stares. Budgie's painted mouth drops open. For a long moment no one says anything.

Stonechat is the first one to start laughing.

Ten

Forty-five minutes later he's still laughing——or at least laughing again. "You should've seen the look on her face when you pulled that scarf out!" he chuckles. "It was tasty."

We are high over Truth or Consequences, still blazing in spite of the hour. Stonechat is, in his very own words, flying me home, as in *Come on, I'll fly you home.*

"Had to be tastier than the scarf," I say. "I'm just glad it wasn't wool."

After the whole questing thing was over, we all sat back down around the fire, and everyone had their chance to thump me on the back and click plastic cups of gossamer. All except for Budgie, who planted herself on her high rock again and toyed with a cigarette. Longbill and Crane tore into her for a while until even I began to feel a little sorry for her. Finally, Scaup gruffed at them to give it a rest.

Which they did, but Budgie's mood didn't improve. Every time I looked up, it seemed like those raccoon eyes were burning into me. Stonechat planted himself right at my side, so close it was impossible for our shoulders not to bump. He even, on two separate occasions, put a hand on my arm, just casually.

His hands are interesting. He has long fingers, and despite the knobby knuckles, they're graceful. It's the way he holds them, like two birds, poised and ready. I caught myself staring at them more than once. I admit it didn't bother me at all when he touched me—once just above the elbow, then a second time on the shoulder.

But I couldn't miss the fact it bothered Budgie. As we glide over the dark waters of Elephant Butte Reservoir, I steel my nerve. "Budgie," I begin, and then give a forced chuckle, "she really doesn't like me."

"Yeah, well," Stonechat says, not looking over, "She doesn't like anybody all that much."

I wait, watching him watch the sky. "Seems like she might like you."

He shrugs a shoulder. "Used to."

"Were you and she...?"

"We were—but it was over a while ago."

"You broke up?"

He nods.

"Does she know you broke up?"

He laughs.

"I'm just curious, you know, 'cause she still seems a little possessive."

"Some people just don't handle rejection very well. And Budgie has got more than the normal amount of bile in her system. She'll get over it. So," he says, in what is obviously meant to be a subject-changing voice, "what happened when you two were on the other side of the Hatchet, anyway?"

"I told you already. I tried to do a cloaking spell. She chased me, blah, blah, blah."

"So the cloaking spell didn't work?" He frowns as if he is trying to diagnose a difficult case.

"Well, kind of—at first, anyway. I had this weird feeling in my hands and knees, like I was sinking into the carpet."

"Yes! The enfolding. That's a good thing. It means you're connecting on a deeper level. Enfolding lets your rug do a whole bunch of other things like cloaking and sheltering. You've experienced some of that already. I mean, how fast d'you think we're flying right now?"

I shrug. "I dunno. Seventy, eighty miles an hour?"

"Try a hundred-twenty. But you'd never know it. At that speed, you shouldn't be able to hang on at all. The wind would be ferocious. But because you've bonded with the carpet, she shares her protection with you. Hey!" He grins. "You ever try one of these?"

He gives a little wobble and then swings up hard. I skid to a stop, watching him soar into the night sky, straight up. At the top of his climb, he slows to a stall, hanging—nose up—not moving at all.

Then he drops.

All the breath rushes out of me. He shoots past, a falling ball of rippling silk. His own scream follows him into the darkness.

Before I can do anything, I see his arms thrown wide, see his carpet wrap about him, hear his cry of terror change into a spray of lazy laughter. His carpet unwraps and for a moment he just hangs, stretched out on a rectangle of moonlit silk. He rises slowly like an elevator. When he pulls level again he sits up, grinning.

I swallow hard, my pulse pounding. "I didn't think you were the daredevil type."

"We're all daredevils—all ruggers are. Misfits and daredevils."

"I'm not."

"Seemed to me you were cutting some pretty daring maneuvers when you were jostling about with Budgie."

I flex an eyebrow. "I guess."

"It goes with the profile," he says. "You wouldn't be here if you weren't."

"So, Scaup? Raven?"

He laughs. "Scaup and Raven might have surprised you in their younger days."

Maybe. It's hard to picture Scaup doing barrel rolls. Or Junco, for that matter. It's funny to think of him rolling across the sky with his maroon vest flapping, a bottle of gossamer in his hand. Still, I can't help liking that guy.

"So, Junco—" I begin.

Stonechat laughs. "He's a piece of work!"

"Does he really collect that gossamer from the clouds, like he said?"

He makes a dismissive sound, pushing air through his lips. "Raven says he probably mixes it up at home in his bathtub." He grins again and gives me a sidelong look. "Good stuff though, eh?"

"You didn't drink any." It's not an accusation. I'm just curious.

"Drank a lot of it back a few years ago. Drank a lot of everything back then."

"Oh."

"Finally decided I better quit before I ended up in rehab."

"I don't usually drink that much. Hardly at all, really."

Stonechat shrugs. "What's the point of having a party if you're not going to celebrate?"

A party. It's funny. I told Lauren I was going to a party, but I hadn't actually been expecting one. Which is exactly what I said to Nightjar while we were all sitting around the campfire.

"What *were* you expecting?" she asked.

"I don't know. Something official, I guess. You know, for the Order."

Crane found this funny. "Ah, the Order!" He raised his cup and donned a fake British accent. "The Royal Imperial Order of Sodders!"

"Oh, please!" Redstart complained. "You know perfectly well it's Scudders."

"It's all the same to me, mate!" Crane said, still mangling the accent. He shot a grin at Budgie, who seemed oblivious.

"The 'Order' doesn't have anything to do with this, Lovebird."

A smatter of tipsy laughter circled the fire. The giggling, and the way Stonechat had said the word *order*, made me feel like I had walked into the middle of an old joke.

"I don't get it. Is there something funny about the Order?"

"There is no Order," Crane said, sounding like himself again.

"Technically, that's not true." Redstart objected.

"Right, right. There's an Imperial Order of Rug Wranglers. Only you've never seen 'em, and I've never seen 'em and nobody you've ever seen has seen 'em..."

"Flo..." Redstart objected.

"Flo is crackers!"

This started Nightjar laughing again, but Redstart only shook his head.

"Well, has anybody *but* Flo ever had any actual contact with the so-called Order?" Crane asked.

"It's not that kind of organization," Redstart began. He broke off with another shake of his head. "This is a very old argument."

For me, of course, it was a very new argument. "But what about the mission?"

This brought even more laughter. Longbill turned to Crane. "Hey, Crane! How's the mission going?"

"Parnell told me there was a mission."

Stonechat put a hand on my shoulder. "There is no mission, Lovebird. We all heard that speech, but it's just a lot of crap. All that ancient tradition stuff—that's just Flo. You know, goes with living in a castle surrounded by volumes of forgotten lore and all that." Stonechat put on his poetry voice again and intoned, "Thou shalt keep secret the secrets of the Arcane Order of Carpet Wranglers, the Fellows of Shaleen—"

"And to the best of your abilities," Nightjar continued, hand raised as if taking an oath, "preserve, protect, and defend the high, imperial Sublime Order of Scudders." She finished with a flourish and a little bow.

"There you go," Stonechat said. "Like a bunch of boy scouts." He held up two fingers in a salute. "On my honor, I will do my best for Order and country, defend fellow ruggers, help the flightless—"

"I've been flying for ten years," Crane said. "If this Order of his needs me sometime, fine. No problem. But in the meantime, *that*"—he jabbed his finger into the darkness, pointing at the stone where the carpets lay piled—"is the sweetest ride on the planet! I've ridden everything. Surfboards, motorcycles, kite-surfing, but there just ain't nothing that compares to riding the wind on a piece of silk."

Redstart, who had been quiet for a long while, spoke up in a quiet, challenging voice. "All right, then. So there is no Order, and Flo is just a nutcase. So what about Mistral, then?"

"Mistral!" Crane scoffed.

"What," I asked, "is Mistral?"

"He's a myth," Crane answered.

"No," Raven said, her voice calm. "He is not."

Everyone turned to look at her. She drew a mouthful of smoke and let it out. "He's real, right enough."

The silence thickened. All the laughter was gone now. I was the first one to speak. "Who's Mistral?"

Redstart drew a deep breath. "About two years ago, depending on whose story you believe—"

"Or if you believe any of them," Crane added.

"—two ruggers were attacked by a gang of renegade ruggers. This was," he thought about it, "somewhere in the Mediterranean."

"Tunisia," Avocet said.

"Right. They were flying around in the desert just doing whatever, and this gang of ruggers appears. They force them to the ground. One of them got hurt pretty badly. They took their carpets and left them stranded in the desert. While they were flying away, one of them shouts, 'Tell Flo, Mistral sends his regards."

Avocet spoke. "That wasn't the only time, either. There have been other attacks."

"There have been other *reported* attacks," Nightjar countered, "Sketchy reports."

"Yeah," Longbill agreed, "Nobody knows for sure. It's all just a lot of rumors, really."

"Carpets are missing," Whimbrel objected.

"People *claim*..." Nightjar corrected.

"Yeah," Longbill agreed, "people can claim anything."

"Okay," Redstart put his hands up. "Fine. But we know there *are* renegades. And something else: ruggers have gone missing *off* the Orb of Descrying, and that's supposed to be impossible. If Mistral can make carpets disappear from the Orb, then he's a power to be reckoned with."

I look over at Stonechat. He's staring straight ahead, lost in his own thoughts. We are flying over some road-less stretch of dessert now, and the moon can't find much to illuminate.

"Hey."

He looks over. "Hmm?"

"That guy Redstart was talking about, the renegade guy. Do you think he's real?"

He gives me a look, head tilted. "You're not still thinking about that?" He smiles, all crinkly-eyed. "I wouldn't take all that Mistral stuff too seriously."

"Redstart made it sound like—"

"Redstart," he cuts in, "is an old windbag. He's almost as bad as Flo. He's always had this notion that he's the heir to the great tradition of carpet flyers because he's Iranian."

"Iranian?"

"Well, you know, Persian. Traditionally, that's where the first flying carpets came from. The thousand and one nights and all of that."

"Oh."

"He's a good guy," he adds, "Just full of himself, you know? Like with great power comes great responsibility."

"Isn't that Spiderman?"

He laughs. "Right first time. That stuff with the carpets being stolen and people disappearing, I mean, I'm sure some of that is true. Stuff happens. But you don't need some super-villain rugger to explain it all. Old ladies get mugged walking in broad daylight. Lunatics go on shooting sprees. No reason why ruggers should be immune. We're bound to have our own share of deviants. Maybe even more than our share, considering what we've got to deal with."

"What do you mean?"

"The secret," he says. "We've all got this great big secret." He waves an arm in the air, describing hugeness with a gesture. "You're pretty new, so maybe it hasn't really hit you yet, but a secret like that can kind of wear on you."

"No. I get that."

"That's why the kettles. It helps sometimes to be with others who are in the same boat."

"So for a while, you don't *have* to keep it secret."

"Exactly."

We fly for a time, not speaking. Then he begins to recite, quietly, as if only for his own ears:

"When shall the stars be blown about the sky,
Like the sparks blown out of a smithy, and die?

Hey!" he says, breaking off the poetry. "Do you want to try a game?"

"A game? It's like two o'clock in the morning. I'm already late."

"We can play while we're flying. I want to see how that cloaking spell of yours is going. It sounds to me like you've got a good rapport with your carpet. Does she sing for you?"

"Yeah. All the time."

He looks impressed. "That's good. I mean, they all sing, but not always at first. So that's a good sign. Does she read you? Your thoughts?"

I nod.

"Sounds like you're ahead of the learning curve to me. Cloaking should be a cinch. Give it a try."

"What, now?"

"Sure. I'm going to go ahead of you a bit, just so I can't see you. You do the spell and I'll try to find you."

He picks up speed and pulls ahead, calling over his shoulder, "Remember: sing!"

It takes me a minute to find something like the tune I'd used back at Big Hatchet. "Ro-sur, Suh-suh, Ob-scuse-ay-mor."

Beneath my palms silk flutters, blooming with warmth. The warmth flows up my arms like current. I let myself sink into the softness.

"Ro-sur, Suh-suh, Ob-scuse-ay-mor. Ro-sur, Suh-suh, Ob-scuse-ay-mor." I hold my hand up in front of my face. It's entirely visible of course. Still, something is happening. Stonechat, maybe twenty yards ahead of me, keeps a constant speed. Moonlight makes silver ripples of his carpet and catches in the curls of his hair. I give Maysa a mental nudge and close the gap.

Sing! I have to remember to sing.

But Maysa seems to be way ahead of me. The feeling of immersion, of connection, is stronger than before. It seems Maysa can keep the spell going even when my mind wanders—at least for a little while. It's like the spell has a kind of magical momentum.

But will it work on Stonechat? I pull up behind him, matching his speed, hanging off his left side. He isn't moving very fast. I ease past, keeping my eye on him. He keeps looking straight ahead. I let myself slide all the way in front of him. His head turns and I brace myself, ready to be found.

He looks right through me. Turning, he stares back over his shoulder, studying the darkness. He smiles. "Not bad!" he calls.

He keeps scanning left, right, above, below. Every time his eyes sweep over me I feel certain this time he'll see me. I speed up and get well out in front of him and then whip across his flight path, right through his field of vision. I cut a tight orbit and then pull even with him again.

He doesn't see anything.

I make a whole series of passes, getting closer each time. Finally, I stop with the whole orbiting thing. I get right in front of him, not five yards away. I turn around so I can face him while Maysa keeps matching his speed. Still, he notices nothing. I let the distance between us dwindle. I study his face in the moonlight. He has a square jaw, and there's a hook to his nose. It's even a little crooked but not in an ugly way. In fact, it's one of his best features. And his eyebrows. He has amazing eyebrows. They twitch and arch as he searches the sky. I let myself get even closer. He stares right at me, seeing nothing.

Then something happens in his big, dark eyes.

"Hey!"

The song!

I'm not really sure what happens next. All I know is my face is mushed up against his shoulder and my arm is pinned against his chest. Our knees are tangled. Stonechat is laughing again. He lifts his face from my shoulder. I pull my knee free. Somehow, we're still airborne. The two carpets fly on, bunched together, as if nothing has happened. I pull my arm out and try to push myself away from him.

He doesn't let me. He slips an arm around my shoulder like it's the most normal thing in the world. He smiles. His face is close to mine. I pull my arms in so they're in front of me, but I don't push him away. I don't want to any more. I just keep them there, the palms of my hands resting on his chest.

For a long moment we just sit in a knot of ankles, of knees, of elbows. I pull one hand free again and hang it on the crook of his arm. He smiles. One hand slides along my shoulder until it finds the nape of my neck. With the other, he reaches up and taps me on the nose.

"Found you," he says.

Eleven

When I finally crawl into bed, I fall straight into dreaming.

It's a different room this time. Beyond the spread of branches and broad leaves, the walls are long panes of glass. So is the high ceiling. It's a glass house—a greenhouse, obviously. I'm standing on a cinder footpath in bare feet. Along the sides of the path, trees grow in beds of mounded earth. They need weeding.

Underneath the branches of one the largest trees, Parnell stands on a small stepladder. His dressing gown is pale purple this time. A green gardener's apron is tied around his middle. He waves me over. "Come and have a look at this."

He's holding a branch in one hand. He pulls it down so I can see. Three white caterpillars cling to the underside of the leaf.

"Ick."

He chuckles. "These are silk-worms, Miss Drake!"

They look like tiny amputated fingers, only with nubby feet and a row of black pin-prick spots along their sides. The leaf is crisscrossed with tiny furrows where the green has been eaten away. One grub gnaws the scooped out edge, making twitchy motions.

"Mulberry leaf," Parnell says, "It is the only thing a silkworm will eat, but they'll eat plenty of it before they're through."

I look up into the canopy. There's another little crowd of white worms on a riddled leaf. Another leaf, now worm-less, is nothing but a network of pale veins.

"They aren't actually worms, of course. They are the caterpillars. Silk moth larva."

Larva is a disgusting word.

"They will need to molt again before they pupate."

And so is pew-pate.

"After they form cocoons, they can be harvested." He lets go of the leaf and climbs down from the ladder. "Silk is a remarkable substance. Very strong, stronger than steel actually. If you could make a fine thread out of steel, it would not have as much tensile strength as plain old silk. Did you know early bullet-proof vests were made out of silk?"

"Yeah?"

"Indeed." We're walking now. He has a limp tonight. His left slipper scrapes the gravel with each step—step, *shh*, step, *shh*. "One silkworm cocoon might produce a thousand meters worth of thread, all wound up in a package the size of a peanut. And silk thread has a natural sheen to it. It reflects light at all sorts of angles so it seems to change color, like an opal. That's why it's so prized."

At the end of the footpath, we pass through a wooden door into a shed lit by skylights. Two large copper vats sit on unlit gas burners. Beside them, an enormous rack stands, hanging with metal rods and wire things. Parnell crosses to a sink and washes his hands under a cast-iron tap.

"Do you know anything about silk?" he calls over the gush of water.

I shake my head.

He switches off the tap and begins drying his hands on a towel. "The process is actually quite simple. Here, sit." A pair of sling-back garden chairs stand near a small round metal table. He gestures me into one and settles himself into the other. "After they have finished their last molt, the caterpillars will spin cocoons." He waves a

83

hand at one of the big vats. "The cocoons are boiled to kill the larva, and then the silk can be unwound, in one continuous, unbroken thread."

"You boil the larva?"

"What did you expect? This is not a silkworm nature preserve. At any rate, the adult moth will only live for a few days after breaking free from the cocoon. Their only purpose is to mate and lay eggs. They cannot fly. They do not even have mouths with which to eat. Do you know what is special about these silkworms, Miss Drake? Nothing. Nothing at all. They are your common, garden variety, mulberry-munching specimens of *Bombyx mori*, known since antiquity to produce that miraculous substance we call silk. Miraculous," he holds a stubby finger up, "but only your normal sort of miracle. Silk is fabulously strong and famously beautiful, but it does not normally fly, of course.

"Now if you want to talk about *flying* silk, that history seems to begin at the southernmost tip of the Arabian Peninsula in what is now the country of Yemen. There, a queen ruled over a land called Saba, or Sheba. She was known by a number of different names: Balkis, Makeda, Mareb. In the west, she is known simply as the Queen of Sheba. It is said that at her coronation some three thousand years ago, a sorcerer created an unusual spectacle: a display of flying fabrics, squares of what we must assume to have been silk that danced in the air. And they must have been quite a hit because that same queen is said to have sent a remarkable gift to another monarch of the era, a king called Sulayman or, more commonly, Solomon."

"Like the guy in the Bible?"

"The very same. The queen had heard of a wise king, the wisest in all the land, and so she paid a visit to wise King Solomon. She brought him the rarest of gifts: a flying carpet. But such a carpet! Of light green silk, set with gold embroidery and precious stones, and so large that his entire retinue could stand upon it. When Sulayman rode upon his magic carpet, the very winds would obey his commands and carry him instantly to whatever remote destination he chose. So great was the magic that a canopy of birds would accompany him, protecting his royal mien from the harsh desert sun."

"Is that true?"

"A canopy of birds? Of course not! The tales of Sulayman's fabulous carpet have certainly been elaborated on over the centuries. However marvelous the Queen of Sheba's gift may have been, I hardly think it could have been large enough for his entire court to ride on. And I think the wind obeying his commands is more metaphor than fact. Over the course of the next thousand years or so, the flying carpet continued to appear in popular folklore. Ben Sherira tells us Ptolemy's great library at Alexandria kept a flock of flying carpets for its patrons to use while perusing the high shelves for the manuscripts they were seeking. The ceilings were so high that readers would often hover aloft, sometimes for days, as they read. There are also legends of a thirteenth century prince who kept a squadron of carpet-mounted archers who would fly over the battlements and rain death down upon his enemies.

"Now we cannot know if any of this actually took place. But the prevalence of the stories, the number of times and places this image of the flying carpet recurs is very suggestive. It is quite possible that the craft of enchanting silk may even predate our stories about Solomon and Sheba. Flying carpets—*real* flying carpets—may have been around for a long time before that. Here's an interesting tidbit, though: those ancient historians had the entirely wrong idea about how a flying carpet worked. They believed that a flying carpet was spun and woven like any other carpet. The only difference lay in the dyeing process. They knew of a special clay that, when boiled in a cauldron of oil, acquired certain anti-magnetic properties. Since the earth is really a great magnet with countless lines of force running all over it, a carpet dyed in this special anti-magnetic dye would float above the ground, repulsed by the magnetic charge of the earth itself. Depending on the concentration of clay in the dye, the carpet would hover above the ground. It would be free to move only in straight lines following the magnetic lines of force that crisscross the earth. An ingenious theory really, but totally wrong of course."

"Is it?" I ask, more to be polite than anything else.

He waves a plump hand, dismissively. "Of course! It is not the dye, it is the silk itself. When you rode tonight, were you constrained to travel in straight lines like a trolley car? Did your carpet hover only at one height? Certainly not. You were free to sail as high and as wide as you wished. The process has nothing at all to do with anti-magnetic dye. The enchantments are imparted during the weaving process. Only a few people in all of history have ever proven capable. I, myself, have met only a handful."

"You don't make carpets?"

He shakes his head. "No, no. It is something I have never mastered. A small number of silkworms have always been raised here—a modest amount of silk harvested and processed. But not by me. I know *how,* of course, but it takes more than knowledge. In some cases, knowledge only gets in the way." He smiles, and fluffs up his beard with his fingertips. "But here I am going on and on! I really want to hear about *your* night, the kettle. Was it helpful? Were all your questions answered? There's really nothing quite like practical experience, and it's been a very long time since I have flown a carpet or done a cloaking spell."

I nod. "Yeah. I think I'm starting to get the hang of that cloaking thing."

"Good. Good. It looked like you had quite the lively crowd?" He stares at me, his bushy eyebrows raised.

"Uh, yeah. I guess."

He just sits there smiling, fingers joined across his belly, like he's expecting details. If he's waiting for me to tell him all about Stonechat and Budgie, he's going to be disappointed. "You could see us, in the globe thing," I say.

"Oh yes! You folks had the Orb all lit up!"

It's odd thinking about him sitting alone in his big room, watching. Odd, and kind of creepy. How much can he really see in that thing? He said he wouldn't spy on us, but when he connected with my fleck, I could see myself sleeping. I get the feeling he can see a lot more than he's letting on.

Then I get an idea, and it's so simple. "Hey. Who's Mistral?"

The bland smile slides off his face. "Mistral?"

I'm thinking about those flakes that had settled on the bottom of the globe, not shining, not moving. "Yeah. There was this guy at the kettle called Redstart. He said there were—" I grope around my memory, trying to find the word,"—renegades. Renegade ruggers. Crazy ruggers, who go around stealing carpets and stuff."

He does a sort of half shrug. "I've heard tales."

"Redstart said their leader was called Mistral. And he said Mistral made their carpets disappear out of the globe thing."

"The Orb," he says. He sounds irritated now, and I don't think it's just because I used the wrong word.

"Right, the Orb. But that's supposed to be impossible, right? Redstart said it was impossible to make yourself disappear from the Orb. And I was just remembering all those little flecks at the bottom of the glass, just sitting there. Are those *their* flecks? Mistral and his renegades?"

He stares at me. Even through his beard, I can see his tongue working around behind his lips. He puts a hand up and rubs it over his face, but when he drops it he's smiling again.

"Goodness!" he says, "Don't tell me Mistral is still the stuff of campfire ghost stories!" He gives me a chuckle. "Those stories have been around for a long time, Miss Drake. I think it's safe to say that they've probably been exaggerated. Things happen—pranks and mischief—but, really, I don't think it's any more than that." He sniffs and yawns. "My goodness we've been talking a long while! I'm surprised you haven't woken up yet. But it sounds like your evening was a success. And I'm gratified that you have your cloaking spell in hand." He wags a finger. "Use it, Miss Drake, from now on. No sense taking chances. Right?" He winks.

And I wake.

I sit up, gulping breath. "What the...?"

I'm in bed. Outside, it's still dark. It's the middle of the night. I let out a breath I didn't even know I was holding in and lay back down.

What the hell was that about? In one abrupt instant, I went from castle to bedroom, from dream to reality, like the flick of a switch. My pulse pounds fast and loud. I can hear it inside my ears.

It's pretty obvious what just happened. Parnell hung up on me. The only question is *why?*

Twelve

"There is one case where the domain has to be restricted, and this one special case is not arbitrary. Does anybody have any idea what I might be talking about?"

Mr. Kemp waits, scanning the room.

"It has to do with fractions," he prompts. "Anyone?"

I check the clock again. Fifteen minutes into a fifty-five minute class. Clearly that's impossible, but it's been a day of broken clocks—of minute hands dragging themselves painfully into the future, second hands barely able to climb the long hill between six and twelve.

"Can anyone tell me what cannot appear in a fraction's denominator?"

Kemp just won't give up. Some teachers are like that. They just keep asking and prompting and giving hints no matter how hopeless it seems. Others don't even try. I can't decide which is worse. Kemp is old school. He wears rumpled suits and calls everybody Mister This and Miss That, kind of like Parnell, only without the inside-my-dreams part. For a minute, I actually look at the board and the problem Mr. Kemp has written there, but my mind won't stay put, any more than it would during English or French. It keeps on wandering, taking me straight back to Maysa, back to the night sky.

Back to Stonechat.

He really isn't like any boy I've ever met. That first kiss led to others, long and lingering, tasting him, feeling his hands on my shoulders—just gently at first, then kneading, working the muscles with those long fingers. When he finally flew me down to my window and perched by the sill, he cupped my face in his big hands and we kissed one last time.

"Can I come see you?" he asked.

"Yeah. I'll be here."

Looking back on it now, I suppose I should've asked when. Tonight? Tomorrow? Sometime in the vague, unknowable future? I run my tongue around inside my mouth, looking for that flavor again, as if it might still be hiding somewhere. His mouth, warm and wet, mashed against mine, his tongue sweet—but also not sweet. I spend a lot of time trying to put a name to that flavor—coffee? honey? maple? gossamer? Nothing quite fits.

It's a lot to try to get out of a kiss, I suppose. But then, those were no ordinary kisses—floating on air, a thousand feet up. I lick the back of my teeth, keeping my mouth shut, remembering. After our longest kiss he pulled back, his fingers still in my hair, and recited some poem about being old and "full of sleep" and a whole lot of other stuff. Something about a crowd of stars. Like the desert sky above us, all around us, crowded with stars. I've never read a poem in my whole life that wasn't assigned in class. But leaning against him, his arms draped over my shoulders, poetry really did seem like something that could matter to somebody. It must matter to Stonechat. He has enough of it memorized.

Yates. Some Irish guy called Yates.

The next desk over, Bryce Fenster brays like a donkey.

My daydream deflates like a sputtering balloon. Everyone is laughing. It takes a moment before I realize they aren't laughing at me. It's Kemp. Mr. Kemp has made a joke and actually gotten a laugh.

Wow. This *is* a special day.

***

That night, I see Stonechat again.

A few minutes before midnight he comes tapping at my window. I'm already dressed and ready to go. I didn't go out flying just in case he might show up, though I spent the whole evening trying to convince myself he wouldn't. I've left the window open, just a few inches. He taps on the glass and calls in a whisper. "Hey, Lovebird?"

Then: "Hey, Wren?"

But by then I'm already forcing up the window sash. Before he can lean in, I'm leaning out, and my words are muffled against his neck, his rough cheek, his lips.

"Hey!"

"Shhh!"

"I'm falling!" he whispers, almost laughing.

He braces a hand against the windowsill, grinning.

"This carpet," he says, "won't hold still. Here."

He steps delicately onto the rooftop and then squats on the shingles, resting his hands on the sill. He beams the magic smile. "You coming out?"

God, what a question! As if I've been able to think about anything else all day. I grab Maysa and climb through the window. He holds out a hand.

"Careful! Watch the gutter."

Beneath his boots, the rainspout clunks.

"Jeez. Nearly knocked the damned thing off!"

"Shhh!" I put my hand to his mouth. "Wow. You're clumsy." I start to laugh. Stonechat stares at me, looking thoroughly perplexed, which only makes me laugh harder. I press my mouth against his shoulder.

91

"What are you laughing at?"

"You."

"You're laughing 'cause I'm clumsy?"

I shake my head, still giggling. It's too hard to explain. It isn't funny that he's clumsy.

It's funny that I like him being clumsy.

We fly out over the Sandia Mountains. I lead him up the arroyo and we park over a bank of clouds, smothered in moonlight. Wednesday night, it's the badlands of El Mapais. Thursday, we watch a street fair from high over Santa Fe. We skim the surface of El Vado Lake and perch in a tall ponderosa pine to watch cars hurry along the interstate. None of it is planned.

"We'll go where the wind takes us," Stonechat says, though really the wind doesn't make any difference. Over the mesas we hang up high in the moonlight and nudge the two carpets together so they form one broad, soft surface. We stretch out and stare up at the stars, talking.

Or not talking. Stonechat talks a lot, but he can manage not talking just as well. Over Cibola, we spend a long time saying nothing at all. I cradle his head in my lap, and we kiss until my neck starts to ache. Finally, I have to sit up. He stays where he is, staring up at the sky. He runs his tongue around in his mouth, and says:

> *"Never until this night have I been stirred.*
> *This elaborate starlight—"*

He scowls. "That's not right."

He sits up and digs in the pockets of his windbreaker. He brings out a tiny book, not much bigger than a deck of cards and begins riffling through the pages. "Ha. That *was* it."

He recites now, in his more typical poetry voice:

> *"Never until this night have I been stirred.*
> *The elaborate starlight throws a reflection*

On the dark stream,
Till all the eddies gleam;
And thereupon there comes that scream
From terrified, invisible beast or bird:
Image of poignant recollection."

He looks up at me and smiles. I ask, "Is that supposed to mean something?"

"It just popped into my head."

"Mmm. I like the other one better—about hiding your face in a crowd of stars."

He turns and lays back, putting his head in my lap again, and does the one about the crowd of stars with his eyes closed. I watch his mouth form the words, listen as each one drops like a stone, rippling the perfect silence. Then I'm kissing him again, despite the crick in my neck.

We do a lot of kissing. Or as Stonechat calls it: necking.

"Necking," I kid him. "Does anybody really say necking anymore? Like since the fifties?"

He buries his grin against my neck, nuzzling in until I start laughing again. I dig my face in against his cheek, holding my breath until I can't hold any more. He squirms under the ticklish pressure and lets go a gust of soft laughter. I roll over on top of him and our lips mesh together. His breath fills my mouth as his hands slowly slide down to my hips. On a sudden, daring impulse I take one of his hands and guide it up under my shirt. His hand doesn't object. He gives a soft, appreciative groan, and I feel his mouth curl into a smile.

Afterwards, I curl up in the crook of his arm. He tips his head so it's resting against mine and doesn't say anything, not even poetry. I'm glad for that. In that particular moment, silence is better than poetry. After a long while of silence and stillness, he plants a kiss on my scalp, pulls his arm out, and sits up. I sit up too, and straighten my clothes. He gives me a smile, one of his best.

I smile back. "I hope we didn't scare the carpets."

He barks a laugh and does up a shirt button. Then he catches me by the elbow and pulls me in. He presses his cheek against mine. "That was really nice."

I nod. "Mm-hm."

"That wasn't—" he pauses to scratch beneath his chin, "—your first time, was it?"

"Oh no. No." I fix my collar. Probably he doesn't expect me to say any more than that, but I do anyway. "It was just a guy from school. We only did it once. It wasn't any big deal. I didn't even like him that much."

He gives me a curious stare. "Why did you do it, then?"

I shrug. "Good question."

Actually the question has an easy answer. Matt Tyler was an experiment, as simple as that. I wasn't swept up in the moment or crazy with desire. Not that Matt was bad looking or especially obnoxious. He was nice enough. We knew each other from school, but we had never spoken until we met at Caddy's house—at a party mostly memorable for a bunch of boys I didn't know who got royally plastered and danced on a coffee table until it collapsed. Matt found them as annoying as I did. I liked that about him. After that, there had been a couple of movie dates and then an evening on the sofa at his house while his parents were conveniently out of town. It seemed like as good a time as any.

As I'd expected, it wasn't any big deal.

"Actually, there isn't that much to tell."

He nods, and we sit for a while just watching the stars. He strokes the back of my hand with long, delicate strokes.

I don't even consider asking Stonechat if it had been *his* first time. He's obviously had some experience in the matter, and not just because he had a condom handy. Matt Tyler had one too. That particular memory is a little cringe-worthy—watching, trying not to watch, but worried that he might not be doing it right.

Nothing about Stonechat worries me. Maybe I ought to be worried, scared even. I really don't know the first damned thing about him. But he smiles, eyes crinkling, and runs a finger through my hair, teasing out a snarl, and I forget to be worried. It all seems so natural. So easy.

How many other girls has there been?

It doesn't matter. It doesn't. I know that's true, but I can't help wondering. Am I just another minor triumph? Like Budgie? I still see those dark, glaring eyes. Budgie was jealous—that much was obvious. But what else was going on? Was it Stonechat's fault? I mean, he dumped her. Tough luck. Shit happens. But was he a jerk about it? Did he get what he wanted and then treat her like crap?

Somehow I can't picture Stonechat turning into a smirking moron because he had his way with a girl. With Budgie. Curvy Budgie with the short skirt and the boots. And wide hips. Plump even, truth be told—but some guys go for that. Maybe Stonechat does too. But then what does he see in me, with my pointy shoulders and bony elbows?

I am going to stop thinking about Budgie. Whatever happened between Stonechat and Budgie is old news. Now is what matters. And now is about us—Stonechat and me. That's all there is.

And as I make this monumental decision, I realize something: that last bit of me, the part of my brain that thought all of this was just a schizoid delusion? It's gone. I'm all in now.

I'm a true believer.

***

Days float by. Every night Stonechat comes tapping at my window, and every night, I go with him. I know it's crazy. The danger of getting caught is very real. It's only a matter of time, but I don't care about any of that. We fly cloaked, high over the rooftops until we're out over the empty desert, and we park in the moonlight. Sometimes I just lie in his arms watching the stars, listening to the melodies he spins with his voice.

"I talk too much," he says one night, "don't I?"

I turn and lean back, pressing into him. "Not for me."

"You don't say very much sometimes."

"I like to listen." And I do. Listening to him read poetry does strange things inside me. It's crazy. I couldn't have cared less about poetry before. It was just one of those things they made you do in school. I snuggle down into the hollow of his shoulder. "Do that one with the white birds."

He does. I feel his voice as much as I hear it, rumbling inside his chest:

"I would that we were, my beloved, white birds on the foam of the sea!
We tire of the flame of the meteor, before it can fade and flee;
And the flame of the blue star of twilight, hung low on the rim of the sky,
Has awakened in our hearts, my beloved, a sadness that may not die."

He stops. I stroke his wrist with my thumb. "A sadness that may not die. What made him so gloomy?"

"Ah, well, he lost the love of his life. Plus he was Irish, so that didn't help."

He digs the tiny book of poems from his pocket and thumbs through. "Here's one." He clears his throat:

"When you and my true lover meet
And he plays tunes between your feet."

"Tunes between your feet?"
"No wait!" He flips more pages:

"He holds her helpless breast upon his breast.
How can those terrified vague fingers push
The feathered glory from her loosening thighs?"

"Come on!" I reach, pawing for the page. "It doesn't really say 'loosening thighs,' does it?"

But he's already let the book slip and he's laughing. When he stops, he takes a breath and recites from memory:

"Half close your eyelids, loosen your hair,
And dream about the great and their pride;
They have spoken about you everywhere,
But weigh this song with the great and their pride;
I made it out of a mouthful of air,
Their children's children shall say they have lied."

I crawl forward until my hands are upon his chest and I stare down into his face. "You know something?" I ask.

"What?"

"Sometimes you *do* talk too much." I settle down on top of him, and our mouths find each other, and after that, we don't talk at all for a good long while.

Thirteen

On Friday he tells me, "There's a kettle tomorrow night, out at
Big Hatchet, if you want to go."

We meet a little earlier than usual. When I tell Lauren I'm
going to bed at ten o'clock on a Saturday night, she doesn't even blink.

"Sounds like a good idea. You've been looking tired lately."

I go upstairs and check my face in the bathroom mirror. She's
not wrong. I look pretty bad, and only some of it is exhaustion.
There's guilt in my eyes, plain as anything. I don't know how Lauren
could have missed it. I run water cold in the sink and take a double-
handful, rubbing it into the black smudges under my eyes. "I couldn't
tell her if I wanted to," I say to the girl in the mirror. "You know that's
true." She stares back at me, looking guiltier than ever.

High above the branches of the ash tree, Stonechat is waiting.
He gives me a grin. "All good?"

"All good."

We make fast time on the way to Big Hatchet—unbelievably
fast.

"That's the way it is with carpets, Lovebird. Once they've been
someplace, they can find it even faster the next time."

98

Lovebird. Wren. He never uses my actual name. I'm not even sure he remembers it. That's okay. I don't know his actual name, either. No one could really be named Stonechat. But I don't ask. I don't even want to know. He's Stonechat, the beautiful boy with the crazy name, a creature of wind and poetry. I like him just like that.

We pass over the crawl of light that is Interstate 10 and plunge into the dark roadless wilderness of the desert, Geronimo's desert. An Indian chief with a flying carpet. Well, why not? No stranger than a seventeen year old girl from Albuquerque.

"There's the Hatchet," Stonechat says.

I catch the gleam of a moonlit cliff, a white face of limestone. In the valley beyond, Redstart is probably talking. Junco is probably pouring gossamer. Budgie, most likely, is sulking behind a cigarette, or at least she will be after I show up. We cross the shoulder of Big Hatchet and slide down into the valley. Moonlight picks out yucca plumes, tamarix shrubs. At the lip of the ravine, I see the white snag of the ironwood tree. Beyond it, fire flickers orange in the stone circle.

"Something's wrong."

He's staring down, his brows creased.

"What?"

"Too quiet."

It is. By now we should be hearing the sound of voices.

"No one's there."

The fire burns, licking up the stacked branches, but the stones are empty. We circle in. Stonechat slows to a hover about ten feet up. I do the same. I can taste the smoke.

"Why would they leave a fire going?"

He shakes his head. "They wouldn't."

We land by the flat stone at the base of the hackberry. There are no carpets piled there. We lay our carpets on the stone and walk back to the fire. Circling the pit, my foot clinks against glass. It's a bottle, corked and half-full. I hold it up for Stonechat to see. He takes the bottle and uncorks it.

"Gossamer?"

For an answer, he brings the bottle to his lips and tries a sip, then swallows and nods. "I guess Junco was here, anyway." He re-corks the bottle and sets it down.

"Who else was supposed to be here?"

Stonechat stares at the fire. He doesn't say anything.

"Stonechat?"

He looks at me like he'd forgotten I was even there. "What?"

"Who was supposed to be here?"

He puffs out his cheeks, then exhales. "No idea. The usual I guess."

We search, reaching into places the firelight doesn't go. We find a second bottle of gossamer, an old tin can and a dusty playing card with a torn corner—the seven of clubs. We take to the air again. When we get to the ravine, we search on foot, poking around, peeping into the scrub and the shadows, keeping quiet.

"No one's here."

Stonechat frowns. "Yeah. But something happened. They wouldn't have just left the fire burning like that."

"Stonechat?" It's a man's voice. In the shelter of a desert willow, a shadow becomes solid.

"Whimbrel?"

"I thought that was you!" Whimbrel's face is pale as ash but his relief is obvious. Behind him, two women uncloak. One is Nightjar. The other has a long hank of silver-blonde hair tucked behind her ears. I've never seen her before.

"What are you guys doing out here?" Stonechat asks.

"It was *them*!" Nightjar says. "I never even..." She draws a trembly breath. "They came out of nowhere!"

"Who?" Stonechat asks. "What the hell are you talking about?"

"They were on rugs." Whimbrel's voice wobbles like it might crack. He brings it low again. "Ruggers. Renegades."

"Renegades?"

"They were cloaked," Nightjar says. "We couldn't see anything until they were right on top of us. It was a good thing we had the fire going or we'd have been done for."

"What happened?"

"It was Longbill and Crane. They were in the air. We heard shouting but we thought they were just fooling around. Then there were other voices—lots of voices. We couldn't see."

"They were laughing," Whimbrel says, "not Longbill and Crane—the others. Then they were on the ground, running. They couldn't fly in because of the fire so they came in on foot."

"We barely made it to the carpets."

"Where are Longbill and Crane?" I ask.

Nightjar shakes her head.

"What about Junco?"

"Here." Picking his way around a bramble of creosote, he comes trudging up the steep slope of sand.

"God! Junco, what happened? Are you okay?"

He steps from shadow into full moonlight. "Yeah," he says, but his voice is beaten and hopeless. "I fell," he waves his hand back over his shoulder a few times. A gash runs from earlobe to jawbone. Blood, dark and congealing, smears his cheek, his chin, his neck. He's caked with dust on one side—one leg, one hip, one side of his floppy maroon vest.

"My God! You look awful!" Nightjar takes his elbow. "Do you want to sit down?"

"I'm okay." He draws a deep breath and forces a weak grin. "Hey, Wren. Hoping you'd show up." His grin falters. He droops, shoulders low, head bowed. When he looks up, he says in a plain voice, "They got my rug."

Nightjar's mouth falls open. There's wetness in Junco's eyes.

"Oh, no. Not really?" Nightjar is near tears herself.

"Wow," the still nameless girl says with flat astonishment.

"Yeah," Junco says. "I went for it but I tripped, and some guy put a knee in my back. I couldn't move."

101

"Wow," the girl says again.

"What did they do?"

"Mostly they just kept me there. Then one of them brings my rug over and they let me up. It was torture. I thought they were going to throw it into the fire or something."

"Jesus!" Stonechat says softly.

"Yeah. They pretended they were going to. There was a whole circle of them—seven or eight—just watching me sweat. The big guy had my arms pinned behind my back."

"What happened?"

Junco sniffs. "They let me go. They rolled up the carpet and took it with them. And then the big one tells me to run. That was part of the joke, I guess. I ran. They we're all laughing their heads off. Then when I get about fifty yards away, I hear them coming. I figured they were going to run me down, beat the hell out of me, kill me—I don't know. I ran hard for the edge of the ravine and I just jumped. I hit the ground and slid all the way to the bottom."

He wipes his eyes, smearing damp grime across his ruined face. "That was it. I heard them flying off, yelling and laughing."

Nightjar leans in and puts an arm around his back. "Poor Junco."

He manages a sad smile.

We begin making our way up the slope, rugs draped over our shoulders. Junco asks about Longbill and Crane and about somebody named Dipper.

"We haven't seen them," Whimbrel answers.

Junco looks troubled. "Man, I hope nobody else got hurt. Those bastards were fucking crazy!"

"Who were they?" I ask.

He shakes his head. "I never saw any of them before. Renegades. Demented renegades. Carpet stealers."

"Why? Why steal a carpet? I mean, it won't fly for you if you don't know its name, right?"

"That's true," Whimbrel says. He sounds miserable.

"And they had carpets of their own anyway."

"It's like I said," Junco insists, "they were just crazy!"

"Do you think they were...?"

But the rest of Nightjar's question dies on her lips. A sound drops down, right on top of us—a wind that isn't wind.

"Oh, God!" Nightjar almost screams.

"Hey!" It's only Longbill.

"Jesus, Longbill!" Nightjar yells. "You scared the crap out of us!"

Longbill descends, flanked by Crane and another woman I don't know. Dipper, I guess.

"Sorry," Longbill says, dismounting, "Weren't sure what was going on. Christ, Junco, what the hell happened to you?"

Junco tells the story again. Longbill shakes his head.

"Well that sucks. I mean, that royally sucks. Doesn't surprise me. Those guys were nuts."

"Where were you?" Nightjar asks.

"Following them."

"Following?"

"Hell, yes! We lost the two that were following us and got cloaked. We were off in the yucca flats, just keeping low and we saw them taking off. So we followed them."

"Nice!" Junco says, with surprising vigor. "Did you see where they took my rug?"

Dipper shakes her head. "No. Sorry, Junco. We lost them in the cumulus." She has dark, olive skin, and wears her hair short. "They were going west."

We all stand for a long moment, pondering this useless piece of information. Then Junco begins climbing the hill again, with fresh determination.

"Junco?" Nightjar asks. "Hey, man, you can ride with me."

"Yeah, okay. Thanks." But he doesn't stop climbing.

"Where are you going?"

"I left two bottles of gossamer back at the campfire," he calls back over his shoulder. "I don't know if those bastards are coming back, but if they do, I'm not leaving any of that for them to drink."

Fourteen

There's darkness.

And then an odd sound: *clink, click.*

Or not so odd, actually: a knife and a fork clunking against a dinner plate. The most ordinary sound in the world.

And chewing. There is definitely chewing. I open my eyes and light crowds in. A pair of hands sit on a smooth table. Those are my hands. Beyond them Parnell Florian spoons gravy onto a mound of something white and lumpy. He looks up.

"Miss Drake. Good evening."

I watch him take a forkful of drippy mashed potatoes, watch him chew, see him wipe his beard. He eyes me over his napkin, his face somber. Leaning back, he rests his elbows on the arms of his chair and exhales. "I believe I owe you an apology, Miss Drake."

"Yeah?"

He nods. "Though you are hardly the first *youthful* flyer we have ever had, I do feel an extra level of responsibility in these cases." He leans forward again. "I would hate for you to think I knowingly put you in harm's way."

I feel my eyebrow crimp. "Are you talking about Big Hatchet?"

"Yes. A most regrettable occurrence. I really should've seen it coming. The meetings at Big Hatchet," he shakes his head, "too

105

conspicuous. There have been kettles there since time immemorial. Everyone knows."

"But who were those guys?"

He draws another deep breath. "Renegades, of course. Followers"—he pronounces the syllables precisely and slowly—"of Mistral."

I squint at him. "You said—"

"I know what I said, Miss Drake," he cuts me off. "The fact is I was not being honest with you. Or with myself for that matter. The renegades are real. Mistral is real. It is more than just a few rebels making mischief." He grips the arms of his chair again and makes himself sit upright. "I think perhaps I need to bring you up to speed. A little history. Oh, don't look so pained! Not ancient history. Recent stuff. It's important you know the whole story." He tugs at his beard and refolds his hands across his belly, "It begins," he says, "with a boy named Algernon Fell."

"Never heard of him."

"No, you wouldn't have." He pulls a hand through his beard again, smoothing the dark bramble. "When I met him, he was just twelve years old. Rather a delicate boy, actually. Young for a rugger, but it was obvious from the first he was an unusual boy. Of course, no one comes to the Order because they are ordinary. But even among outcasts, Algernon Fell was unusual. Wonderfully gifted—not simply his flying, but his understanding."

He tugs an earlobe. "That was fifteen years ago now. I found him living on the street, a runaway. His home life, as I understand it, had been something of a nightmare. I saw at once that he had the potential to become something more than just another rider. After a time, I offered him the opportunity of becoming my apprentice. He accepted and came here to live and study. He had an unusual rapport with carpets, and with the silk itself. For a while, I harbored the hope he might become a weaver. In my fonder moments, I even imagined him taking *my* place one day.

"Have I ever described to you, Miss Drake, the process of weaving an enchanted carpet?" He gives his shaggy head a weary shake. "It takes time—so much time! A weaver might spend a year working on a single rug. A frightful labor. All during weaving the proper sequence of words must be said, the correct series of thoughts performed, the same seventeen syllables repeated over and over, never varying the order or even the pace until she has tied off a row of stitches. I have tried it." He puffs air from his lips. "Hopeless. There is a mental discipline, which I simply do not possess, a sort of a trance state that a true weaver will drop into. Even when I thought I had maintained the proper mindset for the whole time, I would find flaws, places where the incantation had not taken hold. A dropped stitch in a flying carpet may not be visible to the eye, but it will affect its airworthiness.

"As it happened, I had at that time in my employ a woman—a weaver, one of a long line of true weavers. For many years, she was my only reliable carpet-maker. Beata was her name. Her carpets were not the fanciest. Some even called them plain, but they flew. She had the touch all right.

"She also had a daughter, a winsome slip of a thing. Gizella. A lovely child." He pauses. "She never particularly liked me. Her mother doted on her, of course, and taught her the trade of a master weaver. She kept her right by her side, showing her every stitch."

He lets his gaze drift off toward some spot I can't see, somewhere in the past. "It must have been very dull for a young girl. I've often thought if her life had not been so dull"—he dips his head to the side—"maybe things might have turned out differently.

"Well, it was only the three of us at that point. Beata, Gizella, and I. And a cook. I cannot for the life of me recall her name. A fat woman. She lived in the west quarters and prepared meals and cleaned up. Beata and her daughter had rooms near the greenhouse. On moonless nights, Beata would harvest the cocoons and draw the silk. It was exciting work in those days. Every year or so, as Beata completed a new carpet, we would actually expand the number of flyers." He beams. "You know, the Orb is more than a spyglass for members of the Order. It can also reach out to those who have that potential, that innate talent. It functions as a sort of divining rod. I connect to it, and it knows what I'm looking for. With Algernon Fell I knew right away, as soon as our minds touched. He flew like he was born to it. And such a focused mind for one so young! He practiced and studied all the time. I told you he was very good with the silk. He longed to master the art of weaving, the enchantments."

He shakes his head again. "But Algernon was, like me, doomed to fail. I can sometimes darn a small hole or mend a frayed edge. But the ability to create a whole tapestry—which you yourself know is virtually a living thing—well, it is a rare gift indeed. Algernon coveted that gift and he worked at it with a fantastic level of devotion. I would watch his efforts, admire his dedication, and mourn along with him every time he failed and had to scrap another tapestry after months of effort. I understood, having failed at it so many times myself—feeling the stirrings of life in the fabric, then losing it, feeling it slip away. I knew his grief."

He gives a weak smile. "Now, as you might imagine, Beata held a great fascination for young Mr. Fell. Here he was, as learned on the subject of flying carpets as anyone excepting myself, and here was she, who knew nothing of Naser Parvas or Sulayman the Magnificent, yet she could accomplish what he could not."

"He was jealous."

"Jealous. Resentful. And contemptuous. Even as he coveted her natural ability, he reviled her simpleness. She was not stupid, but her intelligence was not of the sort Algernon Fell could appreciate. To him, she was just a crude, ignorant woman."

He digs a finger into his beard and scratches his jaw. "You have to understand, much of this took place without my knowledge. I believe Algernon began to cozy up to the older woman, attempting to win her over by charm. He had charm, certainly. I have said he was delicate, but he was no less handsome for that. By that time he was probably seventeen, tall and fair-skinned. He had black hair, but with pale blue eyes. I am not sure what he hoped to accomplish. Beata's skill was not something she could have taught him. He already knew the method and the incantations as well as she did. He must have believed there was some way he could make use of her, if he could gain her trust.

"But Beata had made up her mind about him long ago. She did not trust him. Nor did she like him. She was impervious to his flatteries. She complained to me about him, told me she could not accomplish her work with his constant pestering. Could I not just make him leave her alone? I promised I would speak to him."

"Did you?"

"Of course. I have to admit, I misread the situation. I trusted the boy too much and valued the weaver's opinion too little. He told me it was *she* who had lavished unwanted attention upon him. He wove a convincing tale, insisting she had mistaken his friendly interest in her work for something more—affection, perhaps—and she had become immodestly infatuated. Her devotion embarrassed him. He didn't want to be unkind, but finally he was forced to tell her, in no uncertain terms..." he waves a hand, as if I can fill in the rest of the story for myself.

"I am ashamed to admit it was his story I believed. After all, why shouldn't the lonely old woman find the handsome young man desirable? And how could the opposite possibly be true? She was more than twice his age and no great beauty.

"I let the matter slide, and heard nothing more on the subject. Things reverted to their former superficial calm, and I believed the incident had run its course. But the course had only begun. For while the weaver may have been immune to the boy's charm, there was another in our midst who was not so invulnerable."

It takes me a second, then I get it. "The weaver's daughter."

Parnell nods. "Yes. I am afraid poor Gizella was all too receptive to Algernon's pursuits. Really, it was almost too predictable. She was a mere girl, no more than fifteen—impressionable, naïve—and lonely. She had no companions, only her mother and the old

109

cook. The blandishments of the handsome young Mr. Fell must have hit her like the proverbial ton of bricks.

"I, of course, was unaware of all of this until Beata came to me again to complain. This time it was on behalf of her daughter. I spoke to the boy, but this time he told me that she was correct. He and Gizella were in love—utterly, madly. He acknowledged the awkwardness of the situation but his heart had spoken. He loved Gizella and she him, and they would not be denied."

Parnell gives a heavy sigh. "I was, frankly, out of my depths. I told myself after the first blush of young love had worn off that they would lose interest. The passion would die. I did my best to ignore the whole situation, but even the walls of this castle were not thick enough for me to hide entirely. Often, late into the night, I would hear mother and daughter, voices raised. Gizella was as headstrong as any young girl would be in the same situation, and the more her mother forbade her, the more she bridled. My young apprentice worked beside me, seeming to take no notice of the unrest he had caused, but more than once I saw a look of satisfaction twitch across his face.

"Then, one morning after a particularly tempestuous quarrel, I was awakened by Beata pounding at my door. Gizella was gone. So was Algernon. A quick search revealed the truth. They had taken their few belongings, raided the larder for provisions, and flown off together on Algernon's carpet."

He gets up from his chair and walks the several steps to the open window. "Beata was inconsolable. She would not work. Would not speak. I feel quite certain she blamed me. If I had done something, listened to her in the first place, perhaps..." He shrugs, leaving the sentence hanging. "She was not wrong. She had warned me and I had ignored it. I chose to believe the boy."

"But you could find him, right? Using the Orb?"

"I tried. Lord, I tried! It was extraordinary. Unprecedented, actually. No one, no member of the Order had ever—" He grimaces and shakes his head. "Time and again, I put my hands on the Orb, calling out to him."

"He didn't want to answer."

Parnell turns. "You don't understand how this works, Miss Drake. It is not a conscious choice to answer or not as you please. Who can refuse a dream? No. This was something else. It was as though he'd simply stopped existing. Somehow, and I still do not know how, he had cut himself off—taken himself out of the reach of the Orb." He turns his gaze back to the window. "It was un*think*able. An impossibility. And it was then I noticed the first of those little flecks lying on the bottom of the Orb. I tried to draw it up where I could view it in detail. It would not rise. It stayed put, just as it has ever since, but I know it was his."

I wait, watching his silhouette framed by dimming daylight. "Did you ever see him again?"

He continues staring out. When he begins talking again, it's as though he didn't even hear the question.

"We were in a bad way after they left. For a few weeks, Beata hounded me, demanding I continue searching, that I do something. But there was nothing I could do. The Orb had failed. Her frustration was as great as my own, but where would I begin? They could've been anywhere in the world, anywhere at all. I told her she had to be patient, that surely her daughter would contact her soon. Gizella was a good girl at heart. But I was just talking. I knew nothing.

"Beata stopped speaking to me altogether. She started taking meals in her rooms. Days went by. I scarcely knew she was there. She did no weaving, of course. I took to tending the mulberry bushes, minding the silkworms. I went to her door on several occasions, offering my sympathy, my apologies. She would not answer.

"Then one day—months later—a message arrived. I was eating dinner when Beata came pounding at my door again. She had a parchment in her hand and a length of ribbon in the other, and she was nearly raving. When I managed to calm her down sufficiently, she said it had appeared on her bedspread. I read the parchment. It said very little. He made the most cursory apology for their abrupt departure and then insisted that she come to them, saying only that

111

Gizella needed her and the reasons were too personal to put into a letter. He had worked everything out very neatly. The ribbon was enchanted. She need only tell it she was waiting and a carpet would appear that would carry her—and only her—to their location.

"She was ready to leave instantly. I counseled against it. I was uncomfortable with the potential danger involved, but I was uncomfortable on another level as well. Sending the letter across god knows what distance, causing it to materialize within these walls, that was an unusual display of skill. Naturally, I could do the same, but it troubled me that he had picked up the ability without my help.

"But what was worse was the notion that he had enchanted this ribbon to summon a carpet upon command, a carpet which would then carry Beata, and *only* Beata, back to him!" He shakes his head, "Now *that* is an extraordinary piece of spell-casting. I mean, I've *heard* of such things. The sorcerer Abrim Chandari was said to keep a whole army of rider-less carpets, which did his bidding. But no one really knows how much of that was real. And Algernon had, after all, made himself disappear from the Orb. If he could do that, anything might be possible."

He turns and trudges back to the table and settles into his chair with a heavy sigh. "Beata, naturally, was not interested in my objections. Her only interest was finding her daughter. I kept the silk ribbon from her. I needed time to think, to gather more information. The other riders might be able to find him given time, and the ribbon might help. Besides, I did not trust Beata. Coming to me when she received the letter was little more than a reflex. She still blamed me, and I had no doubt she would summon the carpet that would take her to her daughter as soon as my back was turned."

He stares down at the unfinished plate of potatoes. "I underestimated *her*, as well. I stayed up very late that night, perusing the Orb, rereading books I hadn't touched in years. I drank rather too much sherry, I am afraid. When I finally succumbed to sleep it was in that very chair." He gestures to the old, overstuffed armchair standing near the bookshelves. "When I awoke late the next morning the ribbon was no longer in my pocket, and Beata was no longer in the castle."

He looks up. His eyes are dark. "That was twelve years ago, Miss Drake. I have not seen any of them since." He drags a hand through his hair. "I waited. Days went by—weeks, months. I recruited search parties from the Order, but they all came back empty-handed.

"For a long time I heard nothing. I had almost put the whole Algernon Fell matter out of my head. But then, just about two years ago, the raids started. Stories began making the rounds of gangs of renegades, swooping down on unsuspecting flyers. They were few at first, but their numbers have grown. Thirteen former Order members, now gone. And each time, a new flake floats to the bottom of the Orb and out of my reach."

"What do they want?"

"Want?" He shakes his head. "I really don't know."

"They steal carpets."

"Yes. And I don't know what they expect to do with carpets they cannot name, cannot control. Perhaps all they care about is creating as much havoc as possible. There have been deaths too, Miss Drake. Two of the raids have resulted in dead Order members." He shrugs. "Maybe they weren't intended. Not a few flyers would rather risk death than surrender their carpet."

He puts his hands together on the table in front of him and stares at them. Then he looks at me again.

"But there is one thing we do know about them. Everyone agrees these renegades are led by a flyer of unusual, remarkable powers. A man who calls himself Mistral. Surely you've guessed by now, Miss Drake. Mistral, the leader of the renegades, *is* Algernon Fell."

Fifteen

Parnell leans back. His chair gives a creak. He yawns, then sighs, then just sits there looking tired. I see it. And I hear it, and there's nothing strange about that.

Except I'm not actually there. Across the table, an empty chair stares back at him.

The dream continues, only I'm not a part of it anymore. I can see the whole room. He's alone. He takes the napkin from his lap, dabs at his forehead, and leans his head back to mop underneath his beard.

This is weird. It's not like having dream meetings with him wasn't weird enough, now I'm seeing him in *his* dreams? But that doesn't make any sense, either. This must be my dream, but it sure doesn't feel that way.

He pushes himself from the chair and stands, and begins pacing stiffly toward the window. There's a sink in the far corner of the room, cast iron and old, like the one down in the greenhouse. He picks up a shiny green watering can. The tap howls and clunks, before finally releasing a gushing, spluttering stream. With difficult steps, he goes from window box to window box, measuring out water into each of the flower boxes.

114

The room has dimmed. Wherever Parnell lives, it's going to be night soon.

Finally he finishes the last flower box and puts down the watering can. From the bookshelf, he takes down a small brown bottle with a fancy label. He uncorks it and pours a little into a tiny glass.

He selects a book from the shelf, then hobbles toward the armchair.

An idea occurs to him. He looks up and says a word: "Najeeba?" From overhead, lilac silk wafts down, falling in darts and swoops until it is perched on his shoulder. Parnell pets the handkerchief, cooing. "Time for bed, little one." He holds open the breast pocket of his robe. The scrap of fabric arches. With a sudden pirouette, she dives into the pocket. Parnell turns to the armchair again.

Downstairs, wood scrapes stone.

Parnell freezes. In the silence, his own breath is noisy and harsh.

Down below, voices rustle, a hushed whispering. He keeps listening, still frozen, the tiny glass clutched tight between his fingers. He shifts his weight, one hip to the other. His knee creaks. There are people on the stairs now, he can hear them coming. His face is crimped with concentration, like he's trying to count, trying to guess.

They enter the room, single-file—a quiet, orderly mob. Six. Seven, now. Why so many? They are his henchmen. His followers.

His audience.

He comes last, wearing a plain charcoal evening jacket, very dignified. Old school. Time has not been unkind to him. The handsome boy has become a handsome man. He bows his head with a demure smile. "Master."

No one laughs. Parnell's gaze goes from face to face. They are a startlingly ugly bunch. One—the tallest, broadest, and ugliest—is missing an eye. It was not surgically removed.

"Are we late for supper?"

"Please, Algernon, whatever it is you want—"

"I think you know." His voice is calm and confident. A second smile curls his smooth features—not cruel, not vindictive, not anything at all.

"I don't have it anymore," Parnell says. His voice is as creaky as his bum knee. "I put it away, for safe-keeping."

"That would've been a smart move," the man concedes, nodding, "but let's be frank. We know each other too well to bother with deception."

Parnell's pushes his lips together. They are dry enough to crack. He lets his tongue edge out to wet them but his tongue is dry as well. "Seems to me," he croaks, "you were always pretty good at deception."

The man laughs, a silky flutter. "Well, you so *wanted* to believe." He reaches inside his jacket and pulls out a handful of silver light. Caught between his fingers, the light becomes solid. He gives it a flick and it snakes out into the room—floating, coiling, sniffing the air. It won't keep still long enough to fix a length to it. Glowing with its own cool light, it sends shadows chasing around the room.

"You always said this wouldn't work," Mistral says.

Parnell watches. "Spider silk?" He tries to sound mocking, but only manages to sound terrified.

The man nods. "You were right, about the carpets. You can't make a decent carpet from spider silk. But you can make some things."

The thing dances a luxuriant, lazy tango, shaping the air into curves and spheres.

"How did you get it to glow?" Parnell asks.

"A distillate of glowworm tail," Mistral answers. "Luciferase enzyme. Pretty, isn't it?"

Parnell says nothing. The slow lashing of the thing holds his eyes.

"Now," Algernon Fell says, "There is really no reason for anybody to get hurt here tonight. I am not a cruel man. I do not take pleasure in preying on the weak. The Orb," he scans the room with a

116

casual gaze, "it hasn't been put away at all, has it? You always kept it handy." His eyes fall upon the curtained alcove. "Ah. Of course. You haven't moved it at all, have you?"

Parnell wheels and bolts for the alcove. The silver rope leaps and darts after him.

"Get the Orb!" Mistral shouts.

The scarf gets to Parnell first. It winds about him, pinning one arm back. He manages to grab a handful, but then it is at his neck, slithering down between his beard and his collar, wrapping a coil around his throat. He wheezes, stumbling forward, letting his weight carry him, reaching out, pawing the soft darkness.

"Don't let him hurt the Orb!"

A heavy hand has him by the shoulder, now. He flails his free arm through the curtain. Mistral is shouting, but all he hears is thick grunting in his ear. Silk tightens, cutting into his neck, sharp as twine. With all he has left, he lunges, flinging his arm out as he falls. One finger finds the Orb. It touches the curved glass and slides, riding down the cool, smooth surface.

Then he is on the floor, on knees and hands. A rough voice swears. Weight bears down on top of him, and he dives down into flat, gray stone.

Sixteen

The world ends.

A giant meteor has hit the earth. A bomb has obliterated Albuquerque. The light outside my window is like the light of a thousand suns. The blare of sirens is announcing our total destruction.

Or it's morning.

Of course it is. The light in the window is only one sun, and that's bad enough. The wail of sirens is just the goddamn alarm clock——*bleep! bleep! bleep!*——shouting its censored curses in my face.

Morning.

I sit up, shut the thing off.

I stumble to the bathroom, and scoop cold water into my face. I look awful. I don't even remind myself of Miranda this morning. My own face is bad enough.

I guess my own brand of crazy is bad enough, too. What's real and what isn't real——that's not even the question any more. Since I can't even make myself *not* believe in flying carpets and magic orbs, I guess this is my reality now. I've made my choice. What's another weird dream, more or less?

But that one was disturbing. And nasty.

I get dressed, drag myself through breakfast, ride the bus to school—but all the while, all through six blurry periods I'm thinking about it, reliving the things I saw, discovering new bits in my memory: the creak of Parnell's knee; the green watering can; the ugly man with a gash where his eye ought to be. But the thing I really can't get out of my mind is that long ribbon of silver light floating in front of me, dancing like something wind-wafted, wrapped around my throat, getting tighter and tighter. Only it's Parnell's throat. Digging through whiskers, cutting into his fleshy neck. He holds out an arm in a lavender sleeve and his thick fingers touch the smooth, round glass of the Orb.

Then the world ends.

That's how the memory always finishes up: a bright flash and a crazy roaring of voices as if a thousand other dreams have just been shoved into my brain. Then it's all gone again, leaving only quiet.

Like I said: disturbing. And nasty.

***

When seventh period ends, I fight my way through the crush out to the front steps. Caddy Gillespie stands with McKenzie Boone and Breanne Mueller. For some reason, I drift on over. All three of them are glancing over the concrete bannister toward the flagpole.

"What's he doing?" Breanne asks.

"Same thing he was doing thirty seconds ago," McKenzie answers. "Just standing there." She shoots me a glance and says, "Bree is stalking Sweater Boy."

"Again?" I'm pretty sure that's exactly what she was doing the last time I hung out with them. Out by the flagpole, I see him: tall and bored, wearing tan chinos and a V-neck sweater. If he's aware of us watching him, it doesn't show.

Bree giggles. "He's picking up his backpack!" She turns away again. "Is he heading for *Phoebe's*?"

"Nope." Caddy shakes her head. "Going the other way."

"Oh." Bree's excitement deflates.

119

"Doesn't mean we can't go," McKenzie suggests.

I almost go with them. For a minute, I experience the desire to sit and listen to them gossip over Cokes and chips, to think about anything but the stupid dream that's been in my brain all day. I even picture myself getting them to ask me about Stonechat. I wouldn't use his name, of course. He would just be a boy. I can almost hear Bree's voice arcing up through the octaves. *You're seeing someone? Oh my God! Who? Is he cute?*

But I don't go. Technically, they don't actually ask me to go, and I can't really blame them. I'm the one who's been blowing them off for the last few months. I go home instead.

Bad mistake. The blare of Gretchen's TV show hits me from the living room as soon as I open the front door. I head for the stairs to try and get some sleep before dinner, but Lauren heads me off.

"Renny? Can I talk to you, please?"

I stop, hand on the bannister. She comes in from the kitchen, and she's not smiling. "I got a call from Mrs. Helms this morning."

My stomach drops. Helms. Guidance counselor. "Yeah?"

"She says you failed a history test, and never turned in a research project for science."

"Oh."

"Yeah, 'oh.'" She waits, but I really don't have anything to say. She is right about the test. I had already forgotten about it.

"And it's not the first time. Apparently you failed a test in chemistry and haven't turned in the last two labs."

"I'm gonna turn those in. And the project. It's no big deal. He accepts late work."

"Have you even started them? Did you do the lab work in class?"

"Yes!" I try to sound outraged, but it's probably not the most convincing display. I also never mention it was mostly my lab partner, Del Enwright, who really did the labs. I was, more or less, present.

Lauren moves in a little closer, drops her voice a notch. "Mr. Munson says you've been nodding off in class."

"Mr. Munson is boring! No one could stay awake in his class!"

"This isn't about Mr. Munson, Renny." Her voice stays quiet. "And he's not the only teacher who's noticed."

I stare. She stares back. I let my eyes drop to the floor.

"What's going on, Renny?" She pauses, waiting for me to produce an answer. When I don't, she says, "Look, I know school isn't always interesting." She pauses again, apparently reconsidering her approach. "Is something else going on?"

"Something else?" I fake a sort of dull incomprehension, but I have a pretty good idea what she's building up to.

"It isn't just happening in school. We've been seeing it at home too. You always seem exhausted. And you hardly ever say a word to any of us. You're always up in your room—"

"Maybe I just need time to myself. Is that a crime?"

"No, Renny, it's not a crime." She's trying to keep her voice steady, but the rough edge of exasperation is already rubbing through the calm. "I'm not mad at you, I'm just concerned."

"I'm fine."

"No, pardon me," she snaps, "but fine is not failing tests and nodding off in class. She didn't come out and say it, but she's probably seriously wondering whether you're going to class stoned."

There it is. I stare down, letting my eyes burrow into the bland hallway carpet.

"Renny," her voice is quiet again, "look at me, please."

I do. Her eyes are full of that dead-serious mother confessor look. "Are you doing drugs again?"

"W-What?" I manage a pretty convincing splutter. "No! Of course not!"

"Because we had an agreement. After last time—I mean, we want to trust you, but you know what we agreed—"

"I'm not doing drugs! Really! I haven't smoked pot in two years. You can test me if you don't believe me."

121

She puts a hand up. "Renny, calm down. I'm not trying to accuse you, but these reports from your teachers worry me. We want to trust you—"

"I've never been good at school. You know that. I can't help it if I'm dumb."

"You're not dumb, Renny."

"Yeah, right. I'm a genius."

"Look, Ren," she puts her hand on top of mine. "You know you can talk to us, right? I mean, if something is going on that's making you unhappy or uncomfortable. If any of your friends are trying to get you to do drugs, or if some boy is trying to pressure you into having sex—"

"None of those things are happening."

"—you can tell us. We only want you to be happy, but we need to know what's going on in your life."

"Nothing is going on!"

"I've always tried to respect your space. I don't rifle your belongings or—"

"Lauren. I'm not doing anything. I just need to be alone. I know I suck at school. And I'll try harder. I will."

Finally I escape up the stairs. I dump my backpack on the floor and flop on the bed, face down. What the hell do I need school for anyway? They're always going on about college and careers and all that crap, but what college am I ever going to get into? And what do I even need college for? I can already say *Would you like fries with that?* perfectly well.

Besides, I already have something no college could ever give me.

I lean over the edge of the bed and pull back the cover. Maysa's still there. I don't even really need to look, anymore. I'm so in tune with her it's like I can touch her with my mind. That enthusiasm she always has bubbles over and I can feel it too—at least when I'm flying.

Or with Stonechat. He seems almost as impossible as Maysa. Sometimes being with him is almost better than flying. His hands, his mouth, the way the moonlight can turn his hair into a crazy nest of silver curls. Why do I need anything else? Me and him, riding the night. Like the poem he does about the white birds on the foam of the sea. That's us. I already have that. I'm not free from the incredible pain in the ass that is school or from Lee and Lauren, but at least I have something—something that makes getting through the day bearable.

I make myself sit up. I suppose if I want to keep that, I'd better stop blowing off school. I can't have Lauren deciding she needs to start searching my room or checking up on me in the middle of the night. I drag myself off the edge of the bed and drop onto the floor, and begin rooting around in the horrible backpack for my science notebook.

***

Day turns into evening at a dreary pace. Dinner is a rare meeting of the entire household. Lee is just back from a three-day convention in San Antonio all ramped up with what he calls *positivity*. "There's nothing wrong with us that can't be fixed by what's right with us."

It's godawful. I spend the entire meal wondering if I've done enough time yet, and if it's all right to excuse myself and go back upstairs. But I stay. Lauren has already complained about my always being up in my room, never talking to them, so I wait. I don't talk, but I wait.

After dinner, I tackle the lab write-up on acid-base, studying the strange column of numbers I'd copied from Del Enwright's notebook. I have no earthly idea what any of it means. I even consider trying to find Del's phone number and calling him up for help, but I really don't know him from a hole in the ground. I have no clue who his friends are or who might know his phone number.

There's nothing else to do. I dig my science textbook out of the backpack and page through it until I find the chapter called 'Acid and Base' and prop myself up against the pillow. I'm just going to have to work through it from the beginning.

***

"Hey, Wren!"

His voice is a soft thing. The tap of his fingernails on glass is like a little bird pecking at the window.

I open my eyes. My notebook slides off my stomach and over the edge of the bed. I follow it. Stumbling, I make it to the barely open window and wrench it up.

"Stonechat!" I whisper. "Jesus! What are you doing here! It's—" I have no idea what time it is. How long have I been asleep?

"I had to come early," he says, his voice hushed, "Something's up."

I crane around for a glimpse at the bedside alarm clock. "It's only nine o'clock! Are you crazy?"

"I know, I know. It's really important. It can't wait."

I pull back a little. "What's wrong?"

"Hopefully nothing, but we're going to find out."

"What are you talking about?"

He leans in a little closer, resting his elbows on the jamb. "Last night, did you have a dream about Parnell?"

I stare back. "Yeah?"

"With Parnell and Mistral, at the castle—"

"—and that silver ribbon thing!" I finish for him. "Yes! I had that dream!"

"We *all* had that dream. I did. Raven, Nightjar—"

"The same dream?"

"Yeah. Raven's got a theory about what it all means, but I'm going to let her tell you herself."

"We're going to see Raven?"

"She's already here. Raven, Nightjar, Whimbrel—they're all waiting about two hundred yards over your rooftop."

I feel my mouth drop open. "You're kidding!"

124

"Nope. Hustle up and get your shoes on, Lovebird. We're ready to go."

"Going?" My voice squeaks. "Going where?"

He stares right at me. "We're going to find Parnell."

Seventeen

Now *this* is crazy!

I say it over and over to myself, as if I need convincing. I don't. I feel like I've become sort of an expert on accepting crazy things in my life the last few months. But this is *really* crazy. Sneaking out my window at nine o'clock at night? Especially with Lauren on the lookout for delinquent behavior. Good chance she'll come and talk to me before she goes to bed, just to buck me up and show how much she cares.

But I have to go. I just *have* to is all.

And that means I have to do something else as well.

Lee and Lauren are watching television in the living room. Lauren's propped half asleep in the easy chair, a wineglass on the reading lamp table. Lee is in his usual place, sprawled back on the sofa, stocking-feet resting on the coffee table, and hugging a sofa pillow across his mid-section. I'm pretty sure he always sits this way because he's self-conscious about his waistline, though compared to nearly every other dad I know, he is thin and fit. It's all part of the obsessive-compulsive maniac that is Lee Teller. Neither of them look up until I clear my throat and speak.

"Hey."

Lee sits up and puts his feet on the floor. "Hey, Ren. How's it going?"

He means my homework, of course.

"Okay," I lie, "I'm done for the night. I just wanted to say goodnight."

Lauren gives me an odd look. "You going to bed already?" Gretchen isn't even in bed yet.

"Yeah. I'm tired. I guess I haven't been sleeping very well."

Lee stands up and puts his hands on my shoulders. He uses the 'face-space' posture from one of his seminars: *"Sometimes, you just have to get right in their face. No one can ignore you when you're this close. And then,"* he always adds, *"speak softly."*

He speaks softly. "You know you can always talk to us, right? We just want to know you're all right."

I look in his eyes, then away again. "Yeah. I'm okay. I mean, I know I've been blowing off the school. And I'm going to try harder."

"But you're really okay? There's nothing else going on?"

"No. Really. I'm okay."

He pulls me into a hug and then lets me go. "All right, Renny. Sleep well."

"Yeah, okay. Goodnight."

"Night."

And that was all there was to it. I go upstairs, slip on my shoes, unroll Maysa, and turn off the light—

"Hey, Wren. What are you thinking about?" Stonechat, flying eight feet away, is looking at me.

I shake my head. "Nothing."

"Worried?"

"Hmm?"

"About getting caught?"

"Yeah. I guess." That's certainly a part of it. I really don't know how Lee and Lauren would react if they found out I was sneaking out every night, but it wouldn't be pretty. I've kept a low profile since coming from Tucson. I'm not that interested in trouble anymore. It

127

lost its appeal a long time ago. And I really don't want to go back into foster care. The Teller's may not be the greatest family ever, but at least here, I know what I've got.

"It's more than that," I say. "I guess I'm just weirded out, you know? I mean it's not like I haven't lied to them before, but it's such a lot of lies. It feels different." I pause again. I'm still not sure what I'm talking about. "I'm not sorry about sneaking out," I add quickly.

"There's a reason it feels different," he says. "In the past, if you lied to your folks about something, you could always make it right in the end by 'fessing up and then taking the consequences. Bear the brunt of their disappointment and then move on. Group hug, all forgiven. But you can't do that anymore. Not about this."

He's right. It is different now. I couldn't tell them the truth even if I wanted to. I'd just have to make up more lies. "How does that work?"

"How does what work?"

"The whole contract thing, where we have to keep the secrets of the Order secret. Why does that work, anyway?"

He leans his head back and scratches his jaw with two long fingers. "It's just magic. It's like a regular contract, only enforced by magic."

"I don't believe in magic."

He grins. "Yeah, neither do I."

"What happens if you try to tell someone?"

"I don't know." He shakes his head. "I've never tried."

I try to conjure up the image in my mind—telling Lee and Lauren everything, showing them Maysa, letting them see me fly. It's impossible. I literally cannot picture doing it.

"Maybe, that's why we all go a little crazy sometimes," Stonechat says. "It's the loneliness of the thing."

We've been flying for about an hour. I didn't wear a watch or bring my cellphone, but I have the feeling they wouldn't have helped much anyway. We've been heading due east all the way, flying very high, and already we are over the ocean. The Atlantic Ocean.

This too, is an impossible thing.

"That's the way it is with Tempovolution," Whimbrel says. "Remember the story about Sulayman and his carpet. According to the legend, it could carry him great distances in a brief period of time. Some of the legends even say it was instantaneous."

"What's it called again?"

"Tempovolution," Nightjar chimes in. "Time-fold. Pretty advanced spell. Personally, I've never quite got the hang of it."

It's Raven who's working the spell for all of us, casting a wide net of something called temporal displacement. And it's Raven who knows where we're going.

"An island," she says, "in the Seychelles. I don't think it has a name."

An island in the seashells. That makes about as much sense as anything else.

"We'll be going through about eleven time zones, so it'll be daylight when we get there. Hopefully there'll be nobody looking out for us. Still, better remember to cloak up before we drop in."

I don't exactly pride myself on my knowledge of geography, but eleven time zones has got to be pretty far.

"Off the east coast of Africa, fledgling."

And that's when she explains about tempovolution, because you obviously can't fly to Africa and back again in one single evening.

"It's all an aspect of enfolding," Whimbrel says. "Just like with cloaking."

"Yeah. I'm not really all that great at cloaking yet."

"Raven can bring you along," Whimbrel says. "She can bring the whole flock along. Don't worry about it."

"I really need to get back before morning."

"Raven'll take care of it," Stonechat says. "She can do this."

So Raven casts her net and we climb into the clear night— higher than I've ever gone before. I brace myself for the cold, but it never gets any colder. The wind doesn't blow any harder. The air doesn't feel any thinner. All in all, it's as comfortable as sitting on a blanket at a moonlight picnic.

It is also about the strangest thing I've ever experienced.

"Time runs funny in a fold," Stonechat tells me.

It doesn't take me long to figure out what he means by that. The land below us stretches and oozes like oil on a puddle. When I look at it sideways, without really looking at it, it all goes by in a blur of light and flickering shadow. Stare at it, and it barely moves at all—a creeping muddle of color, like molten crayons cooling to solid.

I give up staring at the smeared landscape. I look at the stars instead. They, at least, seem the same, though the moon is climbing across the sky at an unsettling rate.

"Spooky, isn't it?"

Raven, who has barely spoken a word for the whole first hour of the trip, flies only a few yards away. She eyes me from beneath the brim of her battered Stetson, chewing on her pipe.

"Yeah. I'll say."

She takes the pipe out and knocks the ashes loose. They drift away on a too-slow wind. "You get used to it." She opens a drawstring pouch, shakes loose the shaggy mix and thumbs it down into the bowl of her pipe. "Better," she says, retying the pouch, "if you don't look at the ground too much."

"Yeah. I figured that out."

Raven ignites a match behind cupped hands. Embers flare into grey smoke. Her hair, wiry and white-streaked, curls about her shirt-collar. Her brows are as heavy as Stonechat's, and except for the crinkles about her eyes, her face is smooth. She sits cross-legged on a red and gray carpet, her pipe resting on her knee. "Your carpet," Raven says, "she's quite the songbird."

"Can you hear her?"

I had only just begun to notice Maysa's singing was a little weird. It wasn't entirely different but it had changed. The same song, only with a new harmony.

"I can hear them all," Raven says. "Because of the net. Can't you hear the others too?"

"Others?" That's when I get it. What I thought was harmony is really a whole new melody, running along with Maysa's usual clanking bells. But the new melody has made her song change. It's like they're combining to make something new. And now I can hear another tune below that, an eerie sort of walking bass line, only vaguely related to the others.

"They're singing together?"

"It's a thing they do when they're all netted like this. They all have their own tunes of course, but when they're linked up—"

"They sing together!"

"It depends on the carpet," Raven says. "Some hardly sing at all. And some aren't very sociable." I close my eyes and listen harder, following one tune, then another. I can hear a fourth as well. Maybe even a fifth. All different, weaving in and out, but all part of one big thing.

When I open my eyes, Raven is watching me. She pulls a mouthful of smoke from her pipe, and lets it ooze away.

"You know," she says, "I wasn't planning on bringing you along on this little jaunt."

"Oh?"

"I'm not intending any offense against your flying or anything like that. Only, with you being a novice and all—"

"Yeah. You were probably afraid I'd just get in the way."

She takes a long puff. "Something like that."

"So why *did* you bring me along?"

She points with her pipe-stem. Ahead, Stonechat flies alongside Whimbrel, talking. "Stonechat insisted. He seems to think you've got something special to offer."

I wait, expecting more, but she doesn't say anything. So I ask the next question. "What do you think happened to Parnell?"

She licks her lips. "Pretty much like in the dream. You had the dream, right?"

"Uh huh. How did that happen anyway? How did we all have the same dream?"

"He touched the Orb. That was the how. The Orb connects all of us, everyone in the Order. Parnell doesn't normally try to reach everyone at once, but it was a dire situation."

"He just brushed the Orb for a second, with a fingertip."

Raven nods.

"So in that second he talked to every rugger in the world?"

"You're thinking about it the wrong way. He didn't talk to anyone. He just sent a message—like opening a window and yelling for help. And he didn't make contact with every rugger in the world, only those who happened to be asleep. In the half of the world where it was daytime I don't imagine he reached anyone at all, unless they were napping."

"So do you think he's all right?"

Raven shakes her head. "No. I think he's all kinds of not all right, and I think we are too late to do anything about it."

I nod. She's right. Whatever happened, it can't have been good. Mistral. Algernon Fell. A funny name for an unfunny guy. I say it out loud. "Algernon Fell."

Raven stares. The pipe-stem clings to her lower lip even with her mouth open. "Where did you hear that name?"

"Parnell. Just last night, in a dream meeting. He told me a whole long story about Algernon Fell. He was Parnell's apprentice—"

"I know who he was," Raven interrupts. "Parnell told you about Algernon Fell?"

I nod.

"Well, well." She puts the pipe stem back between her teeth. "Maybe Stonechat was right about you. Parnell didn't tell that story to many people."

We fly in silence.

Then, without any kind of warning, the sun rises. It blooms furiously over the black water, turning it to a sludge of muddy, blurred-out blue. The eastern sky goes gray, then mauve, then crimson. Stars vanish in the rising light, and a massive white sun heaves itself above the horizon and lurches upward.

"Hey, fledgling!" Raven is right beside me again. "Don't stare at the sun."

I look away. Snakes squirm and drift, dragging unnameable colors across my field of vision.

"It doesn't look as bright when you're in time-fold, but it is."

"Oh. Yeah, okay." I blink away the demons. "Thanks. Are we getting close?"

She puffs more smoke. "Pretty close."

Beneath us, muddy blue gives way to brown and gold.

"That's Africa," Raven says, without waiting for the question.

I stare until I'm woozy. Africa. I'm looking at Africa.

"Something, huh?"

I look up again. Whimbrel is at my side now. "Raven is amazing. I couldn't do this. I can do a time-folding spell all right, but only for me. I couldn't cast a net like she can."

Almost too soon, the rusty brown land gives way to blue again. "We must be somewhere around Mozambique," Whimbrel says to no one in particular. "Out there" he points, "beyond that stretch of ocean is Madagascar and the Seychelles."

"How long 'til we get there?"

"Soon. Take a look at Raven."

I do. Raven has stowed her pipe. Her head is bent, her eyes squeezed shut, like maybe something is wrong—*seriously* wrong. But when I look at Whimbrel, he's smiling.

"Better brace yourself," he says.

Time lurches. All around us wind churns, chasing back and forward.

"Hang on!" Stonechat yells. There's glee in his voice.

We drop straight down into the teeth of the wind. I throw myself flat on Maysa's back. A great snarl of blue and black shatters beneath us like a big glass bowl.

A moment later, it's ocean. White wave-tops toss, dazzled by the morning sun. We've stopped falling. All around me, ruggers sit hovering, wind-whipped in the chill air.

"Jesus!" Nightjar says, with considerable feeling. "A little warning next time, 'kay Raven?"

Raven sits in perfect calm. "Come on then," she says. "Let's get down out of the cold."

She leads us in a sweeping turn to the north. The day warms up as we drift lower. The wind quiets. Soon, an island appears, an oblong sandbar like a footprint in the waves. Then another. New islands appear as the ocean unrolls, each one in its own nest of water.

"Which one, Raven?" Whimbrel asks.

She doesn't answer. An island, far larger than the rest, blooms ahead. There are trees, foggy hilltops, little coral islands. And, strangest of all, an airplane rising.

"Better cloak up," Stonechat says.

"Where are we?"

"That's the big island," Raven answers, "Mahe. We're not going there."

We sweep west, skirting along the coastline of the big island, running cloaked. I try to focus all my attention on the spell, letting it sing inside my head. Warmth spreads into my fingers and up into my arms. Maysa's song is a solo again, restless and excited. She knows something is happening.

"Which island are we looking for?" Whimbrel asks again.

Raven shrugs. "Hell if I know. I haven't been here in years."

Whimbrel chews his lower lip. "It's a big ocean, Raven."

"Jesus, Whimbrel! The carpets will find it! Think you'd know that by now. Parnell is the carpet steward. Every carpet in the world's been there one time or another."

With Mahe at our backs, we head out across open water again. It's only minutes before the carpets prove Raven right. A glint of rock shows itself, bobbing in the surf. Again Maysa shivers. Not just anticipation this time: recognition. She knows this place.

134

We come fast, dipping low. Creased cliffs slide down into the sea. Red rock rises up to the hillsides. We clear the ridge and swoop low, skimming a green-stubble hilltop in tight formation, then plunge into a deep canyon of gray granite and crumbly red sandstone. The hillsides are scattered with clusters of fleshy leaves, stiff papery fronds, spiked palms.

"Over there," Raven says.

Nestled in the lap of the hillside a stone building sits. It's taller than it is wide. There's a tower on top, with a roof of dull greenish metal. It's a castle. With the tower and the thick stone walls and the arched windows, there really isn't anything else you could call it. But it's such a small, plain castle, it hardly seems worthy of the name. The stones are as drab as concrete. The tower roof is marked with popped rivets and streaked with bird droppings.

I bring Maysa in until I'm hovering near the ground and step off.

Nightjar, staring up with an appraising eye, speaks first. "It's quiet."

Raven folds her carpet twice and wraps it around her narrow shoulders. "You were expecting a party?"

The entrance is set back between two pillars on a broad, stone stoop. The heavy wooden door is not closed.

"That can't be good," Stonechat says. He looks at Raven. She nods.

The door gives a raspy scrape as he pushes it all the way open. It's dark inside. High windows let light into the room, but not enough to actually reach all the way to the ground. In one of the shadows, something skitters. We all freeze, stone-still, listening.

"Mice," Raven says in a normal voice. "Let's check his bedroom."

She leads us down a hallway lit by a pair of dirty skylights. Raven passes by the first two doors and pushes open the third without knocking.

The room is dark and warm. The only light comes from a small window hung with gauzy curtains. The bed is oversized and overstuffed, with a dark wood headboard and a patterned comforter. A high-backed armchair stands in the corner and, beside it, a dresser that matches the bedstead. The dresser door is open but everything hangs neatly inside. The bed doesn't look like it's been slept in.

"Well," Raven says, "no surprise there. We better go look upstairs."

We trudge up the spiral stone staircase in single file. This part I know. Parnell's handkerchief led me up this staircase once, in a dream. At the top of the stairwell there'll be the room with a dining table, high arched windows, flower boxes...

The table is still there—and the chairs, all tucked in. But a bookshelf lies on the floor now, books strewn everywhere about the wide paving stones. Bottles have been broken. Glass shards lie about like curved daggers. The green metal watering can sits near a window. One of the flower boxes has been overturned and kicked about, scattering dark soil and broken violets.

I look for the alcove where the Orb sits—or where the Orb *used* to sit. The little wooden table lies on its side. The silk curtain dangles from a single ring, spilling jasmine blossoms and purple butterflies all over the stone floor.

"Fuck!" Nightjar says—a soft, heartfelt curse. No one else says anything. Raven picks her way among the scattered books, glass fragments, uprooted violets. Halfway across the room, she drops to her haunches and picks up a bottleneck of dark glass, examining the broken edge. "Gutierrez," she says in a low voice. Then, "for the love of God, Montresor," which doesn't mean anything at all. She sets the bottleneck on the floor again.

"Do you think there's any chance he got away?" I ask. My voice sounds tiny in that high-ceilinged room. "Maybe grabbed a carpet, went out a window?" I look at the open windows. It would've been a tight squeeze.

"Parnell hasn't flown in years," Raven says. "Decades." She stands.

"Why not?" Nightjar asks. "Fat people can fly."

"It wasn't because he was fat. He was afraid of heights." Raven scoops up a violet and tucks it into the soil of one of the undisturbed window boxes.

"Looks like he put up a hell of a fight," Stonechat offers.

"This wasn't a fight, Stonechat," Raven says. "This was a bunch of hooligans, making merry."

Stonechat and Whimbrel put the bookshelf right again, and we all reshelve books, smoothing pages and brushing away dirt. When we finish, Raven stares, scowling.

"The Hafiz is missing."

"The what?"

"The Hafiz," she says. "Hafiz' Compendium. I know Parnell had one. It was the essential collection of ancient writings on flying textiles." She works her tongue behind her lips. "Gilderscott too."

"What is—?"

"Books, Stonechat! Parnell had the finest collection of ancient books on carpet-craft anyone ever saw. Those books are gone now. At least the important ones. The ones you couldn't find anywhere else."

"Mistral," Whimbrel says "stole his books?"

"He stole the Orb," Raven says. "I'd imagine he just took the books for good measure."

"And Parnell?" It's Nightjar who speaks. Her voice is small and fragile.

We search everywhere—the greenhouse, the other bedrooms, the kitchen, but long before we're through, we already know.

It isn't just the Orb and the books. They took Parnell too.

Eighteen

Raven recasts the time-folding spell and we head for home. No one says much. Somewhere over the western coast of Africa, I gather my nerve enough to ask Raven if there are any spells that would help us find Parnell.

"Fledgling," she says, "leave me alone and let me work this spell, would you?"

As we make our way west, we overtake night again. Over my shoulder, I watch the sun set, hurrying toward the horizon, dragging every color with it, snuffing itself in a black ocean.

Near Albuquerque, Raven breaks the spell and everyone goes their ways. Except for Stonechat. He sits with me for a while, side by side, high over the rooftops, but even he can't find much to say.

When I finally climb through my window, the bedside clock reads two o'clock in the morning. Five hours have passed. We flew all the way to tomorrow and back again before yesterday found out we were missing. My bed is just like I left it: rumpled—almost, if you didn't look too closely, as if someone might be sleeping in it.

I pull off my shoes and peel off my sweatshirt and climb between the covers still dressed.

***

It's another two nights before Stonechat shows up at my window. He looks the way he always does, handsome and wind-tossed, but there's something off about him. It's his eyes. Stonechat usually has what someone's grandma might call a twinkle in his eye, like he's constantly entertained by the world around him. There's none of that about him now.

"I'm worried," he admits, as we hover over the rooftop.

"About Parnell?"

"About Raven. About Parnell too, but right now I'm more worried about what Raven is going to do."

"What can she do? Is there some kind of spell she can use to find him?"

He shakes his head. "Not really. It all comes down to the carpets. A carpet can always find a place if it has been there before. But that doesn't really help in this case."

"Raven knew Parnell. Can't her carpet find Parnell?"

"Carpets don't find people, they find other carpets. You have to know the name—the carpet's name. You can't ask your carpet to go find so-and-so's carpet. Doesn't work that way."

"Oh."

"And that wouldn't help with Parnell anyway. He doesn't fly a carpet anymore. And even if he did, he was kidnapped. He didn't fly away on his own."

"Oh, yeah. Right." Clearly he has this all thought out. "Well, so, what can she do? I mean, it doesn't sound like she can do anything."

He shakes his head. "I don't know. But I'm going to see her tonight. She's fit to run off and do something crazy. She needs stopping. You want to come?"

"Really? Where?"

"At her house. In Boulder."

"Colorado?"

"Sure, Colorado. Can you get away?"

I chew my lip. "Boulder is pretty far away."

"Not as far as Africa."

"Yeah. But we were in that time-folding thing. Can you do the time-folding thing?"

"Not as good as Raven, but I can get us to Boulder."

We climb a little higher and take a heading north. "Don't worry about it," Stonechat says. He pats his carpet. "She knows the way."

I nod, waiting for him to cast the spell. Instead, he says one word: "Shirin."

"What?"

"My carpet," he says, "her name is Shirin."

I stare at him. "Shirin," I say. I repeat it two more times. Then, I take a deep breath and say, "Mine is named Maysa."

He smiles. "Nice." He reaches across the gap between us. At first I think he's reaching for my hand but instead, he places his palm on Maysa's back and lets it rest there. "Maysa. Hello, Maysa."

***

The effect of the time-folding spell isn't so dramatic this time. "We're only covering a few hundred miles, and there's just the two of us. The time distortion isn't so great."

"How long will it take us to get there?"

"Not long. I've done this so many times now, I can just let Shirin handle it. She'll pull us out of the spell when we get close."

"You do this a lot? Visit Raven?"

"Oh, yeah. Me and Raven go way back. She lets me crash at her place when I'm in town."

I chew on this odd revelation in silence, watching Colorado pass in a curdled blur below us. After a few minutes, Stonechat calls out, "Hold on! Here we go!"

Again it's like we're falling, but when the wind stops tossing, and the oozing landscape turns back into normal night, it doesn't seem like we're any lower. A four-lane highway runs with headlights below us. Beyond that, a city glows, lighting a grainy sky. We fly in over a big black reservoir, then cut west toward the city.

"Better cloak up," Stonechat says.

Cloaked, we sweep down over the rooftops of sleeping neighborhoods.

"That's the one." He leads us to a little cottage with a steep-peaked roof and a high dormer window. We land on the roof.

"The attic window is always open." He wrestles the unlatched sash up. "Careful. You have to step on the desk, and then climb down to the floor."

I toe the darkness, feeling for a level surface. A pencil skitters away and drops to the floor. My other foot hits crumpled paper.

"Yeah, don't worry about all that stuff. Just push on through so I can put a light on."

The light is a single bulb with a pull-chain, hanging from a cord. I can't see anything until it snaps on. Then I can't see anything for the sudden light.

"Stow your carpet on the hammock," he says, "then we'll go downstairs and talk to Raven."

I put Maysa down beside Shirin on a wide hammock strung between a post and a wall-stud. It sways under the new weight, tossing shadows on the plywood floor. "This where you sleep?"

"When I'm in town." He looks around the room with its unfinished walls, every two-by-four exposed, and grins. "Pretty rustic, huh?"

I take in the rafters and the crossbeams. It's too dark to see much beyond the stark blare of the light bulb. Pages litter the desk. A book lies open. A whole row of books stand propped against the back edge of the desk. Another half-dozen are stacked on a chair beside the hammock. Through the open window, a breeze carries the soft rumble of the interstate and the whispering of tree branches.

"I like it. A lot."

"Yeah, it's all right." He takes my hand. "Let's go find Raven."

141

I follow him into a small hallway and down a flight of stairs into a dark house.

"It's after midnight. Think she might be asleep?"

"Raven's a total night-owl," he says. He doesn't whisper, but he keeps his voice low. "I guess she might have fallen asleep."

It's a small house. The kitchen is barely big enough for a stove, a small refrigerator, a chopping block, and a white porcelain sink. Pots and skillets hang along the wall. Two high stools stand beside the chopping block.

The living room has a rocking chair pulled near the fireplace, a sofa with faded, flower-print upholstery and a plush easy chair. Raven isn't in any of them.

"I'm going to try her bedroom." He hurries off down a dark hallway. I hear the soft rap of his knuckles on a door.

A moment later, he's back. "She's not there." There's a hard edge to his voice now. "She's gone after Parnell. She's trying to find him. I knew she would do this!"

"You said there wasn't any—?"

"I don't know. She figured something out. She's a cunning old witch. If anyone can—" He stops. "I have to go after her."

"What?"

"Yeah." Stonechat nods, confirming his own decision. "I have to find her."

"But—"

"I have to, Wren. Look, you don't have to come with me. I can take you back to Albuquerque before I go."

"Of course I have to come with you!" I almost shout. "Do you really think I'm going to let you go alone?"

He doesn't say anything.

"Stonechat." I try to make my voice sound a lot calmer than I feel. "Think about this for a minute, okay? I mean, how are you even going to find her?"

"I can find her. That's not the problem."

I stare. "You know her carpet's name?"

He nods. "Yup."

I feel my eyebrows go up. "She told you?"

He shrugs. "She was pretty drunk at the time. So was I, probably. But I remember it. We were sharing a bottle and she just up and tells me. Says if I ever need to find her, just ask Shirin to find Ma'shooq."

"Ma'shooq? What kind of name is Ma'shooq?"

"I don't know. Listen, Wren, I really don't want you to come. You're only going to slow me down."

I keep staring. His long, lean face is expressionless from the nose down, but his eyes have a dark, guilty look. He's lying, and he's embarrassed because it's such an obvious lie. "You don't mean that. You're afraid of what we're going to find. You're trying to protect me."

His face slides down into a scowl. "You're being dramatic. I just need to find her."

"Stonechat! You saw the dream. It isn't just Mistral. There's a whole gang of them. Seven, eight guys at least. Big, ugly, mean guys. What are the two of you going to do against that?"

For that matter, what are the three of us going to do? "We need more people," I say. "The whole flock. Longbill, Avocet..."

"I don't know how to reach them."

"Well, when's the next kettle? They'll be there."

"The next kettle? Christ! The next kettle isn't for over a week. We need to go tonight."

I draw a breath and let it go. "This is a really dumb, crazy idea."

"You don't have to come, Wren. I already said—"

"I know what you said. I'm coming with you. It may be the dumbest thing I've ever heard of, but I'm coming with you."

We collect the carpets and head for the rooftop again. A breeze has come up, rippling beneath us as we rise. I give it one last attempt. "Isn't there any place else she could've gone? A friend's house? An all-night grocery store?"

"Wherever Ma'Shooq is, that's where the spell will take us. You better cloak up again, just in case we do end up in the freezer aisle at the *Safeway*."

Right now, the freezer aisle at *Safeway* is about the best place I can imagine us ending up.

Nineteen

We fly for some nameless length of time. Lights pass beneath us—specks, globs, stretching out in slow streamers—cities melting in the dark. Then, all at once, the lights stop, leaving only darkness.

"The ocean?"

"Uh huh."

"The Pacific." I'm not asking, just saying.

Stonechat breathes heavily, but doesn't speak. Holding the spell together is obviously a lot harder than hopping from Albuquerque to Boulder.

I've seen the Pacific Ocean before. Lauren has a sister Claire who lives in San Francisco. We visited her a couple of years ago—just Lauren, Amy, and me. I can almost see a younger version of myself tagging along across Union Square, a gangly kid, hair pulled back, slumping when she walked. I still slump when I walk. Lee has a thing about posture. *Walk tall: confidence shows in how you walk.*

Or lack thereof.

"Don't sneak through life," he tells me, "as if you're hoping no one will notice you."

I close my eyes. When he's right, he's right. But right now, I'm mostly worried about Lauren noticing that I'm missing from my bed night after night. It's just a matter of time until she does. Then what?

145

Call Ellen, the mighty social worker: *I'm sorry, Ellen, but we can't do this anymore. She's incorrigible. She sucks at school. She sneaks out at night doing God knows what.*

I couldn't really blame her.

Well, fine. I don't really need the Tellers anymore. I have Maysa. I have Stonechat. There's plenty of room for two in that cozy little attic room of his. Of course, maybe Raven doesn't want to run a halfway house for runaway ruggers. Maybe Stonechat wouldn't want me around that much, either. A girlfriend is one thing, but a full-time, live-in roommate?

"Hey!"

I turn. Stonechat is watching me, his face worried. The worry fades into a grin. "You okay?"

"Yeah."

"Looked like you were nodding off."

"No. I'm okay." Now that he says it though, I'm not so sure. I dig my fingers into my scalp and pull them through my hair. "Where are we?"

"Don't know exactly." His grin returns. "I was right. You were almost out, there."

"Maybe."

He grunts. "Light'll be coming up soon." There's a faint blush of red on what might be the horizon, like a thin line of rust on old cast-iron pot. Even as I watch, the smear of red spreads upward, painting low clouds. The light is rising fast.

"Wherever we're going," he says, "can't be long, now."

I knuckle sleep from my left eye. "How do you know that?"

"Listen," he says.

First I don't hear anything. Then I do. Above the sound of Maysa's bells, there's another melody, restless and winding. That's Shirin's song. I've heard that one before, intertwined with Maysa's when we fly together. But there's another sound beneath those: a moaning scrape, like a bow pulled over heavy strings. It plays a strange sequence of notes, straining against the other two as if it's not quite willing to stay in tune.

"Is that Raven?"

"Ma'Shooq. Yeah. I've been hearing it for a while now."

"That mean we're getting close?"

"I hope so."

I give him a look and he laughs. "Don't worry." He gives Shirin a fond pat. "She'll let me know."

About a minute later Stonechat cocks his head. "Hey. Something's happening." He's listening, his eyes looking down. "Do you hear that?"

Deep in the weave of melodies, something *is* different. But I can't tell which part of what song has changed.

"It's Shirin," he says. "She's—" he bends his head again and shuts his eyes. An instant later his head pops up. "Hang on," he says, "I'm going to break the spell."

I clutch onto Maysa and close my eyes.

When I open them again, we're hanging in an early evening sky. A gull shrieks, irritated at our sudden appearance. Stonechat draws a long breath and lets it out again. He looks even more tired than I feel, and I know it isn't just lack of sleep. A steady wind ripples the cloths between us.

"Great job."

He gives me a confused look, then a weak smile. "Thanks." His voice breaks, and a yawn swallows the word. "It's really Shirin who's doing it."

"You're a team."

Stonechat nods. "A partnership. Raven calls Ma'Shooq her life-partner."

We hang in the breeze like a couple of laundered sheets. Sunset is still pink on the horizon, though the sun itself has gone. Above it, a moon hangs high, soap-white and almost transparent. "What time do you think it is?"

"Local time? Maybe eight o'clock? Maybe earlier."

Wherever local is.

"South Seas." Stonechat guesses.

"Hawaii?"

He frowns, using only one eyebrow. "Farther south." He rubs his nose.

"How do you know?"

"You get a sort of instinct for it after a while. Comes with being connected to the carpet, probably. She reads me, I read her. Not sure why she stopped us here, though. Must be an island."

Turns out, the ocean is littered with islands. As we drop lower we can see them—coral rings and sandbars, rocks scattered across the waves like steppingstones. Shirin leads us to one that is thick with forest and ringed half way round by a narrow strip of white sand like a crescent moon. We make a high loop looking for signs of life.

"There! What is *that*?"

We cut back over the forest and drop down to treetop level.

"Wow," Stonechat says.

I'm as amazed as he is. "What is the deal with ruggers and castles?"

It *is* a castle, like Parnell's, but also not like it. There's nothing plain about this place. The walls are made of huge, close-fitting stones. Windows taper to high dagger points. A gapped wall surrounds the tower top, with little turrets at the corners. There is even a banner on a flagpole. Red on black, furling in the offshore breeze, it shows a gorgon's face, cheeks puffed, and a tiny Earth cowering in the squall.

"Damn!" Stonechat breathes.

"Is it him?"

"It's either him, or some kind of damned pirate!"

"Hey!"

A shadow beneath the tree's canopy hisses at us. "What in the name of Morrigan are you two doing here?" The shadow has an angry brogue. "Get down here, and quick!"

Perched on a tree branch, Raven is now entirely visible. Even in the dim light, the fury on her face is obvious. "You idiots! Who gave you the right to follow me here?"

"But Raven—"

"You've got a lot of nerve poking your nose into my business. And you!" she wheels on me, "Your cloaking spell needs a lot of work! You were flashing like a beacon. The both of you just high-tail it back home before someone sees you."

"We want to help!"

"I don't need your help." she sucks at her gritted teeth. "Christ! You'll only be making this harder. All I need is a lot of fool kids getting under my skirts. Get the hell back home and mind your own business."

Stonechat, his eyes nearly as angry as Raven's, waits for a chance to respond. "You *do* need help," he insists. "He's got a bunch of goons in there. I suppose you're just going to fly in under cloak and take Flo out of there?"

"Something like that," Raven snaps.

"Brilliant plan."

"It'll do."

"It won't do. You're going to need lookouts, maybe a diversion. Wren and I—"

"Stonechat—" she begins.

"We can help! We can do this together."

Stonechat waits, letting the silence grow strong. "Your chances are better with us than without us. You *know* that's true."

Raven chews, grinding her teeth. Several objections seem to rise up in her mind, but one by one, she lets each one go without saying anything. Finally, she gives a long, irritated sigh. When she speaks again, her voice is quiet. "You fledglings, you'll do what I say? *Exactly* what I say? And when I say it?"

"Absolutely."

"I mean it, Stonechat! No wrangling about this. We aren't just playing around here. I need your promise."

149

Stonechat goes quiet. He nods. I do the same. Raven gives us a sour look. "All right. We'll go over and check the place out. I saw two of those morons flying around earlier and I'm sure they'll be back. Just follow close and keep your mouths shut. And you,"—she turns to me again—"pay attention to that cloak!"

Raven goes first, hugging the wall. We go window to window. In one large room, the floor is strewn with mattresses and tangled blankets. Near the door, a large pot sits. In the next window, there's a bed with a brass-headboard, the covers smooth.

The next shows us a room littered with the remains of old furniture—splintered table legs, broken-backed chairs, unidentifiable limbs of wood.

The next one takes us around the corner of the building.

"All right," Raven growls. "Stay here. I'm going to check it out."

We hang back and watch as Raven works her way across the face of the building.

"What'd she mean we stay here? Why are we supposed to stay here?"

"There's still too much daylight on this side," Stonechat says. "It makes cloaking harder."

The windows on this side are small and plain, not the pointed arches of the other three sides. Raven goes quickly from the first to the second, hardly pausing. At the third, she stops. She peers in for a long time, cupping her hands around her eyes, pressing her face against the glass.

She raises a fist and raps her knuckles on the windowpane.

"What's she doing?"

Stonechat bites his lip. "She's found him."

He darts forward. I go right after him.

At the window, Raven glowers at us. Her voice, even hushed, bites. "I told you to stay in the shadows!"

Stonechat ignores her. "Is he in there?"

We crowd around the too-small window, each jockeying for a view. Inside, a man lies on an iron-framed cot. Despite Raven's tapping, he isn't moving. His belly makes a mound beneath the blanket. The beard is unmistakable.

"That's him!" Stonechat declares.

"I know that's him," Raven hisses. "Why do you think I'm rapping on the damned window?"

She taps again, three sharp pecks. Parnell doesn't stir.

Stonechat tries, louder. He rolls his tongue around in his mouth, and takes a breath. With his face against the window, he undoes his fist and gives the glass a slap with the flat of his hand. The window rattles.

"Stonechat!" Raven barks.

On the bed, the fat man rolls over on to his side, pulling the cover over his shoulder. Stonechat raps again, more quietly this time but insistent. *Tap, tap, tap! Tap, tap, tap!*

Parnell turns again on to his back. His hand goes up and touches his face.

"Parnell!" Raven hisses, and pecks again at the glass. Parnell bends his shaggy head toward the window. He pulls the blanket away, swings his legs over the edge of the bed. For a long while, he just sits, elbows propped on his knees, hands holding his own head as if it were a fragile thing. Raven gives another insistent tap and he looks up. Finally, he pushes himself to standing and stumbles forward.

"Good lord!" Raven says.

His beard is matted flat on one side. His skin is blotched and red. An oblong bruise stains his cheek purple, smudging a swollen, red-stained eye.

A metal latch holds the window from the inside. Parnell fumbles with it until it squeaks open, then heaves up the lower sash. It inches away from the jamb. Stonechat wedges his fingers into the gap and both of them pull.

"It's no good," Parnell says. "That's as far as it goes. I've tried before." He turns to Raven. "How on earth did you find me, Maude?"

151

Raven just says, "Najeeba."

"Ahh," Parnell nods, his face sagging all the more.

"What's that?"

Parnell's eyes flick to mine. "My handkerchief, Miss Drake." He looks at Raven again. "I had forgotten I ever told you her name."

"Long ago."

"Good you remembered," he says.

"Do you still have her?" Raven asks.

Parnell looks down. "No, they took her, first night I was here." He shakes his head again.

"What?" Raven asks.

He fixes his eyes on her again. "I believe it was meant to impress me with the lengths he would go to get what he wanted. Algernon, Mistral—whatever you want to call him. They made me watch while he—" he sniffs, and coughs into his fist, "—dangled her over a candle flame. Very *dramatic*." He emphasizes the last word with an arch of his eyebrows. "Najeeba, she was always so trusting. She kept twisting out of the flame's reach, and he kept bringing her closer." He looks away. When he speaks again, his voice is quiet. "I guess the fact you were able to track her here means they did not destroy her after all. So, I guess that's something."

His eyes—one dark and swollen, one pale and damp—seem to glaze over. He reaches up and rubs his fingers against his chest, and gives a phlegm-rattling cough. "It was, actually, a most effective demonstration. I have no lingering doubts about whether Algernon Fell is cruel enough and insane enough to carry out what he has planned. I've been such a fool, Maude. How could I have not seen this coming? The Orb. I should've kept it safe." He shakes his head. "This is all, all my fault."

"I don't get it. What is he going to do with the Orb?"

Raven tells me. "He can invade our dreams. Plant his ideas in our heads. He can make us do pretty much anything he bloody well wants."

"But you said you couldn't control our dreams. You were just a part of them."

"Technically," Parnell says, "I said I wouldn't, not couldn't. Given the desire to manipulate and control the dreams of others, I'm afraid actually doing so would be all too easy."

"But he can't, can he?" Raven asks. "He hasn't worked it out yet."

Parnell's mouth is a grim line. "No doubt you have deduced that from the fact I am still alive." He swallows, leaning his head back, fingering his jaw.

"That's why he brought you along. To show him how to use the damned thing."

Again Parnell nods. "Yes. I am afraid so. I have tried to convince him that it will not work for him, that it won't do what he wants, but he knows better. The Orb does not have an ethical sense. Given the right incantations, it *will* do what he wants."

He draws a heavy breath and swallows. Swallowing looks painful. "I shall not tell him, of course. But he has already, more than once, proven himself capable of working out some very complex magic for himself. It may only be a matter of time."

Overhead, there's a flash of movement.

"Damn!" Raven barks.

I whirl around. Stonechat is already rising up the side of the castle wall chasing the fleeing shadow.

"What is it?" Parnell demands. "What's going on?"

"Damn!" Raven curses again. "We've got to get you out of here. Now!"

"It's a fine idea, Maude, but I don't see how you're going to do it."

There's another rustle of silk from above. It's Stonechat. "Lost him," he says, looking grim. "I'd say we've got about a minute before the air is full of ruggers."

153

Parnell waves his hand, shooing us away. "Don't be a fool, Maude! Get out of here, all of you! They'll kill you, you know. They'll take your rugs."

"We're not leaving you here!"

"It's not me, Maude! It's the Orb you have to worry about. He's got it in the tower room. Get into the woods and get cloaked before they come, and maybe—"

"Look out!" Stonechat calls.

Two flyers appear over the parapet wall.

"Into the woods!" Raven shouts. "Now!"

Maysa whips hard about and plunges for the trees. I barely have time to throw myself flat and grab hold of the fringe. We go in hard, but it's too late for a clean escape. The two ruggers are close behind.

"You have a plan?" Stonechat shouts. Wind and branches whip his words away.

"I plan on flying the hell away from here and losing those bastards," Raven shouts back.

My heart is beating so loud I can hear it throbbing in my ears. "And then?" I yell.

"One thing at a time, girl."

Raven leads us deeper into the green murk. For what had looked like such a tiny island from the air, the trees seem to go on and on. She's leading us in circles, weaving a trail through the layers of branches and leaves. I hear surf and think for sure we're about to break through into open sky, but Raven doubles back into the thicket, into jungle again.

"Hey!" Stonechat calls, "I don't hear them anymore."

"I know," Raven calls back over her shoulder. She leads us spiraling up around an enormous, smooth-barked tree. We all find perches on a high, stout branch. In the sudden silence, the pounding of my heart is almost deafening.

"I think we've lost them for now," Raven says, keeping her voice low.

"Do you think they've gone back to the castle?"

Raven sucks at her cheeks. "Maybe. Or they might take a high vantage point. Wait for us to break cover."

"We wouldn't break cover without cloaking," Stonechat says.

Raven scowls, chewing on nothing. "A cloak isn't always reliable. But I'd guess they've gone back to the castle. Might just as well wait for us there."

"So what'll we do?" Stonechat asks.

"*You* two will go home," Raven says. "I'm going back to the castle."

"But—"

"No, Stonechat." Her voice is stern. "I didn't want you along in the first place. I can work a cloaking spell that will hide me just fine, but I can't be bothered trying to hide the two of you as well."

"You can't fool them long. This guy is no ordinary rugger."

"I'm not so ordinary myself. Maybe I can fool him, and maybe I can't, but I plan to try."

"But, you—"

"Get gone, Stonechat! You'll only bog me down."

Before he can say anything more, she slips from the branch and drops into thick shadow. Stonechat watches her go, long after she is entirely lost to view. I watch too. "This is really my fault."

He looks at me, eyebrow crimped. "How do you make that out?"

"My cloak, back at the castle. I know I let it drop. After we found Parnell, I wasn't thinking about it at all."

"No," he says, sounding half-annoyed. "There was still some daylight out there. It's like Raven said, cloaks aren't always reliable."

"Yeah, she meant *my* cloak wasn't always reliable."

He shakes his head. "Cloaks can fail. It was a tough situation. It could've just as easily been my cloak that slipped."

"Yeah, right."

"They were bound to be aware of us. I mean Parnell was talking to us out his window. And soon as they noticed that, the spell was going to break anyway."

I don't say anything. It doesn't matter now. We've been found out. We didn't get Parnell and by now Mistral knows we're here. We're worse off than when we started. I look at Stonechat. He's staring off again, as if he can still track Raven's progress through the trees.

"So," I ask, "what *are* we going to do?"

He tips his head and smiles. "Lovebird, I just don't see any choice in the matter."

Shirin, tucked beneath him, billows as if suddenly full of wind. Then he's aloft, drifting upwards. He swings back so he's facing me again and offers me a crinkly-eyed smile.

"I'll understand if you want to wait here," he says. "It's just something I have to do."

My heart makes a strange skip. I swallow hard. Without a word, I let Maysa lift me up until I'm level with him. "She's going to be mad," I say.

He grins. "There's nothing new about Raven being mad."

Twenty

As soon as we clear the canopy, we drop down low and circle the castle at ground level. If there are patrols out looking for us, they're elsewhere—or cloaked.

"So what can they do to us? I mean, are there spells like for blasting us out of the air?"

"As long as you're on the carpet, you'll be okay. She'll protect you. Rugs are almost indestructible."

"Right. Except for fire." Suddenly, I'm seeing Parnell's friendly lilac handkerchief hanging over some flame, writhing in the smoke. I shake the image away. "Where do you think Raven is?"

"She has to get inside somehow. Don't know how. An open window, maybe. Forcing a door would break a cloaking spell for sure."

"What do you want to do? Go back to Parnell's room?"

We circle back. The window is still open. The room, however, is now empty.

"They've taken him."

We have a pretty good idea where.

***

The roof of the topmost tower is flat and ringed with battlements. No ruggers stand guard. Under the flagpole where the banner hangs, there's a skylight of considerable size.

"Stay cloaked," Stonechat whispers.

157

"I know."

The skylight looks down into a big room with a dark wood dining table and a single high-backed chair. The room is lit by lanterns set in notches around the walls. Standing, hands resting on the chair back, Mistral is alone. He looks a little bored, actually, but his hands knead the top-rail of the chair in way that suggests he maybe isn't so relaxed.

Three people enter the room. One is a blocky, bald-headed man with florid red eyebrows, wearing a patched army jacket. Another—taller, leaner—wears a leather vest over a grungy purple T-shirt. Despite the long, stringy hair, it takes me a minute to figure out this one is actually a woman. She has the biceps of a body-builder and wears low-slung, grime-shiny jeans.

The third person isn't walking. It's Parnell. They have him, each by an elbow. His feet drag the ground. He doesn't struggle. When they let him go, he slumps at once to the floor. The glass of the skylight muffles all the talk. We follow the silent scene. Mistral leans casually, one arm resting on the chair-back, the other hanging at his side. Parnell doesn't look at him. He seems barely awake.

"He looks terrible." His face, so blotchy before, is chalky now. The bruise on his cheek stands out like burgundy on a white tablecloth. The rugger with the army jacket nudges Parnell with a boot-toe and says something. It isn't hard to fill in the words: *"Hey. He asked you a question."*

Parnell shakes his head, just once, like it's heavy and hard to move. Mistral shrugs, and gives his own head a sad shake. He says a bunch of stuff. Nothing changes in his expression. Then, he gives the bald man a single nod.

The rugger shoots a hard boot into the middle of Parnell's back. Parnell sprawls forward, arms splayed. I feel a yelp leap to my throat. I clench my teeth and force my eyes shut.

"Bastards!" Stonechat spits.

The bald rugger gives a crooked smile. Parnell struggles to his knees again, his hands pressed to the floor. Mistral, watching, doesn't smile, doesn't grimace, doesn't even look angry. He speaks again.

Again, Parnell shakes his head.

"We've got to do something! They're going to kill him!" Stonechat chews his lip. "There's only three of them, against two of us. If we got the jump on them—"

But in that same moment, the odds change. Two more ruggers enter the room. A weedy looking youth in an old flannel shirt joins Mistral near the table. They talk. The other stays near the entrance with his back to the doorway. He rubs his remaining eye with a big grubby finger and yawns.

Stonechat exhales, loudly. His breath clouds the dirty pane.

"Hope to God she just stays cloaked and doesn't try anything."

"Do you think she's in there?"

"She's in the castle somewhere. No way she's hanging by a window watching this go—" He stops.

"What?"

Stonechat hisses. "I think she's *in* there! There, over near the door. Just behind that big creep with the one-eye." He shakes his head. "I thought I saw something."

The one-eyed man slouches just inside the doorway, chewing, like he's found some stray bit of dinner in his teeth and is savoring it a second time. It's dark behind him. He casts a big shadow. "I don't see anything."

Stonechat studies the doorway. "No. Maybe not."

Parnell is on his hands and knees. Mistral walks forward until he's only a few feet away and drops down to a squat. He speaks softly to Parnell, and I almost think he's going to put an arm around him or offer him a hand up.

He doesn't do either of those things. After a minute, he rises. Parnell never even looks up. Mistral walks away. The rugger in the army jacket doesn't need more of a sign than this. He steps forward until he is directly behind the old man, and pulls back his heavy-booted foot.

That kick never connects. From the doorway, there's a sudden movement, and the bald rugger turns to look. The one-eyed man steps forward, face clenched, teeth gritted. His big hands grip his head as he stumbles forward, his mouth stretched in a roar I can hear even through the glass. He staggers, blinks once, and hits the ground face first. Behind him, feet planted on her red and gray carpet, Raven stands. In her hand she holds a black iron coal shovel.

Raven swings again two-handed, and clips the female rugger with the biceps across her outstretched arm. Everyone is shouting. Two men who had apparently been there all along come rushing from the far side of the dining table. Another comes in through the hallway door.

Raven wrestles Parnell onto her carpet, and the next moment, they're both in the air. Mistral waves his arms, pointing and shouting—but it's already too late. Raven is through the door and vanishing into the dark hallway beyond.

The room empties. The last one through the door is Mistral himself. The one-eyed rugger still lies face down on the floor.

Stonechat springs up. He wraps Shirin about him and steps through the skylight window, and falls in a shower of shattered glass.

"Stonechat!"

He doesn't look up. Climbing to his feet, he unfurls Shirin, leaps on top, and disappears out the hallway door.

"Stonechat!"

I push out a couple of the larger pieces of glass and let them drop to the floor. "Okay," I center myself on Maysa's back. "Go! Go!" Maysa sweeps through the broken pane, down to the floor and out into the hallway.

I find myself at the top of a winding stone staircase in a narrow tower. A lantern in an iron bracket oozes dusty light. Below, voices collide. If Raven managed to wrap Parnell in her cloaking spell, they might be all right—hidden in a corner somewhere, waiting for the crazies to pass them by.

I take a breath and chant silently. "Ro-sur, Suh-suh, Ob-scuse-ay-mor! Ro-sur, Suh-suh, Ob-scuse-ay-mor!"

We rise and ease out over the bannister. It's getting quiet at the bottom of the stairs. A calm voice says, "Spread out. They have to be here."

We drop, feather-silent. The room is very large, a sort of grand foyer with stone walls and a rough-paved floor. Lanterns are set into the walls but they don't throw very much light. Shadows hang everywhere. An enormous stone fireplace is unlit. Over it, an equally enormous set of antlers hangs—moose or elk, maybe—only ridiculously huge. Cobwebs drape the points like rags.

A half-dozen men are prowling the shadows, searching. Mistral, at the room's center, stands very still. "Now, now," he says, gently scolding, "You can hide, but you cannot fly."

A door opens from under the stairs and three more ruggers stomp into the room. Mistral motions to them. "Guard the stairway."

Everyone goes slowly, methodically, feeling the ground with their feet like in a dark room. But it isn't as dark as that. Only Raven and Parnell are in darkness—their own fragile darkness made of silk and magic.

"They're not on the stairs," a voice says from right underneath me.

"Don't let them double back, Borascu."

Mistral turns slowly about like a lighthouse, peering into the darkness. "Come out, come out," he calls. "Come now, Parnell. Aren't you going to introduce me to your lady-friend?"

"What if they're in the air?" someone asks.

Mistral nods. "It's a thought. You and Tramontane get your rugs and check the ceilings."

Two of them turn to leave. A thick-set man with shaggy black hair stumbles against a baseboard. "Hey!"

Everyone stops where they are.

"Taku?"

The man stands up straight and toes the dark corner with his boot. "Hey!" he shouts, now sounding pleased. "Found sumding!"

A familiar voice, female, snarls. "Get away!"

I can't see what happens next. A crowd gathers. Raven curses—loudly, repetitively. Someone hollers, and a shirtless rugger staggers away, clutching his face. When Taku dances back from the fray, he has Ma'Shooq and he's waving it like a banner.

Mistral, who has been standing and watching from the center of the room the whole time, walks over. The ruggers give way. Raven and Parnell are sitting hunched, backs against the wall. Raven glares up. Parnell—eyes closed, leaning against her—isn't moving at all. Mistral stares hard. He even squats down so he can examine them at eye level. Finally he leans back, "Fantastic," he says. "I know you."

Raven eyes him with hatred. In an acid voice she says, "And I know you, Algernon Fell."

He turns his eyes to Parnell. "What happened to him?"

Raven, stony-eyed, says, "He's dead."

Mistral sounds genuinely surprised. "Dead? Not really?"

Raven's face, if anything, grows even colder. "He had a bad heart."

Mistral tilts his head back and laughs. "Ah, yes. Parnell's heart! Well, then. Couldn't be helped." He reaches out and puts a hand on Parnell's splayed foot and gives it a shake. "Pleasant flight, old bird."

He stands up. A bright smile lights up his face. "A sea burial, I think. That ought to give the authorities something to wonder about, if they ever find him. Fat old man in a silk dressing gown."

A woman—the same one Raven clipped with the coal shovel in the tower—says, "Don't we need him? To show how to work the Orb?"

Mistral swings toward her, still smiling. "Yes, yes Kadja. We did need him. But,"—he brings his hands together as if readying a prayer—"the beautifully ironic structure of the universe has shown its face again." He claps his hands once and turns to face Raven again. "Hasn't it, Maude? You don't mind me calling you Maude, do you?"

Raven says nothing.

"Do you know who this is, Kadja?" He laughs. "It's—it's too perfect! Think of it, Kadja. In the very moment when this"—he pushes a toe at Parnell—"sack of guts, this pathetic lump, dies—" he pauses, relishing the moment,"—the one person in all the world who could replace him is delivered, right into our hands." He shakes his head. "Welcome, Maude." He makes a low bow. "I am humbled by your presence."

Raven gives him a contemptuous scowl. "You're as barmy as you ever were. I don't have any idea what you're talking about."

"Maudie." He raises a hand, looking pained. "You insult me. And, I might add, you insult the memory of the man who lies dead beside you. I remember my days on the island very well. If I close my eyes"—and he does—"I can picture the greenhouse where the mulberry bushes grew, the tower room, the African violets." His voice is wistful now, as if he he's losing himself in his memory. Then, he turns and faces Raven again. "And I remember you too, Maudie. You were there rather a lot in those days."

His eyes study the corpse heaped beside her, then come back to Raven. "You were just like him. His equal."

He lets his hands drop to his sides and speaks to the whole room. "There is no real structure to the so-called Order. Just a loose affiliation of flyers, scattered about the globe. The only thing keeping them connected"—he points at the stairwell, pointing right through me—"is up in that tower room: the Orb of Descrying. For the last three decades the Orb has been in the possession of the late Parnell Florian. There are two people—and as far as I know, two people only—who are capable of manipulating the subtle functions of that globe. I have, on numerous occasions, seen both of them do so— always, of course, in the service of the noble and ever-praiseworthy Order of rug-wranglers. One of them is this sad specimen that lies before us. The other, of course, is you, Maudie."

163

He stares at Raven, his eyes no longer soft or laughing.

"Wait," a heavy-set rugger in a brown jacket speaks. He wears one side of his face bearded and the other clean-shaven. His words are slow and thick. "You mean she can work it too?"

Mistral fixes him with a look. "Good, Squall! Glad to see you're following this. Yes, she can work it too."

"But—" Squall raises one eyebrow in confusion, emphasizing the asymmetry of his face.

"Oh, for the love of the four winds, Squall," an angry voice calls, "She's one of them: a keeper!"

"Yes," Mistral says. "And they have *kept* that particular piece of knowledge to themselves for long enough."

Raven, who has hardly moved the whole time, finally speaks. "I will never help you. I will not tell you how to make the Orb work. If you let me near it, I will smash it the first chance I get."

Mistral laughs. "Well, we'll have to avoid letting you get too close, won't we? And as for helping us, you will—for the same reason Parnell would have, eventually. It will be a simple matter of finding a hostage. You will not stand by and watch the innocent suffer. Not when you have the power to make it stop."

Raven says, "A lot more will suffer if I do cooperate than if I don't."

Mistral dips his head to one side. "In theory, yes. But human nature doesn't operate quite that way. Certainly your cooperation may result in greater suffering. But all that future suffering hasn't happened yet. It's still theoretical. Abstract. The theoretical suffering of uncounted millions pales in comparison to the very real suffering of even *one* individual, someone right in front of you. Especially,"—and his face brightens again, like a wonderful idea has just occurred to him—"someone special. Perhaps even someone you *love*. I'm sure we can find someone who fits in that category." He casts a narrow-eyed look at the corpse of Parnell Florian. "Which is more than I can say for this sorry tub."

Mistral turns to the black-haired rugger who is still clutching Ma'shooq like a big blanket. "Now, Taku, let's see what she has brought us."

Taku hands over the carpet. Mistral drapes it over one arm and gives it a close examination with his eyes and his fingers.

"Very nice, Maudie. Syrian, no? The brocade is distinctive." He holds the rug up and presses his face into it. "Perique?" He chuckles. "I forgot about that pipe of yours." He hands the carpet back to Taku, who tosses it up onto his shoulder like half of a serape.

"It will make a fine addition," Mistral says, "to our fleet."

"He'll never fly for you," Raven tells him.

"Ah, not so well as for you, perhaps, though once we are properly introduced—"

"You'll never learn his name."

"Of course I will. You will tell me, for the same reason you will tell me how to work the Orb."

There's a moan, and then a thick cough, right behind me. I scoot sideways until I'm pressed against the wall. Out of the darkness, the big rugger with the one eye lumbers to the top of the stairs. He leans against the bannister, his hand pressed to his face. His nose is a lump, still trickling black blood. He passes right beneath me. The top of his head, where the hair is thin, blazes with a bright red weal. He stops at the bottom step and the crowd of ruggers standing around Raven and Parnell turn.

"What the fuck happened?" He roars.

Someone laughs. "Ey, Whittle! What happened to your face?"

There's more laughter. Whittle shuffles forward. He fingers the welt on his scalp and winces. "Who hit me?"

A man grins and jerks a thumb at Raven. "Grandma here clunked you with a shovel."

Whittle wades through ruggers until he's standing over Raven. She stares up, not moving. He glances at the body of Parnell Florian, still leaning heavily on her shoulder, then back at Raven. "Get up!" he says.

Raven only stares back, cold hatred in her eyes. Whittle takes a long breath. He leans in. "Get up!"

Raven glares up at him and says two words. She spits them in his face.

Whittle shouts and disappears behind the crowd. When he stands, he has Raven by the shoulder. She's thrashing, an angry toy in his meaty paw. He raises the other hand into a big fist and brings it crashing down into her mouth. She falls, dropping out of sight again, but he snags her by one arm and yanks her upright. I see her face, just for an instant. A dark smear oozes her lip. Her free hand shoots up and claws his face. He hollers but he doesn't drop her. His fist catches her a backhand blow across the skull.

Just then, I hear another sound—something no one else has noticed: a rattling. I look up. The great antlers over the fireplace are moving. A shadow sweeps up toward the ceiling, scattering tattered cobwebs in gray flurries. The shadow becomes Stonechat. He streaks across the ceiling and dives down into the crowd.

I don't stop to think. I hurl myself across the room. Feet first, I crash into a rugger in a long jacket, catching him high between the shoulder blades. He sprawls forward. I swing sideways, and throw all my weight at a tall man. He flies back, grabbing at nothing.

Stonechat shouts, a snarl of meaningless words. His face is white, his eyes crazy. He throws an elbow into the nose of a square-faced man, swings his other arm wildly. A man with a tattooed face grabs Shirin's fringe and brays. Stonechat whirls about and crunches his boot-heel into the man's ugly mouth.

I lurch sideways. A beefy arm heaves across my shoulder. Foul breath grunts in my right ear. "Nuh yu don't!"

The arm tightens. I brace myself against him and push for all I've got, but it isn't enough. My knees buckle under the weight of him. His arm across my throat chokes the wind out of me, but it's his breath that's really making it hard for me to breathe. I jab the fingers of my free hand over my shoulder, stabbing at his face, again and again. My third jab hits something soft and wet.

166

"Nah!"

He yanks his head back. Whiskers rasp my cheek. The arm across my chest tightens even more, and his hand gropes my face. I swing my head hard, left and right, my mouth open. All of a sudden, I feel one of his dirty fingers in my mouth. I bite down.

"Arrgh!" He screams, but he won't let go.

Neither do I.

"Uhng! Graah!"

I bear down, grinding a knuckle, until wetness floods.

"Grarrgh!" He snatches the arm away. I duck and spin. Taku is standing right behind me, his bleeding hand pressed to his mouth. Ma'Shooq hangs from his shoulder. I grab it and launch myself toward the ceiling.

"Wren!" Stonechat is in the air now too. Raven clings tight behind him.

"Here!" I unfurl Ma'Shooq and Raven clambers on. Beneath us, ruggers are scrambling for their own carpets. The room echoes with shouts.

In a moment we're flying up the stairwell. The door to the tower room is still open. We make straight for the shattered skylight, but Raven pulls up.

"The Orb," she hisses. "It was just here. We can't leave without it."

"They'll be here any second!"

Raven, scours the room with her eyes. "Close the door!" she shouts, "Hold it shut!"

But it is already too late for that. A bolt of silver comes shooting in through the doorway, making straight for Raven. It snakes around her ankles and loops her knees.

"Raven!" Stonechat yells.

She's still clinging to Ma'Shooq—half on, half off now—hanging eight feet off the ground. The ribbon winds about her, pulling itself taut. Footsteps and loud voices fill the hallway, coming fast.

She looks up at Stonechat. "Get out of here! Now!"

"Like hell!"

He dives. I follow. Together we drag Raven higher into the air, but the big silk snake pulls harder, wraps itself tighter.

"Stonechat! Go!"

He tears at shimmering fabric. "We didn't—" he grunts, "—come all this way—"

"Stonechat!"

"—just to—"

"Jacob!" she barks.

He goes silent.

She speaks in a quick, quiet voice. "I know I haven't been much of a mother to you," she says, "but I have been a friend." She licks a trickle of blood from her lip. "So take this—one friend to another."

She raises a fist high above her head and yells a word I've never heard before. With a smack, she brings the fist down on Ma'Shooq's brocaded back.

Maysa billows like a sail full of wind and I fall flat, my face buried in soft silk. Stonechat screams one word—"No!"—but the wind tears the word away. I raise my head up, just for a moment.

The world drops away beneath us.

We fall into the sky.

Twenty-One

There is a moment where I can see everything through the frame of the wrecked skylight: Raven's face as they pull her off her carpet; the crush of their arms and shoulders; their ugly, braying mouths; and Mistral, standing directly underneath us, staring up, watching us go. His face is calm and curious. He looks, maybe, even a little bit amused.

Then it's all gone. We fly upward at unreal speed, like we're moths pinned to corkboard. Castle, forest, and island all pull away into the dark of the ocean. I manage one last downward glance, then everything turns into one big seamless, horizonless darkness.

**

I wake up.

A few feet away Stonechat, on Shirin, snores. High above us, three quarter's full, the moon creeps across the star-spattered sky.

I sit up. "Stonechat."

I clear my throat and say it louder. "Stonechat!"

He moans and turns over, but falls back into sleep. I edge Maysa closer to Shirin until their fringes touch and lean over to shake his shoulder.

"Stonechat. Wake up."

He opens bleary, reddened eyes. Slowly, he sits up. Below us, the world is ocean, thick and blurred. We're in time-fold. I don't know how we could be, but it's unmistakable.

"Raven," he says without looking at me. "She did this."

It comes back to me in pieces. The island, the castle, Raven, Parnell—*Good God! Parnell is dead!* I gulp, swallowing hard. My head is spinning, and not because of the altitude or the time fold. He's dead! And Raven is still there. I see her in my mind's eye, wrapped in that horrible silver scarf, big hands pulling her down out of the air.

"A whipcrack," Stonechat says. "That's what she called it. I've never seen her do it before."

"A whipcrack? What's a whipcrack?"

"She sent us here. Threw us into the sky. Sent us on our way. Even put us into a time-fold." I can tell he's speaking as much for his own understanding as for mine. The sleepy confusion leaves his eyes. Understanding—and irritation—takes its place. "We've got to get back there." he says. "They still have her."

"Can you do it? I mean, do you know how to reverse the—?"

He's already trying. His eyes are closed, his face tensed. For several moments he sits there, muttering under his breath, words that don't mean anything to me. As he goes on, the words become plainer, simpler—familiar words: stop, go back, finish, end. It's pretty obvious he doesn't have any idea how to undo Raven's spell. When he opens his eyes, we're still in the time-fold, still heading in the same direction as before. Shirin and Maysa have ignored him completely.

After a while, the long shoreline appears, rolling up the horizon. Then we're over land again. We're running backwards, going deeper into last night.

"How long—?" I clear my throat and try again. "What time do you think it is?"

He shakes his head. "Don't know."

I try to think of something to say, something positive, something hopeful. Nothing comes to me. Raven worked her magic well. There is nothing for us to do but wait for the ride to be over. When I look at him again, he's staring at me.

"You've got blood," he says, "on your face." He stretches a hand out and touches a spot on my left cheek.

"Oh. Yeah." I resist the impulse to lick my lip. I scratch at the spot with a fingernail, then rub it with my sleeve. "I don't think that's mine. *You've* got blood on your leg."

A smear of rust runs from mid-calf to ankle. "Yeah. That's mine. Got it going through the skylight."

There is more silence, a conspicuous amount of it.

"When—" I clear my throat again, trying to sound casual,"—when Raven said she hadn't been a very good mother..."

"Yeah," Stonechat gives me about half a smile. "She never was the maternal type."

I feel my mouth drop open. "She's your *real* mother?"

Another weak smile twitches at his lips. "It's a long story."

"Looks like we've got time."

He looks me square in the eye for the first time, and he nods. "Raven, Maude Byrne." He licks his lips, as if the name has a funny, unfamiliar taste. "I can remember from when I was little. We had a house in Connecticut. My father taught at university. Quinnipiac. Molecular biology. My ma was—" he stops again, and stares off. "I remember her taking me to story hour at the library." He smiles and shakes his head. "Don't know why I remember that. That might be my oldest memory."

"Sounds like a good memory."

"I don't really have any bad memories of her. Up until I was nine years old, I thought we were all happy. I mean, as much as a nine-year old thinks about that kind of thing."

"What happened when you were nine?"

"She left."

171

"Oh."

"Yeah."

I look away. When I look back, he's staring off at nothing. "That sucks."

"Yeah, well, you know. When you're a kid, you get used to stuff. I spent a lot of time in after-school programs and the like while my dad was at work, but I hated stuff like that, especially as I got older. I hated school bad enough without having it all day long. So I started cutting out. After a while, I started cutting out of regular school a lot too. I got very good at forging my father's signature."

"Where did you go when you cut school?"

He tips his head to the side. "Probably you're expecting me to say the pool hall or some street corner, but mostly I went to the public library."

My eyebrows go up. "The library?"

"Yeah. It was a place where I wouldn't attract a lot of notice. I told the librarians I was home-schooled. So long as I was quiet and didn't bother anybody, they didn't care. Anyway, it was close enough to the truth, because I learned a lot more reading library books than I did at school. Of course, eventually my dad found out."

"What did he do?"

He shrugs. "He was really decent about it, actually. He tried to find me a different school, but they were all pretty much the same, and I started cutting again and the whole thing started all over. It was the beginning of the end for us. My dad was a good guy. He tried to do right by me, but he couldn't get past the school thing. Finally, he says 'Look. Is there any sort of school you *want* to go to? Art school? Boarding school? Military school?' And I tell him I think I'd like to go to school in Ireland."

"Ireland?"

He grins. "That look you've got on your face is almost exactly like his when I told him."

"Why Ireland?"

"Well, you know all that time sitting in the library, I wasn't reading comic books. I was reading real stuff. Anything at first, but particularly about Ireland. First, mostly folk-tales and so forth, but also history. And poetry. Yeats, and George Russell, and Patrick Kavanaugh."

"You read poetry when you were nine years old?"

"More like twelve." He grins again. "What can I tell you—I was a weird kid. But something about all those old Irish guys really got to me."

"Because of Raven. Because she was Irish."

"Yeah. Pretty obvious, I guess. My dad saw it too. Funny isn't it? Here my dad was—decent guy, always there for me, all that, and him I treated like crap, like I thought my ma leaving was his fault. It wasn't, but I guess I wanted to think it was. She was unhappy, and she was never one to do things by half ways. She didn't just leave, she disappeared. Clean break."

He puts his hands together in his lap, and begins methodically cracking knuckles, one long bony finger at a time. "Raven always said I was too hard on my dad, and she was right. He did every damned thing he could think of, even sent me to Clarkes College for boarding school in Ireland."

"Is that where you met Raven again?"

"No, no. Clarkes is in Cork. Raven lived in Dublin. I didn't know that at the time. Didn't even know she was in Ireland, though I suppose I always thought she might be. Anyway, you're jumping way ahead. I went to Clarkes when I was thirteen. I stayed for three years. They were pretty good years, all things considered. I wasn't exactly anybody's favorite student, but I got on all right. It was way different from Connecticut—uniforms and haircuts, monitored study halls and dormitories. They kept us under lock and key pretty nearly."

"Sounds awful."

"Well, at least you always knew where you stood. I figured out exactly how much I had to toe the line in order to be otherwise left alone. And I was good at the class-work, so that helped too. Anyway,

173

so it's the night of my fourteenth birthday. Someone in the dorm—a guy named Stevie—has gotten his hands on a bottle of gin. Since it's my birthday, he pours a slug in a tumbler and says: 'There you are, boyo. Many happy returns.' Awful stuff. Don't know where he got it. But I managed to gag it down. And then, after a little while, I'm feeling like I might like a little more. Stevie obliges me, and pretty soon I'm in the bog, as the locals say, praying to the porcelain. Finally, when all that's through, I crawl off to bed and that night I had my very first meeting with Parnell Florian."

"Ahh."

"Naturally, I thought it was just a strange dream brought on by the gin. But there were more dreams after that. Then Shirin arrived. Just sitting on my bed like a parcel from home. You think it's tough for you sneaking out at night, think how it was for me sharing a dorm-room. Fortunately, there were woods not far off. I'd sneak off evenings with Shirin rolled up under my arm, get in some air-time, and still get back before bed-check. Usually."

He looks up at the moon. "You know how it is. Like a free pass to heaven, every night. Really, I think Shirin was the main reason I bore up at Clarkes as well as I did. It was dodgy sneaking out and all but just knowing she was there, waiting for me, made wading through Gaelic Cultural Studies and Intermediate Latin more bearable."

"You took Latin?"

"Ita vero, puella volatilis," he drones in a serious voice.

"What's that mean?"

"It means 'It is so, flying girl.' At least I think it does. I'm a little rusty. Anyway, there I am: schoolboy by day, sky-rider by night. But something happened a few months later that changed everything again. Parnell, in one of our little dream visits, suggested I attend a kettle."

"He did the same thing to me."

"Yeah. Apparently he likes to get the fledglings mixing with the old birds. Anyway, this particular kettle was a major event. An all-night party at the Isle of Man. Ruggers from all over the world were there. I saw all types. Gray-beards in hermit drag, posh young urbanites, soccer moms—"he draws a long breath, and looks at me,"—and Raven."

He lets his head droop to the side and stares down at Shirin. "I recognized her immediately. I could hardly have missed her. Even smoking that pipe, which I'd never seen her do in Connecticut."

"What did you say?"

He shakes his head. "Nothing. She didn't see me at first—it was pretty crowded—but I kept following her and finally she noticed. When we locked eyes, she knew me. She stared for a long time, then she said, 'I was wondering if you'd be here.'" He gives a big laugh.

"Did you know? I mean, did you have any idea?"

"Until that moment there wasn't the slightest inkling in my mind that my own mother might be a rugger. I'd lay odds my dad had no idea either. I mean, she had been flying since she was nineteen— she told me that—but that's just the way it is with ruggers. No one ever tells anyone, except for other ruggers."

"But she was expecting you. She knew *you* were coming."

"Well, she was an insider. It was like Mistral said. She was Parnell's equal, his partner. Parnell must have told her I had been called."

"Did you know she was an Orb-keeper, like Parnell?"

"No. Not at all. I knew she knew Parnell pretty well, though usually she talked about him like he was a bit of an idiot. And I knew she was an unusual flyer. She knew enchantments that I never saw anyone else do. I mean, you saw."

"Yeah. I saw. So what did she say? After that?"

"After that?" He uncurls his long fingers from his lap and scratches under his collarbone. "She asked me how I was. Was I flying a lot? How were things at Clarkes? Mundane stuff, really."

"She hadn't seen you in like six years, and—?"

"I know. You think we would've had some kind of big scene. But we didn't. We just didn't, is all."

"Didn't you ask her about what happened, where she went? Why she—?"

"Why she ran off and left us?" He drops his head back and stares at the sky, then looks at me again. "You're not getting it, Wren. I wasn't angry with her. I loved her, even after she left. And I understood her, better than I ever understood my old man. I mean, she did exactly what I would've done—what I *did* do, eventually. People have to be who they are. Anything else is just a lie."

I shake my head. "I don't buy that. How could you not have been mad?"

"I'm telling you, plain as I can. When I saw her again, it was like neither of us was the same as before. She was still my mother, but I had gotten over needing a mother. I had made my own life. Nothing she could've said was going to rewrite the past, and I didn't want her to rewrite the past anyway. I wasn't really all that interested in the past. We spent most of that evening together, me tagging along after her and meeting people. That's when I got the name Stonechat."

"Why Stonechat, anyway? What's a Stonechat?"

"That's what I said when I heard it. A bunch of them were talking about someone named Stonechat, and I asked, 'What's a Stonechat?' One of them said it was a little bird that makes a clacking noise, like two stones knocked together. I liked the name. The Stonechat they were talking about had died just that year, so they said I could have the name. I was the new Stonechat.

"After that, me and Raven got together fairly often. When I passed my exams after third year, I left Clarkes. She was sort of fed up with Ireland and wanted to move back to the States. She bought the little house in Colorado and told me I was welcome to stay with her whenever I wanted. It was funny. I suppose some of it was her trying to make up for the past, but she was never like a mother to me. If we had tried to be mother and son, we'd have driven each other crazy probably, but all we were was friends, so we got on great. We knew how to be together and we knew how to leave each other alone and we never had a moment's confusion."

He stops talking. He's leaning to the side, staring off at nothing, and it almost looks like he's going to drop off to sleep again. I slide over until I can get my arm around him. I can feel him breathing, his chest swelling and collapsing. I put my hand up behind his head and twist a finger in a thick, black curl and let my eyes close.

He reaches up and scratches his nose. "What about yours?"

"Huh?"

"I've told you about my so-called parents. What about yours? You never talk about them."

I take a long breath. His head is still bent down against my collar. "Real," I ask, "or FPs?"

He squirms around and looks up at me. "FPs?"

"Foster parents. Lee and Lauren."

"Foster parents?"

"Yup. Three years, now. There were others before that."

"Wow." His voice is both small and amazed.

"My birth-mom lives in Kansas." I make an elaborate display of smiling and shrugging. "What can I tell you? She's fucked up." My forced smile feels like it's squeezing my face.

Stonechat struggles back to sitting, but stays close. His hands find mine, and he holds them in his lap. "What do you mean?"

"She's crazy. Schizo. Drunk too, but mostly crazy. I got placed in my first foster home when I was seven, then back with my mom, then back in a home, etcetera, etcetera. It's a long, dull story."

"I want to hear it."

I shake my head. "Naw. You really don't. It's pretty typical stuff—you know, coming home from school and finding her passed out, being left alone in the apartment for days." I give another little laugh. "She *did* used to lock me in the closet. That was kind of classic."

"A closet?"

"Yeah. A little broom closet in the hall. It was a game. She'd put down pillows, blankets, then she'd stick me in there. She'd bring me food. Not like food on a plate—just random bits of food, like one grape, or a Ritz cracker. And I wasn't allowed to use my hands, I just had to open my mouth and let her drop it inside. Once she didn't bring anything but leftover spaghetti, just one strand at a time. She'd watch me chew it up, and then she'd run off and bring me another."

I look at Stonechat. His stare is grim, almost horrified. I laugh again. "It was pretty strange. I mean, at first it was like she was just playing around. I guess she got some kind of weird buzz off of it. I didn't even mind that much. But then sometimes she'd forget about me, or get drunk, or go out..." I stare up at the moon again. It's sliding, melting its way down the curve of the sky. "Once she forgot me and I was stuck in there for a couple of days. That wasn't so pretty."

Stonechat doesn't say anything. His fingers lace around mine, drawing them tight.

"I got fostered out after that. For about a year. My mom got back on her meds, convinced them she had stopped drinking, that she'd cleaned up her act, but it didn't last. It never lasted."

He kneads the back of my hand, his thumb pressing my palm. He says, "Wow,"—but so soft that it's more like a little puff of breath. I force a yawn and lean in, snuggling against his shoulder, and his arm goes around me. "I'm tired of talking about it. Feels like I spent my whole life talking about my bat-shit crazy mom. Lee, my foster-dad, was all gung-ho that I should talk to a therapist, so I did."

"Yeah?"

"Yep. Good old Doc Gananian. He tried to unpack my brain for six months. He couldn't crack me either."

His fingers venture up my spine, find the nape, and squeeze gently. I shiver. "It just got kind of boring after a while." I speak directly into his collar, letting his closeness muffle the words. "He wanted me to talk about my feelings, about my mom, but I didn't want to talk about all of that. I just wanted to move on."

He pushes his fingers higher, kneading the ridge at the base of my skull. I let my head lean back.

"You ever hear from her?"

"Mmm? No. Not for a maybe a year now. She used to send letters, like how she was making progress and going to meetings and all that, and she wanted us to be a family again. That'll never happen. But they never terminated her rights."

"Rights?"

"Sure. She's got rights, I got rights. That's part of why Lee and Lauren couldn't formally adopt me. I mean, not like they would anyway. They used to talk about it three years ago, but that ship has sailed." I sit up and drape my hands on his shoulders. "It really doesn't matter. Either way, I'll be on my own in another year. And Lee and Lauren will have done their civic duty."

He takes my face in his hands and dips his head so our foreheads touch, then he shakes his head, just gently, rolling my brow against his. We kiss. No groping or tongues touching, just a kiss, but it lasts a long time. When he pulls away, he's smiling. "You've really been through it, haven't you?"

I laugh. "Hey, the best might still be yet to come." I point a finger at my head and circle my ear a few times. "Schizophrenia runs in families you know. Could be my turn next."

He doesn't laugh at this. He squints one eye and frowns. "You seem pretty sane to me."

"Wouldn't be too sure about that. You ever hear of windsprites?"

He shakes his head.

"There are these voices I hear sometimes when I'm flying. They talk to me. Mostly they just giggle, if you want to know. I asked Parnell about it. He said they were called windsprites—merry spirits, or something like that. But nobody knows whether they really exist or not. Some crazy old priest who was a rugger wrote all about them. Apparently, he thought they were prophetic, like they could tell the future or whatever. Actually, they're kind of annoying most of the time. But *some*times—" I shrug, frowning, and shake my head"—I don't know. Sometimes it almost does seem like maybe they might know stuff, before it happens. Once, anyway."

"What kind of stuff?"

179

"At the kettle, with Budgie. They tipped me off. They warned me she was coming. At least, I think they did."

He lifts one brow and holds it there. "Voices from the great beyond. Neat."

"Yeah, maybe. Or maybe I'm just as crazy as my mom."

He shakes his head. "I wouldn't bet on it." He pulls me in again and leans his head against mine. His crazy hair tickles my ear. "But if it was me, and I was hearing voices from the great beyond, I think I'd make a point of listening."

The carpets make a gradual swing to the south. The lights of cities appear and vanish with unnerving speed and the moon drops behind us. Stonechat is so still, I would've thought he was asleep, but I can see his eyes, still open, staring off into the sky. When he finally speaks, his voice is casual. "The spell is breaking up."

I feel it too. The wind is rising, getting colder. The sky around us slides into normal night, and the carpets begin their long descent. Maysa and Shirin begin to pull away from each other, and we each scrambled on to our own mounts. I can see the speckled trail of lights along the highway. Ahead, Albuquerque glows.

We ride all the way to my rooftop and hover, crouching together about five feet from the window ledge. His face is lined with worry. "I need to go back," he says. "I can't leave her there."

"I know. But you can't go alone."

He doesn't say anything.

"We can get help. Find the flock. If you explain what happened, they'll come."

He doesn't answer, doesn't even move. He seems like he could stay there, just like that, floating until morning.

"You have to promise me."

He mumbles something. I can't tell what he says. Then he lifts his head and looks me in the eye. "He'll kill her if she doesn't cooperate." He says it quietly, without panic, without anger. "And she won't cooperate."

"He won't kill her. He needs her. He told us what he was going to do—find a hostage of some sort." The words come back to me. *Perhaps someone you love.*

He looks down again. "I can't leave her there," he says again.

"I know. Just wait, until tomorrow night at least. Give yourself a chance to think. There's nothing we can do tonight."

He sits, not saying anything, looking worn and miserable. I want him to promise, but now something else bothers me. "Does he know about you?"

He fixes me with a puzzled look.

"Does Mistral know you're her son?"

He shakes his head. "Doubt it." He puts a hand up and kneads my shoulder in an absent way, staring off into the tree branches. "Hardly anyone knows."

I sit, savoring the press of fingers against my shoulder. When he stops pressing, I lean into him again, sliding my hands around his skinny waist until they can lock behind his back.

"That's good," I say, rubbing my face against his shirt. "That's a good thing."

Twenty-Two

The next thing I really remember is Lauren pounding on my bedroom door. I drag myself up to a sitting position.

"Renny! What's taking so long? Amy's ready to leave."

"Yeah. Okay."

7:40. Either I turned my alarm off in my sleep, or I never set it in the first place. My shoes are off but I'm still dressed.

I stumble to the bathroom. My head is full of dull ache. There's still a smear of dry blood on my cheek. I rub at it with a wet cloth until it's gone, then dunk my whole face in a sink full of water from the cold tap. I check the mirror. I look like the victim of some kind of advanced interrogation techniques—red-eyed and haggard, my skin almost gray.

I don't have time to change clothes. I grab my backpack and charge down the stairs. Amy already has the car running.

"God!" she says, "What happened to you?"

I don't even try to answer.

The day is a waking nightmare. I catch myself dozing in algebra, and get excused to go to the bathroom. I lean over the sink and rub cold water into my face again, and dry myself with paper towels.

In biology there's a movie on honeybees and pollination. I surrender to sleep as soon as the lights go out, but the whole nap is one tumbled dream of riding Maysa into a gale-force wind, and buzzing against an endless pane of glass. When McKenzie nudges my shoulder at the film's end, I feel less rested than when it began.

"Look alive, Ren."

This can't be what being alive feels like.

English is even worse—a tortuous discussion of *The Grapes of Wrath*. I haven't done the reading and I'm not sure who anybody is, but it sounds like their lives suck unbelievably. There's a family who lives in a crummy old truck, a one-eyed auto mechanic, and a lot of starving children. At the end of class, Albright hands back the papers we turned in last week. I almost don't bother to look at it. Then I do. *D plus* and a red marker scrawl: *Please see me.* I stuff the paper into my backpack and make a quick exit when the bell sounds.

The last period is history. I sit with my elbows on the desktop, my chin propped in my hands, and work my temples with my fingertips, pretending to be listening. I didn't do the reading for history either, and when Kellogg asks me a question about something that sounds like Barbie's ghost, all I can do is shake my head and look away.

When the bell sounds, I stuff my books into my backpack and make for the door.

"Renny? Can I see you a minute?"

I pull up and turn slowly back. I make my way against the tide of departing students until I'm standing at the teacher's desk. I don't smile. Neither does she.

"Is everything all right, Renny?"

I give a weak, one-shouldered shrug.

"At home?"

"Sure."

Kellogg pulls a notebook from a stack of papers and flips it open. "You got a D on the last test. I offered anyone who got less than a C to take a make-up test. Did you want to take the make-up?"

I begin another shrug, then nod. "Yeah. Sure, I guess."

Kellogg's brow wrinkles. "It's up to you Renny. But your grades have been sliding."

"I know. I'll retake the test." Probably I should just leave it there. *Thanks. Sorry. I'll work harder.* Instead I say, "It's just that, well I've been getting mostly Cs all year. My average is still a C, right? So if I get a C on the makeup, you'll average it with the D and my grade won't go up at all."

"Maybe you can get better than a C."

Yeah.

"You're a bright girl, Renny. If you worked at it, I'm sure you could bring your grade up." She lets a long breath out. "Well, if you want to do the make-up you can come in at lunch tomorrow."

***

Outside, the bus is waiting. I slump down in a seat beside a girl I don't know and stare out the window. I can't stop worrying about Stonechat. He won't wait long. Hopefully I convinced him not to do anything without me. We need to stick together, whatever happens. But what can we do? Mistral and his thugs have us outnumbered. And now we don't have Raven anymore. Stonechat can cast some spells, but nothing like Raven. And I can't do anything. Maybe what they were saying was right all along—I *will* only be in the way. But I'm not going to let him go alone. There has to be other members of the flock who can help us. I don't know how to reach them, but maybe Stonechat does.

When I get home I head straight for my room, hoping to sleep until dinner, but Lauren stops me in the hallway.

"Hey, I want to talk to you." She passes me by and goes into the living room. There isn't any choice. I follow.

Lauren sits in the armchair and motions for me to sit on the sofa. I dump my backpack on the floor and perch on the edge of the cushion.

"I got a call from school today. Your teacher, Mrs. Kellogg, says you're in danger of failing history. And English."

My head hurts. I reach up and rub above my right eye.

"Are you all right?"

"Headache."

"Ah. Well, I'm sorry about your headache, but I meant in the bigger sense. Is there something going on I should know about? A problem?"

"We just had this conversation."

"Yes, well, apparently the problem is only getting worse, so—"

"It's only been a week! How much better is it supposed to get in a week?"

"I'm aware of that." She keeps her voice low and calm. It takes some effort. "But several teachers have said you're still falling asleep in class. Now, I don't know why you should be so tired. Seems like you go to bed at a reasonable hour. You never go out. You disappear into your room usually right after dinner. I assumed you were doing homework or talking to your friends on the phone, but it doesn't sound like you've been doing very much homework, and from what I've gathered, your friends don't know what's wrong with you either. I called Bree's mother. Bree says you guys haven't exactly been hanging out at school. And since she hangs out with McKenzie, it's pretty obvious you're not hanging out with her either."

"Lauren—"

"Renny, what's going on? You've had grade problems before, but—"

"Yeah! I always have grade problems. I get C's, even D's. I'm average. Less than average."

"Renny, you are not—"

"I suck at school. That's just the way it is."

185

"Renny!" There's anger in her voice now. "You've never failed your classes before. And I've never gotten reports from your teachers of you falling asleep in class." She makes her voice soft again. "You know you can talk to me, don't you? Even if it's really bad, you can tell me. If there's some kind of problem—"

"There isn't."

"Have you been drinking?"

"No."

"Or doing drugs?"

"No!"

"I have to ask these things, Renny. There's no sense beating around the bush but you seem so tired and preoccupied all of the time. If you've got a problem, we can get you help—"

"I don't have a problem!"

"Renny, I only want—"

"I'm not taking drugs and I'm not drinking!" I take a deep breath. When I start again, I try to get my voice to sound as calm and quiet as hers. "It's not anything like that. I'm just not interested in school."

Lauren stares. "Well, I don't know what to believe. I think something is wrong and you're not telling me."

I look at the wall. I look at the floor. I look at my knee.

"So, I guess we'll just have to say you're grounded until you get your grades up. I don't know what kind of difference it's going to make since you never go out anyway. But if you're not going to tell me what's really going on, then I guess that's the best I can do."

She folds her arms across her chest and leans back like she's waiting for me to respond. I'm so tired of the whole I'm-sorry-I'll-try-to-do-better speech. I look up. "Can I go now?"

She nods.

Upstairs, I flop on the bed and stare at the ceiling. This is only the beginning. Lee will, no doubt, want to *discuss* my problem. My grade problem. I'll do the speech, promise them I'll try harder, all the usual. Even the thought of cracking open a book makes me weary.

Weary. Weary and worn. That's from one of Stonechat's poems. Yates. *Sad souls, weary and worn.* What is he doing right now? Worrying about Raven, probably. Not worrying about some stupid history test.

I roll over onto my shoulder and press my face into the pillow. I'll sleep. For an hour. Then I'll get up and study for the stupid history test.

***

I wake. Something is tapping at my window. The room is dark. I roll over and snap on my bedside lamp. The pecking at the window stops.

It's after midnight. I slept through the whole evening. At some point, someone must have come in and placed a blanket over me. I swing my feet off the bed. Behind the blurry glare of lamplight on windowpane, Stonechat's face hangs in the dark glass.

I cross the room and open the window. He's hovering, close enough to touch. I put my hands out and he takes them.

"You can sleep, girl! I've been tapping for ten minutes. Almost gave up."

"It's all that time-folding stuff. It's like jet-lag." His hands are cold. I rub them between my own.

"I know. I slept nearly all day. It's wretched at Raven's house without her there. I feel like everything is staring at me, accusing me."

"Accusing you?"

"Yeah, like why haven't I gone back for her."

"I'm glad you didn't."

"Well, it's not for lack of trying."

"What do you mean? Did you try to go back?"

"Yeah, but a fat lot of good it did me."

I drop one of his hands, hold on to the other. "What are you talking about?"

"Grab your carpet. I'll tell you out here."

I get Maysa out from under my bed. A moment later we're together. We hug, kneeling. His hands tremble against my back. "Come on," he says, breaking the embrace. "Let's rise a bit."

We cloak up and rise into the darkness. It's a clear desert night—brisk and starry. We rise until we're above the highest branches of the ash tree.

"I tried casting the time-fold but it wouldn't take. I mean it doesn't always work for me but this was different from that. It wasn't like I was messing it up, it was more like something else was messing it up for me. I'll give it another try."

He closes his eyes and dips his chin. A trembling, like a ripple of wind, passes through Maysa. I ready myself for the moment when the breeze grows still and the air gets warm and the world beneath us slows into a calm, drifting dream.

It doesn't happen. Stonechat's face is almost painful with concentration, his lips shaping silent words—but we stay precisely where, and when, we are.

He looks up. "See what I mean? She won't listen."

"Maybe she's right. Maybe she knows we shouldn't be trying to go back there."

He shakes his head. "That's not it. This isn't balkiness. Something—*someone* is blocking the spell."

"Mistral?"

He seems surprised at the suggestion.

Then I get it. "You mean Raven. She doesn't want us to go back."

"Yeah, I don't know whether it's left over from the whipcrack or if she's worked some other kind of hoodoo, but I'd bet this is her work. I don't know how she did it, but it's something she'd do."

He stares down, shoulders hunched. With a sudden groan he slams his fist on Shirin's back and curses loudly. Shirin rocks, rocking Maysa, and we all hang rolling on our own private swell. I put my hand on his. "She doesn't want you to do anything crazy."

"She's an arrogant, raving, mad woman! She thinks she doesn't need anyone. Like she can just go in and..." He digs both hands into his mop of hair and tugs like he's trying to pull off a stuck hat, and gives a groan of pure frustration.

"Maybe someone else. Someone who knows more spells?"

He drops his hands into his lap and tries out the idea, moving his tongue around in his cheek. "Maybe. Maybe Scaup. Scaup is no ball of fire. I mean, he probably knows some stuff, but he isn't a patch on Raven."

"Okay. But he might be able to help."

" Yeah. Maybe."

"So, do you know where he is? Is there some way of finding him?"

"Mmm? Yeah, Budgie would know. I can ask her."

"Budgie?" I can hear my voice go up.

"Yeah. He mentored her, back when. They stay close."

He isn't looking at me. "So you, uh, are you still in contact with her? Your carpets know how to find each other?"

He gives me an odd, heavy-browed look. "No. I was thinking of calling her on the phone."

"Oh." I'm not really sure whether that's better or worse.

"She lives near Phoenix. I'll call her and see if she can scare up Scaup. Outta be a kettle at Big Hatchet next Saturday, but I can't wait that long."

"Come and get me when you find him, okay? We'll go together."

I put my hand out again, and he holds it in an absent sort of way, not even looking at me.

"Yeah," he says, "Yeah, okay."

189

Twenty-Three

But Stonechat doesn't come—not the next night, nor the one after that. Those are long evenings alone in my room. It's unlikely he would show up before midnight, but I can't be sure. He did once before, and I really can't risk him showing up when I'm not there.

So I hole up in my room doing homework. There's plenty of that, anyway. I've got a list of missing assignments from all the teachers. They're all only too delighted for me to make up missed work. Everyone seems ridiculously pleased I'm willing to finally make an effort. It's going to take me forever to get on top of it all. French and math are doable, but there's a research project I'm supposed to be doing for science, and I haven't even chosen a topic. I am officially three hundred pages behind in *The Grapes of Wrath*, plus I have to review for history. I'm not even sure where to begin with that. I make myself sit in my desk chair so I won't fall asleep, but it doesn't help. My mind keeps drifting, and it always goes the same place: Stonechat.

I get Maysa out and sit on her, hoping her link to Shirin might somehow translate into a link between me and Stonechat, but Maysa doesn't seem to get the idea. The only pictures I get when I ask about Shirin or Stonechat are from the past—images of riding the high thermals over Big Hatchet, buzzing the sandstone buttes.

190

I stay up really late on Wednesday night, not studying, just waiting. I toy with the idea of flying to Colorado, trusting Maysa to find Raven's house, but it's too risky. If Stonechat comes while I'm out looking for him, well, that would be too stupid for words. Better to just stay put. He *will* show up, probably tomorrow, hopefully with news.

Hopefully *not* with Budgie.

***

Sitting in first period on Thursday, I get a bright idea: Budgie isn't the only one with a telephone. Most likely Raven has one too.

Not Raven—Maudie. Mistral called her Maudie. Maude. The last name hovers maddeningly out of the reach. What did Stonechat call her? Maude Breyer? Brand? No—Burns. Maude Burns. There can't be too many people named Maude Burns in the Boulder, Colorado area. I can call information. Or look it up online.

I sail through the rest of the afternoon, feeling better than I have all week. I even manage a halfway intelligent comment about *The Grapes of Wrath* in English class, earning a look of beaming surprise from Mr. Carr. Even the vaguest hope I might talk to Stonechat, do something besides wait, lifts me up.

That hope doesn't last very long. Home, tucked in my room with my laptop, I search phone listings for Boulder, Colorado. Maude Burns gets me nothing. There are other Burns—Michael, Marianne—and one that's only listed as 'M. Burns."

I try that one. After three rings, a woman's voice answers.

"Hello?" Elderly, decidedly not Irish.

"Um, yeah, uh, is Jacob there?"

"I'm sorry, but you have the wrong number."

So maybe it isn't Burns. Burris? There's no one named Burris in the Boulder area. Berry? That doesn't even sound remotely right.

Maybe it's something Irish. I dial up a website on Irish names and there it is: Byrne. A common Irish name. It means, in Irish, *raven*.

191

That's too close to be a coincidence. I go back to the Boulder phone listings. There is an M. Byrne.

The phone rings. And rings. After four rings I ready myself for an answering machine recording of Raven's gravelly brogue but the phone keeps ringing. I wait, picturing Stonechat descending from his attic room, looking for the phone.

After the fifteen rings, I give it up.

***

By Friday morning, I am losing it. I hardly notice what's going on around me. When Mrs. Kellogg hands back the retake—*B-plus. Much better Renny!*—I stuff it in my binder like it's just some meaningless scrap.

At home, I don't even think of showing Lauren my improved grade. I sit on the bed, *The Grapes of Wrath* in my lap, open but unread. Hope has flat-lined. There's no way Stonechat has spent the last five days looking for Scaup. Whether he found Scaup or not, he should've shown up by now. Something is very wrong.

Dinner is a dull, quiet meal. Lee is at another seminar. Amy is off with her boyfriend. Gretchen talks nonstop about fifth grade. After fifteen minutes, I ask to be excused and retreat to the bedroom again.

Six-thirty. I stretch out on the bed and study the ceiling. How am I going to get through the rest of this night? I'm tired enough to sleep, but my eyes won't stay shut. Outside, darkness is falling fast. If I lie here long enough, sleep will come.

On the other hand, if Lauren walks in and finds me lying awake in a dark room at six-thirty, she'll probably freak out and decide I really am on drugs. I turn on my bedside lamp, scootch myself up to sitting and open the laptop. I do have a science project to start. I need to choose a topic. With exactly zero ideas of where to begin, I check the phone listings for Boulder again as if they might have changed overnight. M. Bryne is still there. I dial the number on my cellphone.

This time I let it ring nineteen times.

There are two possibilities. Maybe Stonechat solved the glitch in his time-folding spell. Or, maybe he just doesn't care how long it takes him to fly there. Obviously he doesn't want my help. Or my company.

Disturbing as this thought is, there's another possibility that bothers me even more: he's with Budgie. They made up. Maybe the two of them have gone after Raven together. Maybe they're hanging out in Phoenix, getting reacquainted. It isn't hard to picture. Budgie's a pretty girl underneath all the eye shadow. Prettier than me really. I open the website for maps and click on the satellite image, and trace the path following Highway Twenty-Five north toward Boulder. Then I drift west and south, toward the sprawl of Phoenix.

The first time I wake up, I'm still propped against the head of the bed. The laptop still shows Phoenix from low orbit. I push the computer aside and crumple back into sleep.

When I wake the next time, it's after midnight. The house is quiet. Maybe it's the sleep, but a couple of things seem obvious to me now. There are more important things at stake than whether Stonechat likes Budgie or not. Raven is still a prisoner—likely as not, a tortured prisoner. Stonechat isn't off rekindling old romances. Wherever he is, his only thought right now has to be for Raven. She's his mother.

I slide off the bed and go to my dresser. I pull out thick socks and a heavy sweater. I put on shoes, and pull Maysa out from her hiding place. She trembles with excitement. She hasn't flown since Sunday, five days ago.

"All right, girl. Here's your chance."

I inch up the window sash and climb out onto the roof. Maysa welcomes me onto her back and begins rising into the air. The sky is clear, the moon near full. The breeze wraps around me. I speak out loud, "Maysa, find Shirin."

Beneath a gust of wind, I can hear it. It's a little slower than usual. Maybe it's my imagination, but it sounds oddly somber. But that same shifting rhythm is there, those same bells.

I listen a little deeper, and Shirin's song is there too, the high yearning melody playing over Maysa's chorus of bells. And underneath, another familiar voice, the droning grind of a cello: Ma'Shooq. The taste of their combined melodies is bitter, like a mouthful of smoke.

"Maysa!" I speak out loud again. "Find them. Find Shirin."

Maysa turns slowly until the moon is over my left shoulder and begins to accelerate. West. She's taking me west. So not to Boulder, anyway. We're heading toward Mistral's island, which means he *did* go back without me, took it all upon himself with no help from anyone.

On the other hand, Phoenix is west as well.

I try to shake that thought away. It doesn't matter. This isn't about Budgie. Or even about Stonechat. This is about Raven.

Maysa continues to pick up speed. I scrunch silk in both hands and spread myself flat. We're going fast, but we're not in time-fold. Despite the racing speed, the landscape below drifts by in normal time.

"Maysa! Can you do a time-fold? Tempovol—"

It's no good. I have no idea how to do a time-folding spell. I fill my fists with silk, and settle in for a long ride.

The night roars by. I lose track of time. The wind blurs my eyes. The dark land stretches out. Clusters of lights, small towns, trucks on some lonely road—none of it is enough to break up the monotony.

Then, there, at the far end of visible, the horizon begins to glow. It creeps up and over the land, spreading out. Even in the middle of the night, it's lit up like a carnival. A city. A huge city. It goes on and on, spilling out over the landscape. Is it Los Angeles? Could it be already?

I pass over the downtown and into endless rambling suburbs. Curlicue housing developments gradually become fewer, the roads less frequent, and before I know it, I'm sailing over open desert again.

Not Los Angeles. Phoenix, probably. And I'm still heading west. Which means Stonechat isn't in Phoenix hanging out with Budgie, anyway. That's something.

But I realize something else as well. I've been airborne for at least two hours. Two hours and I only just passed Phoenix? At this rate, I'll be lucky to reach the west coast by morning. And after that, I still have to cross the Pacific Ocean. How far? How many hours more? And then there's still the trip back.

I breathe out hard through chattering teeth. What am I doing? This isn't going to work. I have to be back before morning. Besides, my fingers are cramping up, and it's freezing up here.

I'm never going to make it.

Phoenix is behind me now, but I can still see it glowing, shrinking—heading for the horizon. I don't even have to say anything to Maysa. Without being asked, she begins dumping airspeed. Gradually the wind stops tearing at me. I let my fists unclench. High over an empty landscape, Maysa finally slows all the way to stopping and hangs, just waiting.

"Yeah," I answer the unasked question. "You're right. We better go back home."

Twenty-Four

When I wake up the next morning, it's late. Almost noon. If Lee were home, I would've been called to breakfast long ago. Lee believes in Saturday morning breakfasts. It's a Teller thing, like science fair projects. We might not have any plans, might not even see each other again until dinner, but there's still time to sit down to a stack of hotcakes or a mound of scrambled eggs and bacon.

Fortunately, Lee is still in Reno, no doubt leading a roomful of conferees in a discussion on motivation and how to stay upbeat in a downbeat world. So the house is quiet. Lauren doesn't care if we sleep in. She sleeps in herself, and when she does get up, breakfast is usually a pot of coffee and whatever anyone is hungry enough to get for themselves.

I have no particular memory of going to bed. Maysa? I lean over the edge of the bed and look underneath. She's there, neatly rolled.

I fall back onto my pillow. Now I remember. My crazy flight over Phoenix. What a dumb idea!—as if I could fly to Australia and back again in a single night. There's no way of doing that without the time-folding spell.

And for that, I need help.

I swing my feet off the bed and sit up. It's Saturday. There'll be a kettle tonight—unless everyone has decided Big Hatchet is too

196

dangerous now after the raid. It doesn't really matter. I have to try. There just isn't any place else to look.

But there's another problem as well. With or without time-folding, this is going to take some time. I can't afford to wait until all the Tellers have gone to sleep before I head for the Hatchet. I need an earlier start.

And I'm grounded. That makes things even more complicated.

I trudge to the shower and stand for a long time under the steamy downpour, digging shampoo into my scalp. By the time I'm rinsed, dried, and dressed, I have formed a plan. It isn't great, but it might work. I drop on to the floor beside my backpack and begin to dig.

A few minutes later, I'm heading down the stairs. Lauren is stacking last night's dinner dishes in the dishwasher. She looks up. I have *The Grapes of Wrath* in my hand.

"Hey, there. Wondering when you were going to get up."

I smile.

"We're you up late?"

I nod. "Pretty late. Reading."

Lauren puts the last plate in the rack and closes the washer door. "You hungry? I was going to make myself a BLT for lunch. You want one?"

"Yeah. Sounds good."

She crosses to the refrigerator and piles ingredients on the counter-top. "Ought to be enough for a couple of sandwiches. How is *The Grapes of Wrath* going?"

"Huh? Oh. It's okay. Pretty good."

"Is that all the homework for the weekend?"

"No. Science. Research paper."

She spreads mayonnaise on two slices of bread. "What's it on?"

"Uh, I'm not sure yet. I think I might do something on pesticides and pollution."

She cocks an eyebrow. "I could probably give you some pointers on that, you know." Lauren's a sort of expert on toxins in food and stuff like that.

"Yeah. I was kind of thinking along those lines."

She smiles. "Tell you what. You come up with a more specific topic, and we can work on it this afternoon."

She puts the sandwiches on plates and pushes one across the counter.

"Thanks." I take a bite. Food seems like something from another world, an unreal world, like one of my dream meetings with Parnell. It's almost jarring how good it tastes—the salty crumble and the wet crunch of lettuce, tomatoes oozing and tangy. Halfway through the sandwich, I pull the history test from the book and unfold it. *B plus. Much better, Renny!* I slide it across the counter.

Lauren looks at it. "Not bad."

I take another bite. Lauren reads it over, nodding. She looks up. "Good job."

"Thanks."

"Good to see you working."

I finish chewing. I scrape at my gum-line with a fingernail, then say, "Well, I was hoping maybe, since I am making progress—I mean, I know it's only been a week, but—well, Bree is having a party at her house and she kind of asked me if I could help her with it. You know, set things up, clean up..."

This is partly true. There is a party and I was, more or less, invited. Bree and Caddy were talking about it before class a couple of days ago. They misinterpreted my vacant stare in their direction as interest.

"You should come, Renny. My parents have surrendered the whole house to it. They'll be there, unfortunately, but they've agreed not to show themselves."

I'm not even sure now if I answered. Nothing could've interested me less. But a party at Bree's is likely to be a madhouse—the kind of madhouse I can slip away from without anyone noticing.

Lauren frowns and stares at the refrigerator. After a long pause, she asks, "When is this party?"

"Tonight."

I watch her think, half a sandwich still dangling from her hand. It's a good sign she's even thinking about it. If she was going to say no, she would have said it already.

"I suppose..."

"Really?"

"I'm not crazy about it, Renny. But I've noticed you've been working. And to be honest, I'm glad you're doing something with Bree. I thought you two weren't really friends anymore."

"No! Sure we're friends."

"So this is at her house?"

"Uh huh."

"And her parents will be there?"

"Yeah, you can call them."

Lauren nods. The frown that creases her brow is still there, but it's a little softer now.

"Oh, uh, the other thing," I press my advantage, "is it okay if I spend the night? It'll probably go really late, and I said I could help them clean up. I figure that way I don't have to borrow the car, and nobody has to give me a ride home."

She looks as though she might back out on the whole thing. Then she exhales, noisily, through her nose. "Yeah. I guess."

"Really? Thanks. And I promise I'm going to keep on working on my grades. I really am."

She draws a deep breath and lets it out again. "I'm glad to hear it. But do yourself a favor, okay? Make sure I don't regret this."

***

Upstairs I call Bree.

"Well," she says, "sure, you're invited. I didn't think you were interested. I thought you were mad at me."

"No, I'm not mad. Why would you think I was mad?" The question sounds weird. I know perfectly well why.

"Well, you hardly even talk to anyone anymore. You walked right by me and McKenzie last week. We said 'Hi' like three times."

"Oh, yeah. Sorry. I've just kind of had a lot of stuff on my mind."

"Like what?"

"Just stuff. It's nothing about you guys. It's just some things I've got to work out on my own."

There's a moment of silence on the other end. When Bree speaks, there's a shrug in her voice. "If you say so, Ren. Party starts at eight."

"Eight. Okay. Sounds great. Bye, Bree."

I hang up and press my palms against my eyes, rubbing deep, slow circles. I've only been up an hour and a half and I've already told an amazing number of lies, with more lies coming before the night is over. I'm not going to tell Bree I'm skipping out early. The simpler I keep it, the better. I'll slip out, maybe call Lauren first on my cellphone, tell her everything is great and I'll see her in the morning. Say thanks for letting me come to the party—that'll be a nice touch.

Then? Then I'll fly to Big Hatchet, try to find someone who can help me cast the time-fold and hopefully come with me.

I put the vague plan out of my head and open up my laptop. Ridiculous as it seems, I need to start doing research on pesticides and pollution for my science research paper. I told Lauren I would. It will impress her if I actually follow through.

Twenty-Five

At eight o'clock, I take Maysa out from beneath the bed. "Well, girl"—I stroke the lilac fringe—"here goes." I hold up the emptied backpack. "Do you mind?"

Maysa gives no indication she minds in the least. If anything, she makes herself a little smaller, a little softer. Folded and rolled, she fits surprisingly well. Probably it's no worse than being rolled up under a bed for days at a time.

For the first time in weeks, I wear something other than jeans and some old shirt. I don't go so far as to wear a skirt, but I do put on a pair of black cotton pants and a blue and white blouse I haven't worn in a year. I brush my hair and even put a minimal amount of eyeliner on. It isn't much, but it impresses Lauren.

"Renny! You look nice."

"Thanks." On the way to Bree's, we talk about the science project—or at least Lauren does. I nod and make a few half-hearted comments.

At Bree's house, there are already a lot of cars parked out front. Lauren trolls for a curbside parking space, but the nearest is over a block away.

"You can just drop me off."

She frowns. Probably she had been planning on checking in with Bree's parents. Trust has its limits. She circles the block one more time and pulls to a stop. She scans the parked cars, probably trying to tell whether Bree's parents really are home.

201

"You know," I suggest, trying to sound helpful, "I can have Bree's parents call you on your cellphone."

She looks at me and shakes her head. "No. That's all right. You go on. Have a good time."

***

I thread my way through the cars in the driveway and up to the Mauers' front door. I knock. Then I try the bell. The music from inside is probably too loud for anyone to hear. I put a hand on the doorknob but it swings away from me. The music swells, reaching out through the open door.

"Renny! Hey, you look great!" Caddy Gillespie stands there, wearing a silver sequined skirt and a black top that hangs off one shoulder. She holds a plastic tumbler full of some bright red drink in her left hand.

"You too." We do not hug.

"Come on in. Dump your stuff in the closet."

I open a hall closet already piled with coats. I put my backpack off to the side and lay my jacket over the top of it. When I pull my head out again, Caddy is already gone.

There are maybe fifteen kids spread out between the kitchen and living room and into the dining room. Three boys are assembled around a big cut-glass punchbowl. The table is laid out with bowls of chips and dip and a tray of tiny pizzas. Kids slow-dance in the corner, ignoring the tempo of the music. Zoe Henniger sits on the breakfast nook counter, long legs dangling. Two boys I don't know stand at her feet like dogs waiting for table scraps.

The music switches abruptly from Beyonce to the Black Eyed Peas. Some boy, standing near the stereo, begins playing along with the intro on a flamboyant air guitar.

I could leave right now. Who would notice? Who would care? But it'll be better if I at least talk to Bree first. If Lauren calls later, looking for me, at least Bree can say, 'she's around here somewhere,' instead of 'I haven't seen her all night.'

202

I find her on the patio with McKenzie. We exchange a weak hug. "You look nice, Ren."

"Thanks. Nice party," I lie.

"Just the early birds here so far," Bree waves her cup in the direction of the kitchen. "Lot more people coming. You should get some punch. We need to catch up."

The Mauers have a big house, but by half-past eight it's crawling with kids. Most of them I don't even know. The stereo speakers have been turned to blast out onto the patio, which becomes the party's dance-floor. The game-room downstairs is full of boys playing Rock Band on Playstation and watching a big, flat-screen T.V.

Bree's offer to 'catch up' never materializes. She disappears as completely as Caddy, and I soon find myself standing in the dining room, balancing a paper plate full of snacks I don't even want. When a boy named Eric comes over and asks me to dance, I decide to make a break for it. I make an excuse and slip into the kitchen, leave my plate balanced on an already brimming trash-can, and head for the front door. I walk casually, like I'm not going anywhere, but no one is paying any attention anyway. Even when I open the hall closet door and free my jacket and backpack from the heap within, no one swoops down to ask me if I'm leaving already.

Out front, there are kids on the porch as well, but they're all involved in far quieter activities. As far as I can tell, no one comes up for air long enough to see me go. When I reach the sidewalk, I pull my cellphone out and dial home. "Hey, Lauren?"

"Renny? Is everything all right?"

"Yeah, sure. It's great." There's a pause. I hope Lauren can hear the noise of the stereo coming through the windows of the house.

"Renny?"

"What? Oh, yeah. The party's great. I just came outside to call. It's really noisy inside the house."

"Okay." There's just the slightest inflection of a question in the word.

"Well, I just wanted to say thanks for letting me go out tonight."

"Oh. Okay. Well, I think you earned it."

"Thanks." I hear my own voice give an odd quaver. A sudden knot tenses in my stomach.

"So, *are* you okay?"

"Yeah, I'm great. I'm going to stay and help clean up."

"Okay. Call if you change your mind."

The knot tightens, pushing up against my ribcage. I take the deepest breath I can manage, but when I speak again, my voice breaks. "Yeah," I croak, "okay."

"All right, then. See you tomorrow."

"Yeah. Good night."

I pocket the phone and frown at the darkness. It's like Stonechat said, I couldn't have told her the truth even if I wanted to. It's true, but I'm still frowning. I shoulder my backpack and hike up the street. At the corner there's a green space with a park bench and a stand of birch trees where the streetlights don't reach. In the shelter of a tree trunk, I unpack Maysa, put on my jacket, and sling my empty backpack over my shoulders. Maysa trembles beneath my knees when I climb on. "You ready, girl?'

She hums a complicated shimmer of bells. I close my eyes and think the syllables of the cloaking spell. I think of Big Hatchet, of ruggers chasing around like bats, of campfires, of Scaup, of Whimbrel, of gossamer mead, even of Budgie. When I open my eyes Maysa is rising. My heart is going like crazy. She takes me up above the tree line. "Big Hatchet," I say, out loud this time. "Take us to Big Hatchet!"

She hangs high, sniffing the wind, and swings like a compass—first too far south, then back again, zeroing in. She gives a low purr and then flings us both across the night.

***

Maysa ripples through the air, humming, delighted. I'm not feeling the same enthusiasm. Lauren sounded—what was the word?—

204

touched, almost choked up by the idea I would call and thank her. Thank her for trusting me. If she ever finds out...

Well, I can't *let* her find out. And I can't let myself think about it now. I need to focus on what's ahead. First Big Hatchet, find some familiar faces. Then convince them. They hardly know me, any of them. Why would anyone want to help?

They know Stonechat. And Raven. It's them they're going to be helping. Assuming they believe me. I have zero proof. The only proof is in seeing, and only I saw, so only I know.

Know. No.

Syllables flute—whistling, wafting.

Renny knows, another voice chimes.

Good for Renny. Sure, so sure.

Laughter glitters, first in one ear, then the other.

Great. My own chorus of crazies. "So," I say, "You're back."

Yes! Back! Back to yes! Good, Renny!

"Come to watch the show?"

The air gives a quiet rustle. Then one voice declares in bright singsong:

A cloud blown from the cut-throat north
suddenly hid Love's moon away.

I feel my eye twitch. "Hey!"

Another voice continues:

Believing every word I said,
I praised her body and her mind

"Now wait a minute!" I can't remember exactly when Stonechat recited that particular poem but I have a pretty good idea the sort of things we might have been doing. "What are you guys, a bunch of peep-show pervs?"

Peep! Peep!

They all take up the word, tossing it about like a silver ball.

Peep! Peep! Peep!

"Go haunt somebody else! I got no time for this."

They're quiet for a moment. Then one voice chirps up a single word: *ridiculous.*

I groan.

Ridiculous, it says again.

"Ridiculous. All right. I agree. It's ridiculous."

The next words come from directly above me, falling in light drops:

Now that no fingers bind,
That her hair streams upon the wind,
I do not know, that know I am afraid
Of the hovering thing night brought me.

That's a different poem. *The hovering thing night brought me.* Something cold tickles at the back of my neck. I touch it, but there's nothing there. "Hey," I say, "You guys. Do you know what's happened to him?"

There's a hush of breath—of breaths. A hushing.

"Do you?" I wait. "Stonechat," I try again, speaking directly to the darkness. "Is he all right?"

But it's just darkness, now, and it says what darkness usually says: Nothing. Silence.

***

Interstate Ten comes up below me, a gray ribbon on a black land. Headlights crawl, a solitary eighteen-wheeler nosing east. After that, it's empty in all directions. Maysa sails on into that emptiness without even slowing. Within minutes, we're descending.

A bright stretch of silver turns out to be moonlight on the sand. A dark wedge hides the stars. I circle in over the familiar pass, following the tumbled cliff-line, slipping between shoulders of rock.

This time, I smell the smoke before I see the flame. There they are in that same circle of stones. Fire cracks, licking the darkness, but there is no laughter, no voices. I see faces. One of the faces sees me— pale as china, eyes dark, hair a black brush.

"Well, look who it is." Her voice is as flat and dry as the desert, her Eastender's accent squeezed nearly to nothing. I coast in. Others stand.

"Hey, Wren!" someone cries. It's Nightjar.

"If you're looking for Stonechat," Budgie snaps, "he's not here."

I turn to Budgie. "I know. I am looking for him, but I already know where he is."

Budgie tilts her head hard to the right, and scowls. "You're looking for him, but you know where he is. You know he ain't here, but this is where you come. You're a matched set, you two. Him with his crummy poetry, you with your riddles."

"You can't call his poetry crummy," a voice creaks. Scaup, sitting so near the fire that he might have been in it, leers, shadow-faced, at Budgie.

"No one asked you, Scaup! This isn't about you."

"I didn't say it was. I only said Yeats didn't write crummy poetry."

"When's the last time you saw him?" I ask.

Budgie gives me a suspicious eye. "Why do you want to know? I thought you knew where he was."

I keep my voice calm and low. "Did he call you?"

Budgie pouts, mashing her lips together so they purse out. "Yeah. He called. Tuesday. Got the message on the machine at home."

"You call him back?"

"Tried. He wasn't home."

"And that was it?"

She flares up. "What the hell business of yours is it if he calls me or I call him?"

"He's gone," I say. I have their attention now. Budgie looks tensed, ready for things to get ugly.

"I'm here," I say in a quiet voice, "because I need your help."

I'm looking at all of them now, going from face to face. "Raven is a prisoner. Mistral has her on an island—out in the South Seas. Stonechat is there too."

"How do you know?" Nightjar asks.

"I tried to find him last night. My carpet told me they were together. I couldn't get to them. I can't do the time-folding spell. I need someone who can—and anyone who's willing to come along and help."

"Was Raven right?" Nightjar asks. "Did he take the Orb? And Flo?"

"Flo's dead."

A flurry of mutterings scuttles around the fire, passing from voice to voice. Nightjar's eyes go very wide.

"Dead?" Budgie's incredulous voice cuts through the murmur.

"Dead," I say, sounding much braver than I feel. "I saw him die."

"But—?" Nightjar begins.

"They tortured him. Mistral. He needed Parnell to tell him how to work the Orb. And Raven found Mistral, because her carpet could find Parnell. And Stonechat found Raven the same way."

"Wait." This is a new voice. It belongs to a black man I've never seen before. He has close-cropped hair and he's wearing a dark green shirt that can only be called a tunic. He speaks quietly. "I don't understand. You escaped, but Stonechat and Raven did not?"

"No. Me and Stonechat both got away. It was some spell Raven did. Stonechat called it—" I fumble with the memory,"—a whiplash?"

"Whipcrack," Scaup answers.

"Right. She did something and—voom!—we shot up into the sky. When we woke up, we were already miles away, and in time-fold. Stonechat tried to go back, but the spell wouldn't let us."

Scaup grins. "That Raven."

"Stonechat tried the next day too, but he still couldn't make the spell work."

"A residual effect," Scaup says. "Raven didn't want him coming after her again."

"Well, I don't think it stopped him. I don't know whether he got the time-fold thing to work or if he just decided to fly there in regular time, but he's there. I'm sure of it."

I search their faces again. "I'm going tonight, if anyone will help me. If no one is willing to come, then—I don't know, maybe someone can help me with the time-folding spell, get me started. Give me a push."

For a moment there isn't any sound at all except the crack of the fire. Then someone laughs. It's a deep chuckle, but not particularly jolly. I find him among the light-flecked faces. I don't know him. I also don't like him. He wears a scraggly beard and a flannel shirt. A bandana holds his hair behind his ears. "I'm sorry but—*where* are you going?"

"Uh, Mistral's island," I say. "His fortress."

He nods, smiling a thin-lipped smile. "Ah. And just what do you expect us to do? Storm this *fortress* with our rugs? Rescue Raven from the clutches of the evil Doctor Mistral?"

I blink and swallow. My instant dislike for this guy isn't getting any better. "Well, yes."

He laughs. "You've seen too many movies, fledgling."

"Your heart is showing, Rail," a voice cracks, "and it looks a little weak, if you ask me." It's Whimbrel. He stands splayfooted at the shoulder of the man in the green tunic.

Rail turns. "Don't tell me you believe all of this?"

"*I* do." This time it's Scaup who speaks. The old rugger stays seated, his face red from the closeness of the flames. "Whimbrel is right."

"Everyone knows your opinion!" Rail says.

"It isn't an opinion. It's a fact. Things are not right. We all know that."

"Yeah, but where's the proof?" another voice demands. A squat woman with black hair says, "All of this crap about Mistral, we've heard it all before. They're just a couple of renegades."

"Seriously!" Rail spreads his hands apart and smiles, looking almost apologetic. "I mean, none of us have ever even *seen* Mistral! How can anyone believe—?"

"I saw him!" I almost yell. "I was there. I saw Parnell die."

Rail shakes his head. "I've been a flyer for over fifteen years. You're just a fledgling."

"Is Raven a fledgling? She went to get Parnell, but it wasn't just about Parnell. It was about the Orb too. Mistral has the Orb. It's in his fortress. Raven risked her life to try and get it back."

"What's all this deal about the Orb?" This is another woman, younger. She has short hair and one dangly earring. "It's just like how Flo talks to us, right?"

"The Orb of Descrying," Scaup speaks slowly. "Didn't Parnell ever show it to you?"

"Sure," she nods. "Once."

"The dreams," Scaup says. "Parnell touched the Orb and called you to him while you were sleeping."

She crimps a dainty eyebrow. "So?"

Scaup flexes his own heavy brow. "Parnell was harmless. More than harmless—kindly. A good man."

"So?"

"Well what if he wasn't? What if he were a madman? A monster? The purposes of a monster would be well-served by that sort of access, don't you think? Access to your dreams?"

The girl stares, considering his words. All around the fire, faces are grim.

"Parnell told me," I say, "that he could plant suggestions if he wanted to—put ideas in our heads that we would think were our own ideas when we woke up—only he would never do that."

210

"But Mistral would," Scaup says.

Flame spits and sizzles as it splits open a limb. The fire shifts, and several ruggers step back or move aside. Avocet, who has been silent so far, says, "I'll help."

"Thank you."

"You're called Wren, right?"

"Yes."

Avocet tosses her long hair back, and firelight catches the bird tattooed on her cheek. "Okay, " she says. "So what's the plan, Wren?"

***

Not everyone is so willing. The one called Rail stalks away from the gathering and he is not alone. The black-haired woman and the girl with the dangly earring—they walk away too. So does Budgie. But some come forward: Nightjar and Whimbrel, Avocet, Scaup. Scaup can work the time-folding spell.

"Of course, I'm going," he says. "I'm not quite as decrepit as I look."

I'm not arguing. It's only just registering on me how small our numbers are. The black rugger in the green tunic—Shearwater—is coming. But that, it seems, is it. Six of us. I look about from face to face. It's hard not to feel a little disappointed. Probably it shows. I look back at the fire where half a dozen ruggers, the ones who aren't coming, have reconvened.

"Maybe they just need a little more convincing," Nightjar suggests.

I shake my head. "No. They had their chance." I shrug Maysa from my shoulder and smile. I hope I look braver than I feel. "Let's fly."

"Wait!" The voice comes from above. Three carpets drop down. Budgie stops right in front of me and steps onto solid ground. "I'm coming with you."

"Okay."

"These guys too," she adds, waving at the other two. "They were racing over at the ravine. I thought they'd want a piece of this."

One is Longbill. He gives me a grin and holds up a thumb. The other is a man I haven't seen before. He's big, six and a half feet easy, and broad. He takes up a lot of space. Budgie jerks a thumb in his direction.

"He's Knot."

"Uh, not coming?"

"No," the man says. "It's my name. Knot—with a K." His voice is a soft rumble.

"Oh. Okay. I'm Wren," I shake his giant hand and smile, "With a W."

He smiles back.

"Right, then," Scaup says. "If all the pleasantries are over, let's get this show in the air. Some of us aren't getting any younger."

Twenty-Six

We fly over a dark land. Lights from below—a town, a truck-stop—stretch out across the landscape, then wink to darkness again. Scaup stays near the center of the flock, casting the spell. Underneath my hands, Maysa hums. She's not alone. The whole flock, all nine carpets, are singing together, an unearthly choir.

Before long, we pass over a bright blur. Someone says, "There's L.A." Hardly a moment later, it's gone again and we're winging over darkness.

"You all right, fledgling?"

It's Scaup who asks.

"I'm okay." This is the first time he's ever said a word to me directly. "Hey, uh, thanks back there. If you hadn't believed me, probably nobody else would've either."

He sniffs. "Didn't have to tell me something was wrong. Been feeling that for a while now. Sorry to hear about Parnell, though. That's a tough pill."

I consider asking some polite question about how long he'd known Parnell, but something catches my eye. For a while now, the sky has been growing lighter, getting gradually paler above the dark line of the horizon.

Scaup says, "Here's something you don't see every day."

213

All at once, the border between the sky and the sea turns a violent purple. A blazing red sun squeezes up from the water, bloodying the sea, blanching the sky. Purple goes red, then orange, then palest blue.

"Morning?" It can't be morning.

"Evening," Scaup says. "Sunset in reverse. We're catching up with yesterday."

When we went after Raven the first time, we left later, after midnight. It had gotten lighter, but we hadn't seen the unsetting of the sun. "So, are we traveling backwards in time?"

He squints one eye shut. "Not really."

"But it's earlier here. If you keep going, it'll get earlier and earlier."

"Same thing happens if you take an airplane flying east."

"Well, okay. But in time-fold, I mean, it's a lot faster than an airplane. We flew to Africa and back in one night, a couple of hours each way."

He sighs like he knows what's coming. "Yeah?"

"Well, what if we just kept going east? Wouldn't we get back to New Mexico and it would be yesterday?"

"There isn't a rugger who mastered time-folding who hasn't tried that."

"You?"

"Sure."

"Well, what happens?"

He knuckles the bristles of his jaw and sniffs again. "Doesn't work."

"Why not?"

"You can fly around the world all you want, but you can't go back and meet yourself yesterday and tell yourself to bring an umbrella because it's going to rain or to buy a lottery ticket with the winning numbers."

"Yeah, but why not?"

Scaup growls. "You can't go back and meet yourself yesterday because it would've already happened."

"How's that?"

"Look. Did you meet yourself this morning? Did your future-self come back and give you lottery numbers to bet on?"

"No, of course not."

"Well, then obviously you are not going to fly back in time to meet yourself yesterday—because you didn't."

We both sit in silence for a minute. It's early evening now. The sun hangs, plump and orange, just over the gray horizon.

"Okay. So what does happen if you fly all the way around the world backwards?"

He yawns. "Mostly you get tired. And confused. Now let me alone. I've got a spell to work."

I let Maysa drift away. Somehow, the explanation that you can't-do-it-because-you-didn't-do-it isn't very satisfying. What would I do if I could go back? For starters, I wouldn't let Stonechat go off by himself. Of course, who knows how long he's been gone. I might have to go all the way back to Tuesday. What was he thinking, anyway? That place is like a high security prison. Even cloaked, he can't walk through locked doors or squeeze himself through tiny windows. Maybe I could have made him see the craziness of it, though I don't know if it would have made any difference. He already knew how crazy it was. He just didn't care.

"Hey! Do you mind?" It's Budgie. "Sky ain't big enough for you?"

"Sorry."

I scoot aside so she can pass by, but she doesn't. She stays alongside. After a long, silent moment, she says, "So Mistral, what's he got?"

"Sorry?"

"Minions. Goons. Has he got a whole army or just a handful?"

"Not sure. I saw ten or twelve guys."

"So we're pretty even, at least as far as numbers go."

"I guess."

"Tough bunch, though, right?"

"Yeah, tough. And crazy."

She hooks a thumb at the sky. Not far above us, Longbill and Knot are side by side. Longbill is talking, gesturing with his hands, a steady stream of commentary. I can't tell from looking whether Knot is even listening.

"Those two," Budgie says, "good in a scrap."

"Yeah. That Knot's big enough for two."

"He's big. He won't start anything, but he might be the one to finish it. Now Longbill, he's the one who might start something."

I look at Budgie. She stares off toward the horizon. "I'm glad you brought them."

Budgie gives me a brief sideways glance. "They knew Stonechat too—I mean, *know* him."

I try to let that unfortunate slip go by me.

"You know," she says, "he always ticked me off, Flo did. Coming into my dreams and all. I'm sorry about him being dead. He was a good bloke. But it creeped me out."

"Yeah."

We fly on in silence again. It's an afternoon sky now, pale blue. The blurred sea is lacy and nearly lavender. I push my hand flat on Maysa's back. *Are we getting close?*

Something in the roll of the melody, some small lilt, there and gone again, comes across as a *yes*. "I think we're getting close."

Budgie draws a long breath. "Might as well get there and get it over with." She reaches down and digs her fingers into the weave of her carpet like she's scratching an itch. "You know," she says, "I still don't like you."

"Okay."

"Just so we're clear about that." She soars up to fly alongside Longbill and Knot, and I drift along alone, listening to the carpets, watching the sun crawl away from the horizon.

Then the song changes. Maysa starts it: a faster tempo—and brighter, somehow—with anticipation. Soon, the whole flock is singing along.

"Hey! I think it's—"

"Yah, I feel it," Scaup calls back. The spell dissolves all around us and we drop down into the wind. Beneath us, the swirl of purple and gray slows into the sudden clarity of open ocean.

Islands, flecks of black and green, lay strewn across the waves.

"Those are the Fiji's," a deep voice says. I look up to find Shearwater flying at my left side, studying the ocean. "It looks like we're swinging north toward the Solomons."

We're getting lower now, and pulling into a close formation. I give Maysa free rein. She leads the whole flock down, passing a whole bunch of islands before dropping in on one in particular.

"Is that the one?" This time it's Whimbrel, who's pulled alongside on the right.

"Yeah. Think so."

We dive down through the salt-sprayed air, skirting over the wave-tops like a line of pelicans. This side of the island is very different. Instead of cliffs, a forest goes nearly down to the water's edge. Only a narrow strip of sand, tucked under the trees, separates the woods from the sea.

Solid ground makes me stumble.

"Carpet legs?" Whimbrel asks, with a grin.

I smile too. "Pins and needles."

Everyone's on the ground now, walking and stretching.

"Nice little beach," Longbill says, surveying the shoreline. "All it needs is some decent waves."

The sun is behind the shoulder of the mountain, leaving the beach completely in shadow.

"So, what's the plan?"

It takes me a minute to realize Nightjar is asking *me*. "Uh, well—"

"We need to wait until nightfall," Avocet says, "We'll want to go cloaked, right? I don't know about anyone else, but I could use some rest."

"Resting until nightfall seems like a good idea," Shearwater says, "but I want to get a look at the fortress first, while there is still light."

"Yeah," Longbill agrees. "Let's see what we're up against."

Scaup?" Budgie says, "You all right?"

Scaup, his carpet hanging from one hand, is teetering from side to side. His face is pale and greased with sweat.

"What's wrong?" Budgie's voice somehow manages to sound both rude and concerned.

"I'm fine!"

But he obviously isn't. He pulls himself up straight, but his eyes don't look right. Even in the course of two gruff words, his speech has a noticeable slur.

"Maybe you should sit down," Whimbrel suggests.

"Look! If you all just—oh, stop it, Budgie!"

Budgie puts a hand out to steady him. He shakes it off, stumbling. Longbill and Knot catch him. Scaup's eyes go wide. He gives his head a slow shake. "Cripes. I need sleep."

He throws his carpet over one shoulder and shuffles his way to the tree line. There, he kicks himself a place in the sand, wraps his rug around him, and lays down.

"I suppose," Nightjar says, "I wouldn't mind an hour myself."

So I agree to lead Longbill and Shearwater over to scope out the castle. Everyone else settles in to try and sleep until nightfall.

***

Maysa leads us scudding over the treetops. It only takes a few minutes before we're staring out from a canopy of leaves at the castle tower.

"I don't see any guards," Longbill says.

"Probably around, just the same," Shearwater says. He turns to me. "How many followers do you think he has?"

"I saw maybe ten or twelve last time. Could be more, I guess."

Shearwater tilts his head to one side. "It isn't a very big fortress. If he had an army, you'd think he'd need a lot more room."

We circle the castle, keeping to the treetops. Shearwater takes his time, scoping the layout. "How did you get inside?"

"The skylight. Stonechat broke through it."

The skylight has been repaired, badly—a half-assed job with plastic sheeting.

"Underneath there is the room where he was keeping the Orb. There's a big staircase, a winding one—and downstairs there's an even bigger room with a fireplace. That's all I saw."

Shearwater stares at the castle top. "Sounds like the skylight's our best bet. Since they haven't replaced the glass, we might slip in there pretty quietly."

We retrace our flight path back to the others. In the half-hour we've been gone the shadows have grown long. The shade that covers the beach now stretches out over the waves as well.

Nightjar sits curled up against a tree trunk, staring out to sea, her carpet pulled up to her shoulders. Budgie is awake too, scowling upward at nothing. Only Scaup is really asleep. He's tearing off snores in great rattling gasps.

"How much daylight do you think there is left?" I ask.

Shearwater peers out over the shadowed water. There's still sunlight out there, glinting on the rippling surf. "Not much. You should both get some rest. I'll wake everyone when it's time."

"Don't you need sleep?"

"Nah. Pretty early for me. We're only about two hours ahead of my normal time zone."

"Where do you live?" Longbill asks.

"Hawaii."

"Cool," Longbill nods. "I've been there. Do you surf?"

Shearwater shakes his head, looking amused and apologetic. "Everybody asks that. I live in Hilo. I teach high school."

"That's cool too," Longbill says, though clearly not *as* cool. "What were you doing in New Mexico?"

"Whimbrel is an old friend. Seriously, get some rest. You're going to want it."

I don't need more convincing. Whatever time it is in the South Seas, it's late inside my head. There's a fuzzy feeling in back of my eyes. Sleep wouldn't be hard to find. I clear myself a spot in the sand and wrap Maysa around me, but my eyes won't stay shut. I just keep staring upward at nothing in particular.

It's late, past midnight back in Albuquerque. Lauren will be in bed by now— unless, of course, she called Bree's house looking for me and discovered I'm not there. By now there could be a police cruiser parked in front of my house, two officers sitting in my living room, listening to Lauren rant about her missing foster-daughter. Her daughter the liar.

"Take it easy now, ma'am. In most of these cases, the missing child turns up in the morning. Now, has she ever run off before? Does she have a boyfriend?"

My boyfriend. Where the hell is Stonechat? All along, I guess I was hoping we were going to find him first thing while we were scouting the castle, just like Raven found us the first time we were here. Is he squatting in a tree somewhere, waiting for his chance? Or is he inside already? Cloaked, he could hide out for days, maybe.

I roll onto my side and dig my shoulder into the sand. Worrying isn't going to help. Stonechat is all right. Raven too. They have to be. If they aren't all right, I would know. Maysa would know, wouldn't she?

I roll onto my back again. It's getting dark fast. Soon, we'll launch our attack. We'll infiltrate. That's the word they'd use if this was a movie—some big-budget action film about a rescue operation. All we need is a hero. Shearwater? He might do. A high school teacher from Hawaii. How weird is that? What does he teach? Science? Math? For all I know, it could be P.E. or hygiene. But he's got this whole serene warrior-thing about him, like in a martial arts movie. A kung-fu master who teaches hygiene.

"Hey! Wake up!"

My eyes flicker open. Budgie is leaning over me. "Shearwater says its time."

She walks away into the darkness. I can't sit up. Maysa's wrapped about me like I'm some kind of burrito. She's surprisingly snug. If anything, she's more tightly wrapped now than when my nap started.

"Come on, girl. I gotta get out of here."

She loosens her grip and hums a soft, sleepy chord. It's still early evening. The darkness isn't complete yet. Colors hang above the horizon, waiting to fade. The moon's face peeks down. I scan the length of the beach, picking out people. Avocet stands by the water's edge. She's balanced on one leg, the other leg drawn up so the sole of the foot is pressed against her thigh. Her hands are joined palm-to-palm as if she's praying.

Out of nowhere, Shearwater is standing at my left shoulder. "Are you ready?"

I nod. "I guess. Everyone else up?"

"Except Scaup. It seems he can't wake up."

"Is he all right?"

"I believe he is just exhausted. The time-fold is a draining spell when you're spreading it over a whole flock. And he is sixty-eight years old. I think we should just let him sleep. He's not going to be much good to us, the state he's in."

Across the sand, Longbill and Knot are walking, carpets on their shoulders. They're all gathering now. It's Shearwater, with that ninja warrior vibe of his. Everyone has decided that he's our leader. Suits me. But as the circle forms, he makes a little throat-clearing noise and turns to me. His look says it plain enough: this is my party. They're waiting for me to tell them what to do. I look from face to face. They're an odd bunch—angry Budgie, brassy Nightjar, eager Longbill, silent Knot.

"What's the plan?" Whimbrel asks.

I press my tongue against my teeth, waiting for some idea to take shape. "We go. We get inside. Somehow. I don't know yet."

"We'll be cloaked," Nightjar points out.

"It doesn't look like there are a lot of ways into that place," Longbill says. "Not a lot of doors."

"Doors," Avocet objects, "tend to get noticed, opening and closing—even if you're invisible."

"We think maybe the skylight might be our best chance. It looks like it's just been covered up with plastic. We could cut a hole in it if we had a knife."

Longbill draws an ivory-handled pocketknife from a pants pocket and holds it up.

"Maybe we should split up," Nightjar says, "come at it from more than one direction."

Shearwater puts a hand up. "I think we need to stop with the planning and just go. Wren is right. We go. We get inside somehow. Planning is all well and good, but we can't plan when we don't know what's waiting for us. So we go. We improvise."

Twenty-Seven

The castle looks a lot larger by moonlight. We gather in the branches of a tall tree with a clear view of the tower's top. It's no longer deserted. Two men stand looking out to sea. Not so far off, a ship makes its slow way across open water. It's all lit up. The front deck is lined with torches. Over the quiet water, I can hear music: steel drums. Calypso music.

The men on the tower are watching the cruise ship too. One has a pair of binoculars. We can't hear anything they're saying, except for a couple of loud bursts of laughter. The guard on the left hands the binoculars to his companion and points, making descriptive shapes with his hands.

"Not exactly the guard at Buckingham Palace," Whimbrel says. "They look drunk."

"This could work out for us," Shearwater suggests. "If Wren is right, then they've got us outnumbered. Maybe we can shorten the odds a little."

He tells us what he has in mind.

***

Longbill, Knot and Shearwater fly off to make things ready. Everyone else waits in the trees. Avocet stares at the tower top, biting her lip. If I've ever seen anybody having second thoughts, it's her.

"You sure you're up for this?"

223

She gives me a nervous smile. "I suppose. Just hope I'm faster than they are."

"Don't be too much faster than them, though," Nightjar says. "If this is going to work, they have to think they can catch you."

Avocet nods, looking even more nervous. "Right. Fast, but not too fast."

"And try not to let them know you want them to follow you. Just act all helpless and confused."

"You know if you want to do it for me—"

Nightjar laughs. "Come on, Avvy. They might or might not follow a thirty-eight-year old soccer mom, but there's no *way* they won't follow you!"

Avocet crimps her delicate, feathery eyebrows, and chews her lower lip.

"Don't worry," I say. "If anything goes wrong, we'll be right here."

Avocet runs a hand through her hair, pulling out wind-tangles. "Do you think it's been long enough?"

Nightjar nods. "Yeah. Good luck."

Avocet pushes away from the branches and floats down into darkness. We lose sight of her immediately. The guards stand, leaning against the low wall, looking anything but on guard. Beyond them, the cruise ship glides in the moonlit distance. The bright percussion of the orchestra, tinny as a music box, carries an amazing distance.

"Hey!" the paunchy one shouts.

Avocet shoots up over the far wall like she just rose up from the sea. Both guards leap back. One swears loudly and gives a big braying laugh. Avocet tosses her hair back, and wipes her brow.

"Where the hell did you come from?" His voice is thick and gritty.

"Wow!" Avocet skids forward, and comes to a bobbing stop. "Sorry. I mean, I heard—" I can't hear the rest. She is talking a lot, though only random phrases come through: "—heard there was a—"

and "—take a look around—" And then, more clearly, "So what is this place?"

One of the guards—taller, with a softer voice—says something I can't make out at all. He takes two slow steps closer. Avocet drifts back the same amount.

"No, I—" she speaks again with bit of a stammer. "I think— Look, I gotta go. Sorry, I..."

She rises suddenly like she's caught on an updraft and just keeps going, up and over their heads. "Sorry," she says again, drifting backwards. "I uh..."

Then she turns again and heads out over the trees.

"Hey!" One guard pulls a carpet out from a dark corner of the rampart wall and unfurls it. "Wait up!" He climbs on his carpet and grins over at his companion. "I saw her first!"

But the other man has his carpet out too. The sound of their laughter follows them out over the forest and dwindles to nothing.

I look at Nightjar. She holds up both hands, fingers crossed.

"Think they're ready?" Nightjar asks.

"They're ready," Budgie says.

For a while, all we do is wait. I can still see the cruise ship, torches flickering, but I can't hear the music anymore. There's nothing but the dull wash of the sea. Whimbrel sits cross-legged. His hands dangle between his knees, knuckles drumming against silent silk. Budgie shifts from kneeling to sitting. "Taking kind of a long time," she says. "Do you think a couple of us should maybe go and see what's—?"

The rustle of branches cuts her off.

"Ow! Watch it, Knot!"

Avocet materializes on a limb above us. Behind her, Longbill rubs his nose, a scowl on his face.

"What?" Knot asks.

"You let that branch swing back in my face!"

"We did it!" Avocet chirps. Her face is flushed. She's grinning.

"You were great!" I say. "We saw the way they took off after you."

Avocet snorts. "Those idiots! They would've followed me right out to sea if I'd kept going. It was nothing getting them to follow me into the forest. Longbill and Knot were great. And Shearwater."

"Where *is* Shearwater?"

"I am right here." He's about eight feet away, right behind me, hovering cross-legged.

"What did you do to them?"

"We clobbered them," Longbill says. "Knocked them right off their rugs."

"We caught them totally off guard," Shearwater says. "They weren't the sharpest knives in the drawer. Though, it was Longbill and Knot who did the actual clobbering."

"What did you do to them?" Nightjar asks. "You didn't, you know, *kill* them, did you?"

"Naw," Longbill rejects the idea. "Knocked 'em down and took their rugs." He holds one bundled roll of carpet. Knot has the other.

"Brilliant!" Whimbrel says.

"They might make their way back here," Shearwater says, "but it'll take them a good hour at least, I'd think. That's thick forest they'll have to get through. You know, I wouldn't mind trying to reduce the odds a little more. We haven't lost the element of surprise yet."

"Yeah," Whimbrel agrees, "but if we wait for the next watch of the guard, it could take hours. I mean, who even knows if those two *were* guards. They could've just been hanging out watching that ship."

"Right," Shearwater says. "We need to get their attention—without tipping our hand. See if we can get a couple more of them to come out."

"How are we going to do that?" Budgie asks. "Throw rocks at their window until they come out to complain?"

"Not rocks," Nightjar says. She reaches up into the branch above her and plucks a nut about the size of a golf ball. "Nuts. This tree is full of them."

The plan takes shape all by itself. Shearwater flies over for a closer look at the skylight while Nightjar and Budgie collect nuts. The tree branches are heavy with the hard, round fruits. They pull easily from their stems. By the time Shearwater returns, they each have a pile of ammunition.

"Okay," he says. "There won't be any trouble getting through that skylight. All the glass is gone, and we can cut our way through without making any noise. But there's someone in there."

"Mistral?"

"I've never seen Mistral." He turns to Budgie and Nightjar. "You ready?"

They re-cloak and quickly vanish in the darkness. A moment later, the first nut hits the rooftop. It makes a surprising amount of noise, bouncing on the stonework: *pock, tock, pit pat pock.*

Another follows. And a third. After a short pause three more hit all at once, rattling on the rooftop like a sudden shower of hail.

One hits the repaired skylight with a plastic *thwack!*

Still, nothing happens. Budgie and Nightjar go at it again, pelting the rooftop, aiming more and more at the plastic covering the skylight. For two minutes that feel like a lot longer, they keep it up. Just as Budgie winds up to throw her last nut, two dark shapes flit up out of the shadows.

Budgie holds her fire. The two ruggers rise up over the parapet wall and onto the rooftop. Still mounted, they survey the scattering of nuts. One scans the night sky. Her's is a familiar face. The name flashes: Kadja—the skinny woman with the stringy hair and lean-muscled arms. The other rugger starts to speak, and the woman hushes him.

"What?"

"I'm listening, you idiot."

The man listens too. His face is also familiar, with thick-jowled, black-bristled cheeks. His voice is gruff. "I don't hear anything."

Kadja, still scanning, apparently doesn't either.

"Think it was squirrels?" the man asks.

Kadja scowls. "You ever seen a squirrel around here before?"

The man shakes his head. "Never looked."

The woman sucks her teeth and mutters something. She puts her hands together, framing her mouth, and yells, "Chubasco! Samiel!" She waits for some reply. "Where are those morons?"

The man tries bellowing the two strange names into the night. When there's no reply, he glides nearer to the trees and draws breath to shout again. He never gets the chance. Before the words can leave his mouth, Knot materializes from empty air, barreling over the stone wall. The man flies backwards, arms flailing. Thrown clear of his carpet, he crashes to the rooftop. Knot is on top of him in an instant.

"What the—?" Kadja hollers.

But before she can finish, a long arm wraps around her shoulder. Another clamps across her mouth. Longbill is suddenly right behind her, lifting her clean off her carpet and into the air. The two of them rise, locked in a bizarre embrace. She wrenches backwards, trying to get her elbow into his gut. When he clamps tighter she slams her heel down hard, trying to stomp his foot.

"Ow! Stop it!" he hisses. "Are you *crazy*? Stop it!"

She throws another elbow, aiming high this time. When he pulls back, she jerks her head free from his grip and shrieks some meaningless syllable.

She falls forward, arms wheeling. Her breath comes in three short pants: "Huh, huh, huh!"

The sound when she hits the roof stuns everything into silence. Shearwater is there first. He turns her over. Her face is dark with blood, her nose mashed flat. A gash over her eye oozes. Judging from the odd way her hand is joined to her arm, it seems pretty likely her wrist isn't quite right either. Shearwater has his ear to her mouth.

228

"Is she alive?"

It takes him a moment. "She's breathing."

Longbill, nearest to the scene, takes longest to arrive. He floats down, looking ghostly pale. "I didn't mean to drop her."

Knot, kneeling beside Shearwater, stands up. "What the hell, man!" he says, in his usual low voice. "What were you trying to do?"

"I didn't know what to do. I couldn't..." he stammers, "I mean, she's a girl. I didn't want to hit her."

"You'd a done her a hell of a lot less damage if you *had* hit her!"

Shearwater stands up. "Her nose is probably broken, but she's not going to die."

The woman confirms this with a painful groan. Her breath rattles wetly in her mouth.

"We gotta get these two out of here," Knot says.

"Right." Shearwater agrees. He points to Knot and Longbill. "We'll take them down where we left the others. Somebody roll up their carpets and stash them somewhere. They probably heard that, and there could be a whole bunch of them up here any minute, so I suggest you get cloaked and into the trees. Come on, Longbill! Snap out of it!"

Longbill, still staring down at the woman lying on the ground, jumps. "Right. Right. I got her."

He scoops her up on his carpet while Shearwater and Knot wrestle the unconscious man on to theirs. Together they rise wobbling into the air and disappear over the forest.

Budgie and Nightjar gather the renegades' carpets. One of them lies peacefully on the stones, as motionless as a normal carpet. The other floats at about knee-level, waiting. They roll them up and carry them into the trees.

Then, we wait. Avocet and Nightjar sit close together. Budgie hugs her own knees. The castle crouches, silent in the moonlight. It seems impossible no one inside has heard any of that. I shiver, not in the least bit cold. My eyes find Avocet's. She smiles, probably trying to look encouraging. I force myself to smile back, but it feels odd on my face and I let it go.

A low blast sounds. The cruise ship is back and closer this time. There is a splash of far-off music and a ripple of laughter. The on-deck orchestra breaks into a lively calypso number.

"Idiots!" Budgie curses low.

A mosquito whines by my left ear. I wave it away.

"Hey," Nightjar whispers, "I hear something."

In a moment, the branches around us are swaying and bouncing. Knot and Longbill become visible first, then Shearwater.

"Everything okay?"

Shearwater nods. "They're all tucked in. Not too far from the first pair, but not so close either."

"The woman—did she wake up."

"Hell, yes," Longbill says. "Started screaming her head off before we even touched down." He holds up a hand. "Tried to bite me. I almost dropped her again. Only this time on purpose." He turns to Shearwater. "If we have to worry about any of them, she's the one. She'd kill me with her bare hands if she got the chance. The sooner we get on with this and get out of here, the better."

"What's happening here?" Shearwater asks. "Anyone poke their nose out?"

"Nope. First I figured they were just waiting for the right moment. Now I'm not so sure. I suppose they could be asleep."

"It's not that late," Avocet says. "In local time, it's probably only about nine o'clock."

"Yeah, I guess." I repress the impulse to ask, *So what do we do now?* I look at Shearwater. He's studying the castle, his lips tight over his teeth.

"Are you sure he's got a dozen ruggers inside?"

"I only know what I saw last time. There were about a dozen. But I don't know how many he's got there now."

Shearwater stares at the castle again. "I still don't like the odds."

"Look," Longbill says, "we go in cloaked. We look around. If it comes down to a fight—"

"We don't need all nine of us blundering around in there," Nightjar says. "What we need is to draw off the rest of the guard."

Shearwater agrees. "A smaller party is less likely to get caught." He turns to me again, like he's asking for my approval.

"Yeah. I think that makes sense. No offense to anyone, but I'm not sure some of us are going to be any good in a real fight. I know I'm not."

"I've never hit anybody in my life," Avocet says.

"I'd prefer stealth to brawn, personally," Knot says.

"Right," Shearwater says. "If we can get enough of them out here, maybe we can lead them off—cause a diversion. Wren, you're the only one who's been inside, so you'll have to lead the assault team. What do you think? Two, maybe three others with you?"

I try to draw a full breath, but my chest feels all shallow, like not much air is getting in. "Uh, well..."

"Fastest flyers lead the diversion," Longbill says, "Me, of course. Budgie. Avocet."

"I'll go inside with Wren," Knot says.

"And I," says Shearwater.

"I may as well too," Nightjar says. "I never was a fast flyer. I mean, I'm not sure I'm going to be much good to you either way." I know exactly how she feels.

We cloak and gather on the rooftop. The other team collects still more nuts from the trees and begins circling the castle. On a signal from Longbill they all begin pelting the sides of the tower, aiming for windows.

"Mistral!" Longbill bellows.

Whimbrel shouts it too. "Mistral!"

"Mistral!" Budgie shouts. "You bloody coward! We're here! The Order has come!"

Darkness, already deep, doubles. I look up. There's a shadow on the moon, a straight-edge piece of night that cuts across the silver

231

disk. Budgie sees it too, and throws herself forward into a dive, whipping around the base of the tower. An instant later, I see her skimming up the far side of the rampart, a streak in the moonlight. The shadow follows. I look again. A silver snake gathers itself, coiling—bracing itself against nothing but air. It shoots forward, catching Budgie by her forearm.

"Get off!" she shouts, waving the arm.

Whimbrel appears. He catches the flailing scarf by an end and yanks down. It comes loose, floating free—then it coils itself for another strike. Someone shouts, "Here! I see 'em!" Voices dodge about in the darkness.

Then there's another voice. This voice I know. He's dropping down out of the black sky, his pale face shining like a second moon.

"Chubasco!" he calls, "Monsoon! Don't let them get away!"

Twenty-Eight

Metal whistles, slicing the air.

Avocet slams to a stop. A length of rope freezes taut, inches in front of her, and falls slack again. She spins hard about and shoots upward. Below her, the rugger with the red-hair is gathering rope. His weapon, a metal rope-dart, dangles over the edge of his carpet. He collects the rope into a coil and begins spinning it like a lariat.

Avocet whistles a high, fast trill. Longbill answers with a falsetto bark: *Yip! Yip, yip!* In an instant they're all heading into the trees. The ruggers from the castle follow.

"Sirocco!" Mistral shouts. "Back inside! Stay alert!" He goes after the others, his silk serpent carving the air like a chrome kite-tail.

The big rugger they left behind sinks back to the rooftop, muttering. Just as he drops level with the ramparts, a voice says, "Sirocco."

He whirls around. Knot puts a big hand on his shoulder and squeezes. Shearwater appears at the same instant grabbing the carpet fringe in both hands and yanking back hard. The rugger gives a strangled yelp and collapses on to the rooftop stones. Knot is on top of him immediately, a hand over his mouth. Then he stands. "He's out. Must of hit his head."

Without another word, the big man scoops the stunned rugger up onto his carpet and flies off. Shearwater draws Longbill's knife and pries it open. "Let's have a look at that skylight."

233

The room below is empty. Shearwater cuts a long slice along one edge of the plastic sheet, and then another, shorter slice crosswise to that. The plastic sags open. Shearwater cocks an ear. "All quiet," he says.

A flurry of silk makes us all jump. It's only Knot.

"That was fast," Nightjar says.

"Left him down at the bottom of the cliff. We ready?"

One by one, we slip through the slit plastic until we are all standing in the middle of the room. An oil lamp, standing in the middle of the long wooden table, is the only light. In the dark room, the flicker is almost painful.

The door to the hallway is open, but just a crack.

"That way?" Shearwater asks.

"Yeah." Something keeps me from moving toward the door. It's Maysa. She doesn't want me to leave the room.

"Wren?" Nightjar gives me a worried look.

"Something's wrong. May—my carpet." I look around the room. In a dark corner, there's a wooden, glass-fronted cabinet. As soon as my eyes fall upon it, Maysa sings a bright chord in my head.

"Over there. In that cabinet."

We cross the room together. Inside the cabinet, eight or nine carpets stand on end, tightly rolled and tied with silk ribbons. Maysa twitches. I recognize the tune she's thinking.

"Stonechat's carpet!" I stab the glass with my fingertip. "That one. It's right there."

The case is locked.

"Doesn't look very sturdy," Knot says. I step aside and he takes hold of the handle. A hard twist cracks the wood where the latch is, and the door falls open.

I put a hand on Shirin and run a finger down her length. "I guess that's it, then. They have him." The words are thick in my throat. I tug at a ribbon-end but it stays tied tight.

"Here," Shearwater says. He draws Longbill's knife again and opens it. "Use this."

I take the knife. Before I can even point it at the knot, the ribbon unwraps itself in a quick whipping motion and leaps at my face.

"Good god!" Nightjar shouts.

The ribbon wraps itself around my neck, twists, and wraps again. I fall to my knees, and grab at my own throat. I get one finger— one joint of one finger—underneath the ribbon, but it's already cutting into my throat, sharp as wire. Nightjar has her hands at my neck now, trying to wedge a finger in under the silk. The ribbon tightens its grip. I gulp, forcing air in, but it won't go. My finger is a numb knot at my throat. A bigger hand replaces Nightjar's. It's Shearwater. The smooth edge of the knife presses against my neck. He's working the point in under the ribbon. "Try and pull your finger out!"

I tug it free. For a second there's slack, then the ribbon snaps tight again. Shearwater turns the edge of the blade outward and pulls.

A high wail sounds in my head. The ribbon falls in three pieces at my knees. I catch a whiff of burning like a blown out match. One of the bits of silk gives a feeble twitch.

I suck in breath. The others are squatting and kneeling beside me. Nightjar has her hand on my shoulder. "Are you okay?"

All I can give for an answer is a rasping breath. My finger is almost blue.

"Wren?" Shearwater asks.

I nod, gasping. "Yeah. Yeah, I..." Cold dread creeps down my spine. They're all looking at me, but I'm looking at the cabinet. Behind the glass, all the other ribbons are unwinding. A band of yellow has almost wriggled free from two carpets.

"The door!" Shearwater calls.

One ribbon leaps free as Knot slams shut the cabinet door. His big hand plucks the tiny serpent from the air. It wraps and rewraps his fist. With perfect calm, he holds his free hand out to Shearwater, palm up.

Shearwater hands him the knife. "Nice catch," he says.

Knot straightens his hand and slides the blade between two fingers. "Thanks."

He gives the blade an upward flick. Silk breaks with a pop, and there's the same whiff of spent sulfur. Knot lets his fingers open, and the withered bits flutter to the ground. He closes the knife and hands it back.

"Trained attack ribbon," he says. "Neat. Never seen that before."

There's a tap. Then another. Behind the cabinet door, two more ribbons are launching themselves at the glass like angry bugs. The door jumps.

Knot slams it shut again. The broken latch will not fasten. He looks at Shearwater. "Maybe that chair?"

Shearwater hoists a heavy wooden chair away from the table and wrangles it into position in front of the cabinet. When Knot takes his hand away, the door stays shut.

I get to my feet and unroll Shirin. I put her up close to my face, thinking the questions. Where is he? Is he all right? It begins low—a sweet tune in a sad way, but tinged with an eerie, unpleasant, harmony. Maysa sings along but it sounds strange and hollow like the dull thunk of a heavy metal bell. A sick feeling rises in my belly. All at once, I know three things for certain: he's here, he's alive, and he is definitely not all right.

I hang Shirin over my shoulder, on top of Maysa. "He's here."

"Do you know where exactly?" Shearwater asks.

"No. But I bet she'll tell us if we're getting close."

The staircase is dark, lit only by what light spills from the doorway above or wells up from the hall below. The place is dead quiet. It's hard to see how our presence could still be news to anyone, but we creep along, anyway, cloaked and silent.

The great hall is empty. Oil-lamps sit on brackets fixed to the wall. Three flicker low. Others sit unlit in their own little shadows. Around the room there are four wooden doors, all closed. One has a leaded-glass window set above it, glowing with moonlight. The other three aren't even a little bit inviting.

"Got any ideas?" Nightjar whispers.

I shake my head, but it seems that I do. I turn around and search the darkness behind the stairs. There's a fifth door. It looks the same as the others, but for some reason, it's a lot more interesting. It's Shirin. She wants us to go through that door.

"I think it's that one." At that exact moment, a sound comes from behind the door—metal against metal, like the clank of a cast-iron pot.

"Someone's in there," Nightjar hisses, panic in her hushed voice.

"Yeah. Sounds like."

"Well, maybe we should try one where there isn't anybody waiting."

Shearwater says. "It sounds like a kitchen."

"Yeah," Nightjar says. "Why would they be holding prisoners in the kitchen?"

It's a good question, but the feeling is stronger than ever. "I just think that's where we need to go."

Behind the door, metal clatters. There's an odd creaking sound, followed by the gush and splash of water.

"I don't like this," Nightjar says.

"I don't like it either, but what else do you suggest?"

She twitches, a tic in her cheek I never noticed before. "Maybe one of these other doors? A quiet one?"

Shearwater frowns, his lips tight. "If we start opening doors, we lose the element of surprise." He takes a long, quiet breath. "Choose the devil you know. Someone is in there, maybe just fixing a meal or cleaning up. They aren't expecting anyone."

"It really doesn't matter," I say. "That's the door we need to go through. I'm sure of it."

"You didn't seem so sure a minute ago?" Nightjar objects. She's beginning to get on my nerves.

"Well the longer we stand here, the more I feel it. Stonechat's rug wants us to go through that door."

From behind the door there comes the clink of plates knocking together.

"Do we rush in," Knot asks, "or try a sneak?"

Shearwater looks at me. I avoid his eyes and say nothing. I can't make that choice.

Finally he shrugs and says, "Let's try the subtle approach."

We all move in close. Shearwater presses his ear against the door—then he pulls back. The door moves. When he pushes a gentle hand against it, it swings. He pulls his hand back again, and the door eases shut. "No latch," he whispers. "That makes it easier."

And it might have—if the door hadn't squeaked. At the first creak, Shearwater freezes. The noises from within the room stop abruptly. It is a very quiet castle again.

Shearwater catches my eye. He draws another breath, pushes the door open and slips through. The door falls shut behind him.

A few seconds later it opens again, and he waves for us to come inside.

It *is* a kitchen. Skillets and cooking pots hang from wood pegs set in the walls. A heavy wooden counter-top takes up most of one side of the room. A rack of plates sits beside a sink with a hand-pump. Water drips from the spout. The only light comes from a trio of oil lamps hanging from the ceiling.

No one else is there.

The smell of fryer oil and baked bread hang in the air, but it's a stale smell. The plates on the rack are still wet. There's a door on the far side of the room. If someone went out that door in the brief moment between door-squeak and Shearwater looking in, he would've needed reflexes like a cat.

We spread out and search the kitchen, going slowly, feeling our way. I can't help thinking of Mistral's gang of thugs searching for Raven and Parnell, wondering who I might stumble over at any second.

But it's Knot that finds her, and even though she isn't cloaked, she is hard to see. Crouching in the darkness behind a set of metal shelves, hugging her own bony knees, she's about as noticeable as a sack of potatoes. Even when all four of us are standing right in front of her, she doesn't look at us. Her clothes are drab and shapeless. Her feet are bare. The scrap of hair that flops across her face is as dull as the dusty wing of a moth.

"Hey," I try.

She draws her knees in tighter. She doesn't look up.

I kneel down on the stone floor. "Hey. Are you okay?"

She acts like she doesn't hear.

Shearwater tries. "Are you all right, Miss?"

The girl gathers herself like she's ready to leap and run, but she still doesn't look up.

I put my hand out slowly and touch the frail shoulder. She jumps as if she's going to run straight up the wall, but she doesn't actually leave the ground. She swallows a gasped breath and then becomes silent again.

"It's okay. We're not going to hurt you." I put my hand on my chest. "I'm Renny. Wren." I feel like I'm one of those movies, an earthling trying to communicate with an alien. She's that far gone. When she finally looks up, the light catches in her big round eyes. They're brown, almost golden—pretty eyes, but also awful. They're the eyes of someone who's braced for something horrible to happen.

"It's okay," I say again. "We're not going to hurt you."

The words have no more effect the second time. Her eyes go from face to face, as if she's sizing up her chances, looking for the best way to run. She has high cheekbones and delicate eyebrows. A pretty girl—once. Her hair isn't dusty, it's drab brown streaked with ash gray. She's not a girl at all. She's a lot older than I am. It's only her size and her fear that makes her seem like a child.

I switch from kneeling to squatting. "This is Shearwater, Nightjar, Knot." I point to each in turn. "We are looking for someone. Our friends. We think they might be here."

Her eyes dart from one a face to the next. I'm talking to her like she's an idiot or something, but I have no idea if she's even hearing my voice.

"An older woman," I keep on trying. "And a boy with curly black hair." I point to my own hair and draw tight curls with a fingertip.

She still shows no sign of having heard, but she isn't looking at my face anymore. She's staring at my shoulder, at Shirin. Her mouth hangs open. She reaches out and takes a loop of Shirin's fringe between her thumb and finger. Over and over, she draws the same strand through her fingers, and her scaredy-cat eyes go soft and sad.

All at once, the story Parnell told me comes rushing in like water. I grope around, trying to find the name, but I can't think of it. I ask anyway. "Are you her? The daughter? The weaver's daughter?"

The stroking stops. Still holding the loop of fringe in her fingers, she stares right at me. The name comes back in a sudden flash. "Gizella?"

At the sound of her name, her eyes grow even wider.

"It's you, isn't it? You're Gizella."

She doesn't nod, doesn't react at all except for a blink of her big eyes.

"You've—" The awful, obvious thought pushes its way into my brain. "You've been here? All this time?"

Gizella shuts her eyes. She presses them shut, like she's trying to squeeze out tears. But when she opens them, her eyes are dry. I touch her shoulder again. This time, she doesn't flinch away.

Footsteps sound—heavy-booted steps tromping up a wooden staircase. They're coming from the door at the far end of the kitchen. I look at Gizella. Her eyes are fixed on the door, her jaw clenched.

The door swings open and a man steps through, thick and beefy, with fine yellow hair. He's whistling through his teeth, a tuneless set of notes with a bouncy rhythm. He stops whistling when he sees Gizella and he grins. "Oy! You still here?"

Gizella watches his approach. Her eyes burn him—burn him crisp, then disintegrate the cinders. But he isn't affected by the power of her eyes. He keeps on walking—right past Nightjar's invisible feet, almost brushing Shearwater's invisible shoulder—until he's standing right before her, his black boots nearly touching her cringing toes.

"What's ya doin' on the floor, little Sheila?"

His voice is raspy but soft. A voice meant to calm. He squats down, and drops a dirty hand on her upturned knee. Her brows tighten.

He gives a little chuckle. "Silly Sheila, sat on the floor."

I'm closest, only feet away, cloaked, holding my breath. I'm only a step away from the counter where a big cast iron skillet sits, washed, but not yet hung.

"Silly Sheila," the man leans in a little closer. "Give us some more?"

He reaches a hand out to touch her cheek. She slashes at it with her teeth.

Laughing, he snatches the hand back. "Well, all right then little Sheila, let's do it your way then!"

Gizella claws at him with both hands, but he catches them, and mashes them both into one of his own.

"Get off!" Gizella shrieks. "Guhhhnaa!"

Those are the first words, the first sounds, she's made the whole time we've been there. Her voice is surprisingly strong. I don't wait. I don't think. The skillet is in my hands like it jumped there by itself. I step forward, and raise it high over my head, and let it swing.

The sound is amazing—a thunk. Metal crunching against bone. He pitches forward, arms flaying and collapses on top of Gizella. A gurgled scream leaves her in tight, panicked gasps. Shearwater and Knot reappear, pulling the big man off of her. She wriggles sideways, whimpering, rubbing her palms on her face, on her shoulders. She scrambles to her feet and presses herself even deeper into the dark corner.

Shearwater and Knot turn the big rugger over. He's breathing. Blood gushes from his nose. The left side of his face is scraped and bloody from where he plowed into the wall.

"We'll have to tie him up," Shearwater says.

Nightjar looks dubious. "He doesn't look like he's going to wake up all that soon."

But Shearwater has already found a length of cord on the metal shelves. He binds the man's hands behind him, pulling tight.

"All that stuff in the movies about knocking people unconscious, that's not usually the way it works. People usually regain consciousness pretty quickly." He ties the man's feet next. "Unless they don't at all."

The rugger is already showing signs of life. He groans once. His head flops from one side to the other. Then he goes quiet again. Shearwater pushes him up against the shelves and ties his arms to the metal brackets. "Hand me that dishrag."

I do. He takes hold of the man's jaw, forcing his teeth open. The man rears back, suddenly very awake again. "Oy! Whaa—?"

The rest is muffled. Shearwater sits back on his heels. "That should hold him."

The man looks at him with bleary, blood-eyed hatred, but he isn't struggling anymore. Whatever Shearwater teaches at Hilo High School, he seems to know something about knot-tying. He stands up, wiping his hands on his pant-legs, and looks at Gizella. "I don't suppose she'd be likely to help him escape?"

I shake my head. "I doubt it." Gizella is curled up beside the wall again, but she isn't looking at me, or at Shearwater, or even at the trussed up rugger. She's staring at the skillet still dangling from my hand like she's never seen anything like it before.

"Gizella."

Her eyes meet mine.

"You won't, will you? You won't untie him?"

Her eyes go wide. She steals a glance of the skillet again, looks back at me, then jumps to her feet and bolts from the room. We all watch the door swing shut behind her.

"You don't think she's gone to report us to someone?" Nightjar asks.

I finally put the skillet down. "I don't think so."

"Probably gone to hide," Shearwater suggests. He shakes his head. "God! What a miserable life she must have had."

"Where to next?" Knot asks me.

"Huh? Oh, yeah." I'm still thinking about what Shearwater said, trying to picture the misery. Fifteen years? First as Algernon Fell's runaway lover. Then as Mistral's kitchen maid. I shake it off and turn my attention back to Shirin. The answer to Knot's question comes quickly. The door by the cook stove, the same doorway the big rugger came through. I point. "Down there."

Knot eases the doorknob open. The door swings without a sound. A flight of old wooden steps leads down and makes a hard right into a lit basement room. The first step is quiet enough.

The second creaks like a rusty playground swing.

A voice from the bottom of the stairs calls out, "Pali?"

Knot grunts a clipped syllable. "Yeah?"

There's a squeak—a metal folding chair. The voice that comes up the stairs is relaxed, even amused. "Heard the kitchen girl yelling. Sounded like you two was gonna tear up the place. What'd she do, hit you with a frying pan?"

We go down the stairs, light-footed, Knot leading. He doesn't hurry.

"Hope you got some grub," the voice says.

The man is spread out, leaning back on one metal chair with his feet propped up on another. His eyes are fixed on the game console he's working with his thumbs. The only sound is the chirp of the game. Knot says nothing until he's standing right behind the man, looming over him.

"Aw, man! Twenty-thousand life points, down the tubes!" He holds up the game in disgust. "Did you bring any food?"

He looks up.

Knot kicks a foot out. Chair and man collapse with a crash of clanging metal. Knot drops to one knee, his hand on the man's throat. The rugger stares up at him, too amazed even to struggle.

"Wren?"

The voice comes from the top bunk of a bed on the dark side of the room. He leans out his shaggy, dark-curled head over the edge.

"Stonechat!"

I run. He catches me, one-armed. I hang, toes balanced on the edge of the lower bunk. His lips, his chin, a mouthful of his hair—I press closer. Hot tears burn beneath my eyelids.

"Ow!" He winces, pulling back. "Sorry. It's my arm."

His right arm is tucked against his body, bent beneath a hunched shoulder. When he sees Shirin wrapped around my shoulders, his eyes light up.

"You found her! Brilliant!"

"Yeah." I pull the carpet loose and hand her over. "She's okay. What happened to your arm?"

"Broken."

"Did they do that to you?" I stroke his hand.

"He did that to himself." This voice comes from the bunk below. It's Raven. Lost in the shadow of the top bunk, I managed to miss her entirely. "It was his own damned fool fault," she says.

"Not my finest moment," Stonechat admits.

I still have my toes on the lower mattress, an arm around Stonechat's neck.

"You had no business tangling with that bastard," Raven says.

"He left me no choice."

"You had a choice," Raven insists. "You could've stayed in Colorado like I wanted."

He shakes his head. Curls brush my arm, my cheek. "You know I couldn't."

"You came back," I say, "without me. You promised you wouldn't."

"I didn't exactly promise," Stonechat says.

"To be fair," Raven says, swinging her legs off the bunk but not standing up, "I don't guess he really had *all* that much of a choice."

I look down at her. "What does that mean?"

"Algernon. Mistral." Raven runs a hand through her hair and tucks it behind her ear. Her other hand is chained to the bed frame with metal handcuffs. "He sent Stonechat a message."

I climb down and look at Stonechat again.

"Yeah. I was a bit stupid," he concedes.

"What kind of message?"

"It was two days after we got back. You know how I couldn't get back here? Raven did something with that whipcrack spell of hers."

"That's how he found him," Raven adds. "Mistral, I mean. Somehow he traced him using the spell I cast. He must have assumed there was some special connection between us."

"The next day in Colorado, I was pacing around the living room, wondering what the hell I was going to do, and this little bird comes fluttering down. Amazing little thing. Like origami, only made of silk. It spoke to me inside my head, told me it could get me back to the island in spite of Raven's spell."

He gives his head a disgusted shake, and pushes his lips out. "I fell for it, right enough. I thought somehow maybe Flo had left some kind of spell, something." He shrugs one shoulder. "Well, it doesn't matter. I wanted to come back here, and that little bird gave me a way, so it didn't really matter what it was or who sent it. I would have come anyway. Naturally, they were waiting for me. I didn't have a chance."

There comes a sound, a wheezy sort of cackle. The man, still clamped beneath Knot's paw, laughs. "You don't. None of you. You don't have no kind of chance."

"This isn't exactly your party," Shearwater says. "We have you. And your friend upstairs isn't any better off."

245

He laughs again. "It ain't me you gotta worry about. Mistral's gonna have all your rugs before he's through. You'll all be walking back to wherever you come from." He laughs. "Or swimming."

Knot tightens his grip. "Talk nice, little man. I'm getting tired of holding you down. Might have to do something else with you instead."

The man blinks, but doesn't say anything.

Stonechat holds up the hand cuffed to the bedframe and gives it a little shake. "He's got the keys in his front pocket."

After Shearwater unlocks Stonechat and Raven, Knot leads the rugger over to the metal bunk and cuffs him to the frame. He doesn't resist at all. He lies down on the dirty mattress and stares up at the wire mesh above him with complete indifference. Shearwater leans over and speaks in a low voice. "I don't know what good screaming will do you, frankly, and we'll be gone in a minute, so I guess I'm not going to gag you."

The man yawns. "I ain't going to scream. It doesn't matter to me what you do. But if you don't mind helping a fella out, you could do me one favor."

Shearwater cocks a curious eyebrow. "Yes?"

"My game," he says, plainly. "Think I could have it before you go?"

***

We leave him there on the bunk, playing his electronic game, and make our way back upstairs. Stonechat stays by my side, his good arm around my shoulder. In the kitchen, the bound and gagged rugger glares at us as we pass. The blood from his nose has slowed to a dark trickle. Gizella is nowhere in sight.

In the main hall we stop.

"Front door?" Shearwater asks, "Or through the tower room?"

"Front door is right there."

"We still need the Orb," Raven says.

"We were up there a few minutes ago. We didn't see the Orb."

246

"He keeps it in a foot-locker under the table. He's shown it to me several times, trying to get me to tell him how to work it. Besides, my carpet is up there."

I think of the savage little ribbons guarding the stolen rugs. "Okay. Right. I guess we'll never get a better chance."

We climb the stairs. Everything is quiet except for our own footsteps on the stone stairs and the rustle of our clothes. It's only when we reach the doorway that we hear anything strange—but it's just the snap and buzz of those freakish little attack ribbons, still flinging themselves against the glass of the cabinet.

We ease our way into the room. Everything looks just as we left it. Knot and Raven cross to the table where the oil lamp stands, still flickering. From the shadow underneath he drags a box of dark wood and kneels down beside it.

"There's a padlock," Raven says. "If we can't break in we can just take the whole thing."

Knot lifts the hasp. "There is no padlock." He opens the box. Inside, there's nothing.

"That's strange," Raven says.

From the doorway, a voice says, "Not so strange as all that, Maudie."

The air hisses. Knot stiffens, his head jerked back. Without even a groan, he crumples to the floor, his face twisted in agony.

They stand near the doorway. The rugger beside Mistral is already recoiling his nasty metal dart. Knot lies on his side, a heap on the floor. On his forehead, a brutal wound runs with blood.

"No," Mistral says again. "It's really not strange at all."

247

Twenty-Nine

Silver flares from Mistral's outstretched arm and lashes across the room. Shearwater drops to his knees, bright silk billowing around him, wrapping and rewrapping. He struggles upward, growling through gritted teeth, but the scarf only cinches tighter.

"You're wasting your strength," Mistral says.

There are six of them. We must have walked right by them when we came into the room, near enough to feel their breath. But they had been cloaked then, and nobody felt anything. Mistral stands in the front, the Orb of Descrying balanced on his fingertips.

"It was a good chase," he says, "an impressive effort. But it's over now."

No one else speaks. Shearwater and Nightjar are staring at Mistral. Raven leans against the table. Of all of us, Stonechat is closest to the door, closest to Mistral. His face is cold and angry. His crippled arm hangs bent at his side.

Mistral looks straight at me and smiles. "It seems to me we've met," he says. He snaps his fingers. "You're the little girl who took a bite out of Taku's thumb."

Several of the ruggers behind him smirk. Taku holds up a grimy hand, looking amused and strangely proud.

"Algernon," Raven barks. "Talk to *me*. Not the girl. She's got nothing to do with this."

Mistral turns, cocking his head to one side. "Nothing? Really? And yet," he looks at me again, "here she is. Brought her own little army of do-gooders to steal my Orb."

"She doesn't care about the Orb," Raven insists. "She only came because of Stonechat."

Mistral throws back his head. "Ah, yes, of course! The wild, improbable things a young girl will do, all in the name of love."

I feel my cheeks grow flush. I want to wipe that smug look off his face.

"You'd know all about that, wouldn't you?" Raven says. "You were counting on it when you made off with the weaver's daughter."

A smile drifts across his face. "Gizella was hardly abducted. She came most willingly."

"You played her like a tin-whistle."

He shrugs. "It was necessary. I hoped she might prove as adept as her mother at the enchantments, but the poor ninny had no talent at all. Still, she was useful. She brought me Beata."

"But Beata didn't exactly work out either, did she? I don't exactly notice a fleet of original rugs by Beata around here."

He purses his lips, looking almost pouty. "She made a few. Unfortunately, they were not up to her usual standard. I suppose you would say her heart wasn't in her work. No doubt the captivity did not agree with her, though I can hardly see what difference it made. She never once, in all the years I was with dear old Parnell, ever left his castle."

"She was happy there. It was her home. It was your home too."

He laughs loud and long. "Such a lovely home!"

"Parnell took you in. He treated you like family," Raven insists.

Algernon smirks. "I suppose he did, in his own rather disturbing way. But then, I never had much use for families. At any rate, Beata is gone now, and I have more or less given up on the idea

249

of making new rugs. I have experimented myself—made that creature," he flicks a hand at Shearwater, still wound in his silver snare but no longer struggling. "I have had a few successes. But carpet making is so dreadfully tedious. And why make them, when there are so many around for the taking?"

Knot gives a low moan, and rolls over. The rugger with the rope-dart readies his weapon, but Knot remains lying on his back. His eyes are open, and he's staring up at nothing.

Mistral smiles again and continues as though there had been no interruption. "We've been through this before, Maudie. I have been patient. I need to understand the workings of the Orb of Descrying, and you are going to tell me. This little escapade has accomplished nothing except to supply me with hostages. Your resistance has been admirable, Maude. You have a very strong will. But you will not find mine lacking, either. I have been somewhat hindered by your special attachment to this boy. He is too valuable a hostage for me to actually kill, and obviously you know that. But now we have some new players in the game. Are you ready to watch one of them die? Perhaps her."

He points his finger at me.

"No!" Stonechat barks and heaves himself forward. A rugger with the bullwhip steps forward and catches him without effort, bending his good arm behind him, leaving his injured one drooping uselessly. Stonechat hisses, his knees buckling.

Then there's another sound: a low thunk, the dull ring of metal.

For a second, nobody moves. The man who's holding Stonechat, lets him go. Glaze-eyed, the man steps forward. He makes a half-turn to the left, then slumps to the floor.

Behind him Gizella stands, an iron skillet in her hand. She points at me and spits out the words, "Not her!"

"Gizella?" Mistral says. For the first time he seems really and totally surprised.

"Hey, there! Gimme that!" A husky rugger in a flannel shirt and a bandana makes a grab for the frying pan.

Gizella shouts, "No!" She swings hard, from the heels. The man drops. He bellows something meaningless and falls to his knees. His hands grasp at his face, catching the blood from his own spurting nose.

"Now, Gizella—" Mistral begins.

"No!" she bawls.

She flings the pan at his head.

It sails, wobbling through the air like some clumsy bird, unaccustomed to flight. The clang of iron on stone is an impressive sound, but by the time it clatters to the floor, nobody is paying any attention anymore. When the rugger with the bullwhip releases him, Stonechat drops to one knee, good arm cradling his bad. As Mistral twists out of the way of the flying skillet, Stonechat launches himself headfirst. Hugging his dead arm to the side, he slams into Mistral with his elbow, his shoulder, the top of his head.

A burly-armed rugger leaps forward, grabbing a handful of his hair. At once, Raven leaps on top of the man, raining fists down on his skull, gouging her boots into his side.

"Hey! Gerroff, now! Hey!"

Raven hollers something no one could've understood and whips her clawed fingers at his face.

"Yahh! Get off!"

He topples forward. Raven goes with him.

While I stand there watching like I'm rooted to floor, the Orb rolls out from under the pile of bodies and stops, right at my feet: a ball of sparkle-filled glass, glinting in the light of the oil lamp.

"Wren!" Raven snarls. I look up. "Take it," she yells, as a big hand paws at her neck, "and get the hell out of here!"

I don't stop to think. In one motion, I scoop up the Orb, and toss Maysa out in front of me. A second later, we're rising. We hit the skylight and I clamber through the torn plastic. With a last yank, I pull my foot free and I'm out.

The moon hangs high now, bright and flat. The air is cool and free from the taste of oil smoke. I could vanish, put on a cloaking spell

251

and head for the sky. But that's not why I'm out here. They're going to come after me—after the Orb. I need to be seen. I have to let them chase me and give everybody inside a chance to get away.

They come fast, tearing through the tattered plastic that still hangs from the frame. "There!" one shouts. "There she is!"

Three carpets soar upward. I see the red hair of the rugger with the rope-dart. I see Mistral's pale round face. There's no time to think. I tuck the Orb into my lap and point Maysa out to sea.

Voices carry in the calm night. I don't need to look back and see if they're following. I put head down and ask Maysa for more speed. I have a head start. If I just keep moving at full-speed, how can they catch me?

The answer appears directly in front of me. A huge man, his face torn by a ragged scar, materializes right in my path. I pull back, stalling, and twist hard around to the left. But then Mistral is right there in front of me. I veer around again, but another one looms up out the darkness. He leers at me, rope-dart swinging from his hand. I pull up, bucking high, and shoot past him. Behind me, I can hear him laugh, like it's all just a game. I lean in close and dig hard, heading back to the island. I whip around, scanning the sky, but now, all three of them are gone.

Time-fold! They're using a time-fold. How am I supposed to deal with that?

Instantly, the red-headed man appears again. I pull left and call out loud, "Faster! Faster, Maysa!" I'm begging her now. But no matter how fast I go, I can't outrun them. Not in time-fold. Speed doesn't mean anything anymore.

Another rugger appears on my left, and I roll to the right and dive into the darkness. I let myself fall a long way, clutching the Orb tight against my belly. The Orb. That's the only thing I've got going for me. They aren't trying to kill me—not yet, anyway. Mistral's gone to a lot of trouble for the Orb. He isn't ready to see it fall into the ocean. That's their plan—they're going to surround me, force me to land so they can take it from me. They've already got me heading back toward the island.

I pull up again and spin about, skidding on air. I'm not giving in that easy. I lie flat and dig my fingers into the weave. "Come on, Maysa! Go, girl!" She hunches once, then leaps across the sky and out to sea again. The rugger on my tail shoots by going the other way. His ugly face flashes by and then vanishes. At least this time he isn't smiling.

I stay low. The moon is on my left shoulder. It'll only be a matter of seconds before the next one shows. Well, if they want me to go back to the island, I'll do just the opposite and keep on heading for open ocean.

A familiar sound drifts up—music. At first I think it's Maysa. A second later, I recognize it. The cruise ship has cleared the far headland of the island, making its lazy way back out to sea. The party is in full swing. I can hear the boozy laughter, even over the steel drums. Couples are dancing on deck, ringed by torchlight. What would happen if I landed on deck? I could plow right into that crowd with their Hawaiian shirts and their drinks with little paper umbrellas. Mistral and his gang—they wouldn't dare follow me there.

From somewhere out in the darkness, someone shouts. "There!"

Two ruggers are coming up fast. I swing back the other way again. Silk ripples. I look up. A ribbon of silver light coils above me, drifting forward, ready to strike. Not twenty yards away, Mistral floats—arm upraised, conducting the strand, calling it down upon me again.

I drop. I have no plan, no hope, no idea of anything other than being somewhere else. I tumble down. Maysa wraps herself around me like a blanket and everything becomes very quiet. The voices, the wind, they all go away. All I can see now is the ocean, flying upward, reaching up to me. A few more seconds and I'll be a part of it, writhing in the cold, wriggling my way deeper and deeper, into all that sweet silence. I watch the ocean, darker than the sky, getting bigger and bigger.

Something swells inside my chest, clawing its way up, into my throat. "*No!*" I pull up hard. Breath squeezes out of me. I shoot over the waves.

The ship. So maybe I can't show myself, but I can still use it. Like a shield. How close will Mistral get? How much exposure will he risk? They're all cloaked, of course, but in the torchlight?

They are really only vulnerable to a few things. Fire, of course.

The ship lies dead ahead, a hunk of white topped with tiny flames, like a birthday cake with candles. I force the inane thought out of my head. Somebody swears in an angry voice. They're closing in. I lean down, pressing my face against Maysa, begging her for all she has to give.

The white ship looms up out of the dark water. I'm right behind her, riding above the churning water of her wake. I can't hear anything now, except the rumble of her engines. I slide out over to the right side and rise until I'm level with the railing. If I time it right, I can drop down over the railing, and ease right up the corridor toward the main deck.

Silver silk gleams, flying at me fast. I buck high, riding over the thrashing serpent and make a dive for the deck. A hand reaches out of the darkness. I dodge, rolling left, skidding and spinning.

A man in a white jacket fills the walkway in front of me. He's carrying a tray full of skewered meat and cut pineapples. I pull back and throw my weight to the right, clearing the rail again. Back over water, a rugger flies not ten feet away, his red face washed in moonlight. I force myself not to look, but I can see him anyway, matching my movements.

I swerve hard to the left, crossing back over the rail again. The sound of the steel drums, the jumble of voices, it's all around me. There's a torch bracket in front of me at the end of the walkway. I swing around it, and come to a full stop, just long enough to twist the burning torch from its socket. Clutching the thing in one hand, I swing the other way and head back again, out over the wake and into the sky. If any of the passengers happened to notice, what would they have seen? A torch—torn loose by some impossible thing—rising into the night? Probably they were all too drunk to notice or to care.

"It's okay, Maysa." She's trembling. I hold the torch as high as I can, as far as possible from her highly flammable fibers.

"Don't worry. I won't let it touch you."

She takes me up, way high, hundreds of feet. There, we wait. We don't have to wait long. I can see them coming. There's plenty enough moonlight for that. Four of them, climbing in a spiral like vultures riding a thermal. When they come even with me, they spread out, forming a great circle. I hold my position, turning slowly, trying to keep them all in view.

"It's all over, girl!" one of them says. I can't tell who spoke, but he's breathing hard. I spin back the other way. The rugger with the red hair floats past, still keeping his distance. I turn again and find Mistral. His pale face seems to throw back reflected moonlight. The silk serpent is wound about his shoulders, at the ready. He gives a little whistle—two notes falling. One of the ruggers drops down. I tighten my grip on the torch. I'm breathing pretty hard myself. The rugger takes a position directly underneath me, about fifty yards down.

That's in case I drop it. This is still all about the Orb. Maybe. He obviously hasn't given up on it yet. That's positively the only bargaining chip I have left. It isn't much.

I can't watch all of them at once. It's hard to say for sure, but the circle seems to be closing, getting a little tighter with each slow revolution. I watch Mistral again. He's studying me. I raise the torch a little higher, leaning in his direction. When our eyes meet, he smiles.

"This doesn't have to end badly," he says. "I offer you a trade, straight up: your life for the Orb of Descrying."

I don't say anything to this.

"So far none of your people are dead as far as I know. But my people—" he shakes his head and looks apologetic. "Well, you have seen how they are. They will not show restraint."

We keep circling, watching each other. I keep on saying nothing.

"Of course, I will allow them the same amnesty I offer you. In exchange for the Orb, I will grant all of you safe passage from this island. You have the power to end this. You can all simply fly home again."

"What about—" my voice cracks. I sound like a frightened little girl. I guess it isn't far from the truth. I clear my throat and try again. "What about Raven?"

"As soon as she tells me what I want to know, she will be free to go. She knows this. I have made that clear from the beginning."

"She'll never do that."

He smiles again. "I think she will, after tonight. Your valiant little rescue effort may have backfired in more ways than one. If I know Maude Byrne, I think she may have a change of heart after seeing the sort of danger she has put all of you in. At any rate, that is between her and me."

"And what if she won't tell you? Does she die? Like Parnell?"

They've stopped moving, all of them. Now it's only me, slowly spinning in the center of that triangle. Mistral laughs. It's a bitter laugh. "Parnell? I lived with Parnell Florian. I was his apprentice for nearly four years. The things I could tell you about him would make your hair curl up. Do you think he kept me in his house out of generosity? Do you think there wasn't a price for his mentorship? Trust me. Parnell Florian was no great loss."

His voice is so calm, so reasonable. "My offer is genuine. I am perfectly willing to let you go. I'm not the cold-blooded killer you believe me to be. I may be to blame—to some extent—for Parnell's death, but it was not my intention. He was an old man. His time had come. And really, all he had to do was show me how the Orb worked and I would've flown him personally back to the Seychelles and tucked him in his nice warm bed."

Anger wells up like heat in my chest. A hot tear spills on to my cheek. I wipe it away with my free hand. "You just said his death was no loss."

"I'm not sorry the man is dead. I only said that I did not intend it. And that it wasn't necessary. None of this is necessary."

The torch gives a little pop, and Maysa shudders. Two embers snake off into the darkness and wink out.

"May I ask your name?"

I chew my lip. This whole conversation, the mood of it, is wrong. "Wren."

He speaks again with perfect calm. "Well, Wren. Do we have an understanding?"

The torch dips a few inches. My arm is getting tired. I raise a knee so I can prop up my elbow. The flame is weakening. Is that their plan? Wait for the torch to burn out, then attack?

A warning sounds inside my head, a harsh blaring discord. It's ugliest sound I've ever heard Maysa make: a blast of pure panic. I look up at the torch, but it's something dark that catches my eye—a movement, like a shadow across my shoulder. I spin around hard.

"Yah!" A hard hand rakes across my shoulder, groping for the glass sphere.

"No!" I push the torch out, shoving flame into a face I can't even see.

He backs away, coughing, waving smoke. His hands go to his face, to a smoldering beard. He beats at his own face, patting out tiny sparks. He coughs, and waves his hand again. Then he looks down. His watering eyes grow wide.

"No. No, no." His hands drop. "No, no!" His words are short, desperate breaths. "No!" His hands slap his carpet, but his hands aren't enough. He throws himself flat against the fibers, trying to smother the burning, but that's not enough either. Silk withers beneath him. Warp threads snap. He digs his fingers into the weave but there isn't anything to grip anymore. He tumbles through the shreds and ash that had once been his carpet. A desperate, animal howl follows him, tailing away into the darkness.

Far below, flesh smacks water. Not a splash—a hard sound: *smack!* A slap.

Something silver leaps across the dark sky. I spin about, flailing the torch. Mistral's big silk serpent is right there, diving in. Luck is with me. The head of the torch catches the awful thing, and it hangs for a second, gulping flame. Then it rears up, howling, a snake on fire. Flame writhes, tracing figures in the air. Heat carries it higher. It's burning now along its entire length, a twisting tail of fire hanging in midair. Then, everything is quiet again. A faint trail of smoke is just visible in the moonlight.

Mistral stares up at the patch of sky where his scarf has just evaporated. He turns on me, glaring. "You have cost me a very valuable object!" he says, like I'd just knocked an antique vase off an end table. I keep the torch in front of me, turning slowly again. The third rugger has ascended again, his face like bone in the moonlight.

"This," Mistral says, "has gone far enough." His voice is calm again, a forced calm that glows with tamped-down anger. "It is time for you to save yourself, little bird. You, and those you came with. No more talk. No more deals. Give me the Orb."

He doesn't need to say *or else*. The *or else* is packed into crisp way he says the words. I keep turning, going from one face to the next. My options are running out. My flame is dying. Do I run again? Do I give up the Orb? After all, what's the Orb to me?

The Orb is everything. The Orb is the only thing keeping him here, talking to me. My only chance.

My eyes fall on the rugger with the red hair.

That is exactly when it happens. One minute he's peering at me like an ugly toad; the next, he's lunging forward, arms flailing, mouth open, fear filling his eyes. He topples into the darkness. A wet smack brings his screaming to an abrupt end. When I look up, I see Stonechat. He came out of nowhere, cloaked and silent, and he must have been moving pretty fast. His cloaking spell held right up until the moment when his feet hit the big man's back.

He doesn't wait for the man to hit the water. He plows aside the now empty carpet and banks hard to the left. The rugger sees him coming. He doesn't have time to uncoil his rope-dart, but he's ready, braced.

They meet with a crunch—snarling, grunting curses. The man swings an arm at Stonechat's head, but he falls back, ducking the blow. His boot, too big for his skinny ankle, sinks deep in the big man's paunch. Angry breath gushes. The man grabs Stonechat's foot and twists like he's going to wrench it clean off. Stonechat flails forward, and gets his good hand in the man's hair, grabbing his ear and pulling.

The man bellows, and throws his head back, thrashing. Stonechat clings tight.

Then something else has him. There's an arm folded around his neck, and now Mistral's angry moon-face looms over his shoulder. He's got one arm locked across Stonechat's throat, the other gropes for his broken arm.

I shout. "No!"

I heft the Orb and rear back. "Here!" I shout. "Here! Take it!"

And I throw the stupid thing. It follows a flat arc, spinning slippery moonlight. It catches Mistral as he looks up, just below his left eye.

I see the whole thing happening, all at once—Mistral tumbles backwards, still grabbing for the globe. Stonechat pitches forward, headfirst into the other rugger, taking him with him.

Arms wheel, grasping the sky. But the sky will not hold them. With hardly a sound, they fall, all of them, three bodies diving into the darkness.

Darkness swallows them all.

"No!"

Something tears inside me. I shout again—not even a word this time. I throw Maysa into a dive, plunging down, alone with nothing but wind and terror and disbelief. I only pull up when there is no more sky, and the slap of a wave wets my face. I lean out, holding the torch, peering into the lapping waters.

"Stonechat!"

But there's nothing. No hand reaches up from the water. No head, black-haired and drenched, bobs to the surface. I sweep back one way, then the other, searching. I saw where they hit. He has to be close. But each pass shows the same thing—just dark, shiny, water.

On my fifth pass, hope already dead, I see it—so smooth and nearly transparent, it's amazing it catches my eye at all. But the guttering flame of my torch sees it first. I drift right over it, and it winks at me: a ball of glass. I lean down and slide a hand beneath it and scoop it from the cold water.

I don't remember much after that. They said when they found me, only a few minutes later, I was sitting cross-legged, in the halo of a dying torch, just holding the thing in my lap. My eyes were closed. I wasn't searching for anything anymore.

But I was listening. I remember listening very hard.

Thirty

"I have been trying to reach you for a while now," Raven says. "I'm guessing you haven't been sleeping very well."

I'm back, sitting in my usual chair, the same table. The place has been cleaned up—books re-shelved, floor swept, flowers repotted, but Raven hasn't changed anything else. "No. I guess not."

She strikes a match. "I understand." She holds the match to her pipe and sucks flame down into the bowl. Through puffing smoke, embers glow. She blows out the tiny flame and drops the curled, blackened match on the tabletop. "I'm out of practice with using the Orb. I never had Parnell's skill with it in the first place, but it works best when the sleeper is in the middle of a good night's sleep."

A good night's sleep. It sounds so abstract, like something I heard about once. "I guess I must be sleeping right now."

She takes a pull on the pipe and lets the smoke go in a lazy plume. "Exhaustion. It'll catch up with ya." She clicks her teeth on the pipe stem and stares up at the dispersing gray. I wait, but Raven seems happy to let silence linger.

"How is Knot?" I ask.

261

"Better. Has a dandy scar on his temple but otherwise, no lasting damage. Says thick skulls run in his family. I visited him in person in the hospital. He was doing better, but he couldn't stand up without reeling. Said first twenty-four hours, he couldn't remember anything. Didn't even know who he was."

"Really?"

"Post traumatic amnesia. Even now, he says the events are sort of soft and gray in his memory."

I nod. Soft and gray.

"He's out of hospital now." The smoke from Raven's pipe, which didn't smell like anything at first, is beginning to develop its familiar peppery tang. I guess my brain can't deal with odorless smoke.

"What about the others? Avocet?"

"She's fine. Got a bad scratch on her face from a tree branch, but it looked a lot worse than it was." I remember Avocet's lovely face, smeared with black blood, after it was all over. "And Whimbrel is mending."

Whimbrel took a bad fall, broke his ankle, but he dragged one of the renegades down with him, a big bruiser called Squamish, or something like that. The two of them fell together through the trees. Whimbrel landed on top.

"Nightjar got a bad burn on her arm, but it's all right. Could've been worse."

It was Nightjar who had freed Shearwater from the scarf by breaking the top off the oil lamp, brandished the open flame. Self-preservation got the better of the ribbon's more murderous instincts, and it had unwrapped itself from Shearwater's neck and bolted for the sky. Nightjar, who was pretty well worked up by then, threw the lamp at the rugger with the bullwhip, torching his carpet, and setting the cabinet with all the stolen carpets on fire, freeing the savage attack ribbons. They all had to get out of there after that.

"What happened to the girl? Gizella."

"She's here."

I feel my eyes widen. "Really?"

Raven gives a slow nod, puffing. "Temporarily—though I don't know how long that might be. Truthfully, I have no great desire to continue on as keeper, so I hope my residency here is temporary as well. But someone had to step in. And, as Algernon Fell pointed out, there are probably only the two of us who knew how to work the Orb. Someone else will have to be trained."

"What's she doing here?"

"Oh, bit of this, bit of that. She helps with the cleaning up—won't go near the kitchen though. She's been helping reestablish the silkworms. She's good with the worms. Seems to like them. Personally, I'm not sure why we're bothering."

"There isn't anybody who can make new carpets?" The question comes out automatically, just something to say. I have no interest at all in the answer.

Raven shakes her head. "Not so far as I know. We can still do some mending and darning. I suppose that's a reason. But mostly, we're doing it because we always have. And, like I said, Gizella likes them. Seems to do her good. And, after the shambles of her life..." she gives a lazy shrug, letting the end of the sentence drift off with the smoke.

"Yeah. It wasn't her fault what happened."

"No. She was just a child. God knows what he told her, handsome boy like that. And she'd never known anything but this fool castle. She'd have been ripe to believe it."

Just a child. She would've been almost exactly my age, now that I think of it. "You saw her, didn't you, in the doorway? While you were talking to Mistral?"

Raven peers at me, with no readable expression. I ask anyway. "You got him talking. You wanted her to hear."

"I suppose I hoped something like that might happen. Of course, I didn't know exactly what he'd say. I could've been all wrong. She could've been coming to save *him* from us." This time her smile is a little warmer. "Love'll make a lass do strange things. But she had blood in her eye and a skillet in her hand. Somehow, I didn't think she was coming after us. The girl had wrongs to avenge."

"I'll say."

"She'd been living with Algernon Fell for a long time. I'm sure it was all very romantic at first. Whatever else he was, Algernon was an accomplished liar. No doubt he threw himself into his role as the impetuous lover. I'm sure she was only too glad to try and work the incantations, weave the silk." She gives her head a sad shake. "Poor fool. It couldn't have taken him long to realize she was not the one. He needed the weaver, not the daughter."

"Did you find out what happened to Beata?"

She pushes her lips together, flattening them against her teeth. "That part of the story is a little vague. They weren't living on the island yet. That came later. But it was already abundantly clear Gizella had no gift for carpet-making. Algernon became sulky—and then angry. Then one day he announced that he had sent for her mother, and that she was to join them. He made Gizella believe that this was for her, to make her happy. And she was at first. I don't know what Beata thought about all of that. I'm sure she was glad to be back with Gizella, but she never trusted Algernon a bit. And no matter what she might have told herself, she had to know she was his prisoner. She worked for him for a while but like he said, the carpets were not very good."

"Didn't they try to leave?"

"It wasn't as easy as all that. Algernon was already gathering the beginnings of a gang around him—many of the same lot you saw on the island. Misfits, crazies. The ability to fly a carpet is in no way connected to virtue or to sanity. You can have the calling and still be a low-life or a psychopath. Obviously, Parnell tried to weed that sort out, but you can't always tell. And sometimes, it's the flying itself that pushes a person over the edge. Not everyone can handle it. Algernon seemed to have a talent for finding these rogues. I am not altogether sure what happened but it seems that one night, mother and daughter tried to sneak out. They were caught."

"What happened to Beata?"

"I don't know. Gizella doesn't know. There was a fearful row that night between Algernon and Beata. The next morning, she was gone. And with her, every sign that she'd been there—clothes, shoes, whatever few possessions she'd brought. All gone, except for her hairbrush. Gizella found that where it had fallen behind the bathroom vanity. She kept it hidden among her things. She still has it."

"Didn't she ask?"

Raven scratches her chin. "I would imagine she did. And Algernon, no doubt, told her a tale. She wouldn't have been fooled, of course. She can't have believed that her mother just up and left her there without even saying goodbye."

"But, what do *you* think happened?"

She blows out a mouthful of breath, smoke-free. "Nothing good."

"So she hated him for that too. Because of what he did to her mother."

"No doubt. But she may have tried to convince herself, even then, that everything would be okay, that he really loved her and that nothing else mattered. Love dies hard. I believe it wasn't long after that when the real lawlessness of the renegades began to happen. His band of degenerates was growing, and he was making a name for himself. He wasn't Algernon Fell anymore, he was Mistral. I'm sure the notoriety appealed to his inflated sense of self-importance."

Raven brings her pipe about halfway to her mouth, but it's gone out again. Frowning, she empties the bowl into an old coffee mug, and pulls her tobacco pouch from the pocket of her sweater. "When he set up operations on the island," she keeps talking as she fills the bowl with the rough-cut flakes, "Gizella went with him. I don't suppose she had many options, but it mattered less and less to Algernon what she did. She had worn out her usefulness. In time she became what you saw, a scullery maid, nothing at all to him. I doubt he even noticed she was around. It's likely you lot were the first people to pay her any kindness at all in years. I'd also imagine that seeing all of you fighting back might just have rekindled her own fighting spirit. Even after all that time, maybe that brought some glimmer of hope rising to the surface."

There's a question clawing in my chest. The thing Mistral said about Parnell while we floated above the ocean, about the price of mentorship. It seems like a question that needs asking, and if anyone would know, it'd be Raven. But I don't know how to ask it and, honestly, I don't know if I want to hear the answer. So I just sit there, staring at the wall, wishing for something—a wisp of smoke curling toward the ceiling—anything that might take my mind away from the *real* problem, the image I can't shake from my mind, the thing I can't say.

Raven stares at me. "You know," she says, "I did not call you here to talk about Gizella or Algernon Fell or any of the others."

She takes a long pause like I'm supposed to say something, but I don't have anything to say. I don't even look at her.

"Wren—" she begins, then stops. It occurs to me she probably doesn't even remember my name, my real name. She probably doesn't remember how close my rugger nickname comes to the real thing, or that she herself suggested it. She strikes another match and relights her pipe. When she has it going, she says, "I went to see Stonechat's father the other day."

This earns her a glance. "Yeah?"

"I hadn't spoken with him in a long time. I was surprised, actually. Stonechat—Jacob—it turned out Jacob saw his father fairly often, at least a couple of times a year. He stayed with him for a week just a few months ago, around Easter time. He never told me that."

There's really nothing to say to this either, though I admit, it's interesting. I've never given much thought to Stonechat's father. I guess I just assumed they didn't see each other anymore. Raven exhales smoke, and wrinkles her nose. "He was—well, he was a special boy." She puts the pipe back in her mouth, chewing the stem. "You know, if you like, we could meet in person sometime. Not a dream meeting, a real face-to-face. If you'd like."

"The Orb—"

Raven stares, eyes curious. "Yes?"

"It didn't break."

She looks at me like I might be seriously crazy. With a slow nod of her head, she goes along with the odd change of subject. "Obviously it's tougher than it looks. I suppose Algernon, if he had gotten some kind of grip on it, his body might have broken its fall. That's only a guess."

"It floated."

Raven keeps staring. "Yes," she speaks slowly, "that surprised me too. Who knew the damned thing would float."

I don't know what else to say. That thought—some things float, some things don't—bothers me. I don't want to think about it, but the memory keeps crowding back every time I push it away: the glass globe, a shiny eye staring up at nothing—cradled, cold and dripping, in my lap. Heat wells up behind my eyes, threatening tears.

"You know," Raven says, "there was no chance of him surviving a fall like that. He fell a long way. At the very least, he would've blacked out, lost consciousness." Her voice is calm, unbroken. She's trying to be a comfort. A hopeless task.

She lost him too.

"And with his arm broken," she goes on, "he really couldn't have—"

"Yeah," I finish the sentence for her. "He couldn't have swam anyway."

Better that way, really, just to die, to fall into meaningless sleep. That's the way to go. But I can't stop picturing him, plunging through green murk, all that curly hair drifting about his beautiful face. Deeper and deeper into darkness, breath going stale. Stonechat—who sank like a stone. Without meaning to, I reach up and touch a fingertip to the corner of my eye, feeling for wetness. Raven watches.

"Anyway," she says, "It'd be good, I think, for you to stay connected with the flock. Avocet asked about you, and Whimbrel. I can keep you informed of what's going on, through the Orb."

I stare at the tabletop. The light from the window has a pinkish glow. What time is it in the seashells?

"Raven. My carpet, Maysa, can you call her back?"

She cocks her head, looking truly astonished. "Call her back?"

"She needs to fly. She's not going to be happy unless she can fly, and I—I don't want to fly anymore."

She stares, like she really doesn't understand what I've said. I ask again. "You can do that, can't you? Use the Orb to call her home?"

She takes a long time answering, and when she finally nods, it is a slow, slight movement. "I *can.*" She gives the second word a lingering, down-turned inflection. She sighs. "Fledgling, listen, I can't force you to ride, and I wouldn't try. But you should know something. If I take back your carpet, it will never be offered to you again. That would be that. Maybe you don't think you care about that now, but I want you to know what you'd be signing off on."

I nod, but don't say anything.

"It's bitter, what happened to you. And me also. I cast away a son once. Fortune brought him back again, but it was like we were two entirely new people. I was still his mother, and he my son, but Jacob and his ma were like folks from a tale we didn't neither one of us remember too clearly. Stonechat," she pauses over the name, "Stonechat was like someone new, someone who knew me and liked me for who I was, not just because I was his mother." She puts her cold pipe on the tabletop and rubs her face, like she's chasing sleep from her eyes. "It was as though I had two sons, and I lost them both."

She picks up the pipe again and puts it in her mouth. She can't leave it alone.

"Why did you leave him the first time?"

She gives me a long look. "It wasn't Jacob I left. That was between me and his father." She waves her hand vaguely. "Jacob had nothing to do with it. He was just caught in the crossfire."

"But you could've stayed in touch with him. You didn't have to disappear completely."

For a moment, she looks as though she's going to tell me to mind my own damned business. She rubs her chin, pushing her lower lip out, and the unlit pipe rises and dips.

"That's true." Her voice is weary, like a sad old melody. "But I didn't." She pulls the pipe from her mouth and points the stem at me. "Do you remember the first time you flew?"

An odd question. "Yeah?"

"I still remember my first time. Knifing through the wind. Not tethered to the heavy old earth any more. No weight, no gravity." She smiles, her eyes half-shut. "The pure bliss of having every thought, every care, blown free, scattered behind you in the wind." She looks me square in the eye. "I don't know if there's a heaven somewhere, but that was close enough for me. I've been flying since I was nineteen, and I still remember. It changed the way I saw myself, created a whole new world. Do you know what I'm meaning here?"

I nod. I do.

"When I married Jacob's father, I never told him about Ma'shooq. You can, you know. Despite the enchantments against it, some flyers do manage to tell a few select people—a spouse, a sibling. But it always comes down to trust. The same enchantment that binds us, binds the people we trust—they become caught in that commitment. They can't tell anyone either. They may not even understand that it's so, but they're bound just the same."

I put my hands in my lap again. "So how come you didn't tell Stonechat's father?"

She leans forward. She's smiling a full, broad smile. "I didn't tell him because I didn't want him to know. I loved him, right enough. He was a kind, thoughtful man. I don't have regrets for having given a piece of my life to him. But flying was mine. It was only mine, and I didn't want to share it—not even the knowledge of it. I always thought I would tell him. When we were first together and the passion between us was strong, I sometimes felt right on the verge of telling him, but something always held me back."

She settles into her chair. "I was selfish. I have been a selfish person more often than I'd really care to admit. But there had to be something else as well." She tilts her head and gives me a stare. "I wonder if you know what that could be."

I do know, and she knows I do. "You didn't trust him enough."

She nods, looking very serious. "It seems the inevitable conclusion, but I can't say why. There was nothing untrustworthy about him. He was an honorable man. But I *chose* not to trust him. That probably says a lot more about me than it does about him, don't you think?"

Very undreamlike pains shoot along the undersides of my thighs. There's a tightness in my chest.

"Keep the rug, Wren. You and she, you're bound together now."

"She needs to fly," I say. "She can bond with—with someone else." I don't sound very convincing, even to myself. The tightness in my chest pulls again, stretched almost to breaking.

Raven's face grows dark. Her expression doesn't change. She hasn't shifted in her chair. It's the light itself that's changed, gone from clear day to shadow in a subtle slide to gray.

"It's not as easy as you think," she says. Her voice fades along with the light, becoming a distant uncertain thing. "You know her completely. And she knows you too. There are no secrets between rug and rider." She's melting into smoke now, a gray woman blending with the gray walls.

"And certainly she needs to fly." Her face is gone now, but her voice remains. "But give her some credit, Wren. Don't you think she might be willing to wait for you?"

Thirty-One

A few days later, I tell Lee and Lauren everything—not about Maysa or Mistral or any of that, but the rest. I tell them about a boy I loved, about sneaking out, and about how he was gone now. I call him Jacob, of course—a name I never once called him in real life. And when Lauren broaches the obvious, inevitable question, I answer honestly: yes, we did. Several times.

I'm sitting on the end of their bed. Lee stands leaning against the edge of the dresser, his back filling the mirror. Lauren sits beside me, not touching.

"Who was this boy?"

I shrug. "Just a boy I met at a party."

"When?"

"Couple of months ago."

Looks are exchanged. I don't watch their faces. I just keep staring at the floor, but I assume looks are being exchanged.

"So what happened?" It's Lauren's question. Her voice is soft.

"Happened?"

"Did you break up?"

Right. The break up. I could tell them the truth about that too, I guess. He died. Maybe even drowned. In a storm. A fishing boat, maybe, somewhere at sea. But it sounds too melodramatic. The truth just isn't believable. "He left. He moved away. Went to live with his father. In Connecticut."

271

I wait. No doubt, more glances are exchanged, but I keep on looking at the carpet. They ought to be giving it to me soon: the disappointment. They're very disappointed that I could be so selfish, so careless, so inconsiderate. They trusted me, and I betrayed them, lied to them, let them down. The only reason they haven't started in on the big lecture yet is because they're in shock. I've caught them completely off guard.

Lee speaks. "Thank you. For being honest with us."

I look up. He's smiling, just barely.

"Was he someone you knew at school?" Lauren asks.

I shake my head.

"But he was your age, right?"

I nod.

"So," Lee takes up the thread again, "he moved?"

"Yeah. His mom lives around here, but his dad lives in Connecticut."

That's almost true—though Raven, apparently, now lives on an island off the coast of Africa. Another unbelievable bit of truth.

"Maybe you'll keep in touch. Email and whatever."

Lauren again. I try to draw breath, to say something, but it's like I've forgotten how. Wooziness swells up inside me, sudden and awful. The room sways. The whole floor bucks like it's trying to throw me off. I grip the bedspread with both hands. Why aren't they yelling at me? When does that part start?

Lauren's hand is on my shoulder. "Are you all right?"

I nod, and that's the worst lie of all. My face is wet. Lauren slides closer and puts an arm around me, tucking me under her shoulder.

"He's not—" A tear splatters in my lap. "We're not going to keep in touch." A sob breaks up my words. I can't stop it from coming. "I'm never going to talk to him again."

Lauren reaches her other arm around, and I let my face sink on to her shoulder. Everything else I try to say is lost anyway, so I just give up talking. I don't know what they'll make of that last sentence—

that he broke up with me, or me with him, or that it's all just a lot of teenage drama. It doesn't make any difference. It's all fiction. None of it's real—except the pain.

I cry for a while, and everyone stays where they are. Lauren strokes my hair, brushing it away from my face. To her credit, she doesn't try to tell me that everything will be all right or anything like that. In fact, neither one of them says anything. When the crying's over, I rub my face on my sleeves and sniffle for a while. The room is thick with silence. When I can get through a full breath without breaking, I look up. Lee smiles a sad smile, all sympathy.

The next thing he says is almost too predictable: Do I want to talk to Dr. Gananian about it? He's sure he can get me an appointment.

I don't. I really don't.

***

Two days later, Amy stops by my half-open bedroom door. "Hey. Get your shoes on."

"What for?"

"Special treat. We're going over to the mall—get our hair done, mani-pedi—the works."

I make a grim face.

"No arguments," she says. "This is a mandatory. Besides, Mom's paying."

"This was her idea?"

"Nope. My idea. I just talked her into paying."

Amy drives. For a few minutes, there's nothing but silence, which is always pretty unusual with Amy. After she settles into traffic, she says, "Mom told me what happened."

I nod. "I figured."

She grins and changes lanes. "You got some moxie, girl! Sneaking out the window in the middle of the night!"

I can't bring myself to smile. "Yeah."

273

I wait for her to continue, but she's gone back to being uncharacteristically silent. After about half a mile, I say, "I was expecting them to be a lot madder."

"Mad isn't their style. You know that. Dad is all about that win-win, cooperation-conflict, easing resolution or whatever. Besides, Mom has your back."

"She does?"

"Hell, yeah! Didn't you know? She was hell on wheels back in high school—partying, cutting class. She got suspended a couple of times. She drove Grandma crazy."

This is all news to me. "How do you know this?"

"Aunt Claire."

"Oh."

"Yeah, you wouldn't know it now, but she was out of control back then."

I stare out the window. You certainly wouldn't know it now. Lauren, the wild girl.

A blue sedan pulls level on the right side, matching our speed. I have this sudden flash that if I look over at the driver, I'm going to see the rugger with the gash where his eye should be, leering at me. I've seen him often enough lately, usually when my eyes are closed. When the car rolls past us, it's just some random woman who isn't looking at me at all.

"Actually, she's been on your side all along," Amy goes on. "She tried to push your adoption through, you know."

"Yeah, I know."

"Not like Dad was against it," she adds quickly, "It's just that Mom was the real instigator."

I don't react to this at all. It's like listening to someone talk on the radio about people you don't know, things you don't care about. I slump down even farther and stare up at the sky. The sun is small and bleak behind clouds, so pale I can stare right at it. The wind pulls the thin curtain across the little white disk. It seems to be moving very fast.

"She is again, you know."

I look at Amy. A little ghost sun swims in front of my eyes, dancing about. Perhaps the real sun isn't quite as pale as I thought. "She is what?"

"Trying to do the adoption thing," Amy explains. "I heard her and Dad talking about it."

I stare straight ahead again. The bright spot fades, ebbing away, unreal. I can't think of anything to say.

"You know," Amy says, "now that I think of it, maybe I wasn't supposed to say anything about that. Probably they didn't talk to you first because they didn't want you to get your hopes up."

I feel a smile twitch across my face, or almost a smile.

Yeah. There's not much danger of that.

***

The girl who cuts my hair talks nonstop, plying me with stories about her boyfriend who watches football and that's pretty much all she has to say about him because that's all he ever wants to do, but he *did* take her out for her birthday to the Nut Hatch, which was a nice place—not super-fancy but that was okay with her because they had those deep-fried onion things and it was nice to go out sometimes instead of always pizza in front of the tube. It all washes over me in little waves. I probably don't hear half of it, but it doesn't matter. It's restful, the way lapping water is, and all I have to do is listen and grunt the occasional response.

No, I don't watch football.

No, I've never been to the Nut Hatch.

No, I don't have a boyfriend.

"Well, there's no reason to rush. Lot of fish in the sea. You've got your whole life ahead of you."

Amy, who's already finished with hers, wanders over to kibitz on the final snips. She nods with guarded approval. "Looks good. Maybe a little shorter around the ears?"

275

I've been avoiding looking in the mirror. Now I do. It looks all right around the ears, but it's the eyes I really notice. Sad eyes. Not Miranda's sad eyes. My own.

I turn my head and make a show of looking at it from both sides. "No," I say. "It looks fine the way it is."

***

I pass on the manicure-pedicure.

"Aw, come on!" Amy says. "It's all about the pampering. You'll love it."

"No. You go ahead. I'll just wait."

Amy makes a face and shakes her head. "It's no fun unless you share it. But if you won't, you won't. Want to shop for shoes?"

"Not really."

She gives another helpless headshake. "You're a hard person to do nice things for sometimes." We walk past the toy store where a make-your-own teddy bear machine churns up a tiny snowstorm of cotton fluff. "You might want to work on that a little," she says "Eventually people might stop offering."

We stroll past the Tollhouse Shop. Plate-sized cookies with elaborate, multi-themed frosting sit under glass cases like garish clowns, cheap and sad.

"Oh, hey," Amy says, "I wanna go in here and get a card for Mom."

We're in front of the Book Mobile, a completely stationary bookstore which also sells, of course, stationery. "Why are you getting a card?"

"A congratulations card, on the City Council thing."

"The what?"

"She's running for City Council." Amy pushes through the door, which gives a little electronic *bing*. "Didn't you know?"

Obviously not.

"She's been talking about it for weeks, just hadn't made up her mind. Now she has, so I thought a card—you know, something funny."

She heads off for the Hallmark racks, and I wander about, looking at nothing. Lauren is running for City Council? That isn't hard to picture—she's always talking about politics. Somehow I completely missed the transition from talking about it to actually doing it.

I drift into a corridor between two high shelves. On one side it says: Fiction and Literature. On the other: Fitness, Self Help, Parenting. Hanging above the aisle, there's a mobile of brightly colored, oversized, cardboard books, turning in the air-conditioned breeze: *Moby Dick, Crime and Punishment, War and Peace, Gone With the Wind.* At the far end of the aisle, after Classics, there's a tiny section, just two shelves. The sign says: Poetry.

I kneel down. At the very bottom, at the very end of the shelf, there's a little yellow paperback: *Best Loved Poems of William Butler Yeats.* From the cover, a serious young man stares at me through little round glasses. I thumb it open. It's not the same book as Stonechat's. His had lots of poems printed in small type, crowding together on the page. This book is thinner, with larger print and only one poem per page.

I leaf through, not looking for anything.

When you are old and gray and full of sleep—

Stop. I don't want to do this. I am not going to read this poem. I'm not going to think about this stupid, fucking poem.

—and dream of the soft look your eyes had once, and of their shadows deep—

The words come rolling back, flooding out of my memory. My eyelids are drooping and I let them fall. I don't need to read the words. His voice is so clear, his shoulders hunched, his head thrown back against the sky.

—how Love fled...and hid his face amid a crowd of stars.

A shadow falls across the page. I snap the book shut.

"Hey, you ready to go?"

I push a knuckle against my eye, roughing away the wetness. I stand up, book in hand.

"What's that?" Amy asks.

I show her the cover. She squints. "Poetry?" A curious frown wrinkles her brow. "For school?"

I nod, not looking up. "Yeah. For school."

It isn't very expensive: six ninety-five plus tax. I have just enough.

***

That night, after everyone has gone to bed, I dig Maysa out from the dust bunnies beneath my bed. She unfurls herself, hanging at knee level, trembling with readiness. I stroke the long tail of an impossible silk bird, running my thumb along the smoothness.

"Been a while, hasn't it, girl?"

Ten days? Two weeks? I don't want to count back. I pull on a heavy pair of socks and a windbreaker and push open the window.

Outside, we rise until we are clear of the branches of the ash tree. There, high above the rooftop, I pull a flashlight from one jacket pocket, and the little paperback book from the other. It takes me a moment to find the one I'm looking for. By the dim light of the tiny flashlight, I read it out loud. The words are strange. Even though I've heard them before, they're still strange. On the page, they mean nothing:

> *"I am haunted by numberless islands, and many a Danaan shore,*
> *Where Time would surely forget us, and Sorrow come near us no more."*

But out loud—even in my own trembly, stumbling voice— they take on a shape. They rise and fall, like surf, like wind, and it really doesn't matter what they mean.

> *"Soon far from the rose and the lily, and fret of the flames would we be,*
> *Were we only white birds, my beloved, buoyed out on the foam of the sea!"*

When the last line is done, I leave the book open, sitting in my lap. Silence roars.

A silver voice chimes behind my right shoulder. *Ah, very nice, Renny! Yes! Very, very nice.*

"Think so?"

On my left side, another voice gives a frothy giggle. *Yes! Please! Again, please!*

I keep my thumb on the page but let the book fall shut. With my other hand, I click the flashlight off and rub the wet blur from my eyes. It's a cool night. The best sort. The wind has a bite to it—a lovely, crisp tang. I fill my lungs with it and Maysa shivers at the delicious taste.

When my eyes are dry, I click the light back on. I bend down close to the page again and read the whole thing over, straight through from the beginning.

Atthys Gage is a writer and musician with a lifelong love for myth, magic, and books. His second real job was in a bookstore. As was his third, fourth, fifth and sixth. Eventually, he stopped trying to sell books and started writing them. After studying classics at Haverford College, he developed an interest in the ways that ancient stories influence modern storytelling, and has always had a fascination for that cloudy borderline between the normal and the paranormal. He lives on the coast of Northern California with his long-suffering wife, strong-willed children, and several indifferent chickens.

To find out more, visit atthysgage.com

CPSIA information can be obtained at www.ICGtesting.com
Printed in the USA
LVOW07s1255221015

459186LV00042B/1677/P